Enterprise House
A Story of Success

Julian Ashbourn

Enterprise House

Copyright © 2015 Julian Ashbourn

All rights reserved.

ISBN: 1519417187
ISBN-13: 978-1519417183

Enterprise House

This book is dedicated to those who come to understand the true meaning of life and what is really valuable in this world. They are often overlooked by our fast moving materialistic society.

Enterprise House

CONTENTS

1	In The Beginning	Pg 3
2	The Big City	Pg 21
3	Disillusionment	Pg 33
4	The Move to Boggle	Pg 61
5	Rebirth	Pg 75
6	The Conference	Pg 91
7	Meeting Violet	Pg 119
8	A New Regime	Pg 137
9	The Boggle Festival	Pg 151
10	More Disillusionment	Pg 187
11	Enlightenment	Pg 201
12	The New Rising Sun	Pg 217
13	Clouds	Pg 235
14	Love Story	Pg 253
15	Epilogue	Pg 283

Enterprise House

For Joanna who, for a long time, encouraged the writing of Enterprise House

Enterprise House

1 IN THE BEGINNING

Some men are born great, some have greatness thrust upon them and some absorb greatness, by degrees, until they eventually come to tower above their peers. Young Earnest Trubshaw had no great vision or burning motivation as he sat, idly contemplating the world outside the window of Dr Parfit-Twist's Academy for Young Gentlemen at Crinkington, nestled in the rolling hills of the Sussex countryside. Indeed, he had no inkling that he alone among his school fellows was, in fact, destined for greatness. It wasn't a concept that was much considered within the dusty confines of the Academy for Young Gentlemen, that noteworthy institution that perfectly reflected post-war decay and the decline of the British Empire.

The Academy had been formed by Dr Parfit-Twist following his demobilisation from the Royal Corps of Signals where he had served as a storeman somewhere on the Sussex coast. Failing to secure any gainful employment after the hostilities had ceased, he assumed the title of Doctor and decided to set up shop in the house that he had inherited from his aunt Beatrice, at the end of a Victorian terrace in a quiet Crinkington street. Although now well past retirement age, Dr Parfit-Twist continued to run the Academy for Young Gentlemen in exactly the same manner as on the day when it first opened its doors to an eager brood of freckle faced belligerents from the neighbouring villages. The lessons which Dr Parfit-Twist delivered himself were all based upon a book which he carried around from class to class, called 'Tell Me Why'. It made no difference whether he was teaching geography, history or English literature, the source was always the Tell Me Why book and he set the same questions, week after week, term after term. Unfortunately, his copy of Tell Me Why was an aging, dusty old first edition with a tattered spine, much of the contents of which had been somewhat superseded by the relentless march of world politics. Consequently, when Dr Parfit-Twist asked "What is the official language of Patabele Land?", one of his favourite questions, he was blissfully unaware that Patabele Land, actually, no longer existed. Nevertheless, the eager little heads of the incumbents at the Academy for Young Gentlemen were systematically filled with a wealth of similarly invaluable facts with which to guide them in their future years. Dr Parfit-Twist was aided and abetted in this gross distortion of the English education system by his colleagues, Mr Dobbins, who supposedly taught mathematics and science, and Mr Veiberio, whose background was far from clear and who supposedly taught languages. In reality, the scope of Mr Dobbins' mathematics and science started and ended with the Isosceles triangle, endless examples of which were chalked up on the blackboard, whereafter the venerable Dobbins took great delight in highly animated explanations of angles. Mr Veiberio was hampered somewhat in his language classes by the fact that his spoken English was actually quite poor and most of the pupils hardly understood a word he said. He had a little French, and did his best to impart this meagre knowledge to the class, but with very little success. There was a good deal of window watching, dreaming and cartoon doodling in Mr Veiberio's classes.

Unsurprisingly, Dr Parfit-Twist's Academy for Young Gentlemen produced very few notable academics. In fact, it produced no academics at all, and the boys unlucky enough to find themselves deposited there spent the four years or so of their entrapment daydreaming about their future lives. Young Earnest was no exception, drifting through the passing days in a haze of bewilderment. One talent which did emerge was that of attracting life's outsiders to himself. Any students who were considered odd, or who, for one reason or another, didn't quite fit in, seemed to gravitate towards Earnest and, to his enduring credit, he always befriended them. It was a talent that was to stay with him in later years. As always in such situations, there existed a variety of personalities, some less attractive than others. One of the latter type was a precocious young lad by the name of Raymond Black. Raymond lived in a dark, rambling old house in the middle of town with his father, but no mother. His father indulged his every whim and young Raymond had the best of everything. He had the best bicycle in the school, the best sports equipment, the best clothes and a wealth of gadgets and various boyish paraphernalia that all the other students envied. He was an arrogant know-it-all, who was not particularly popular, although this didn't seem to worry him. However, he seemed to single Earnest out as someone he could speak to, and many fairly one sided discussions ensued, usually in praise of some new gadget or other that Raymond had acquired and whose merits he was keen to describe in great detail to Earnest. Interestingly, Raymond had become besotted with the concept of computers and was sure that, one day, computers would run the world and that he, naturally, was going to be a computer scientist. There was something about Raymond's preoccupation with computers that appealed to Earnest. It was clearly a passion with Raymond, who read everything he could get his hands on that was in any way related to the subject, and who seemed to have developed an impressive knowledge of his own, although Earnest was never quite sure whether this was simply bragging on the part of Raymond, or whether he really did know what he was talking about. And then one day,

Raymond casually announced that his father had bought him a computer which he was in the process of assembling and that, if he liked, Earnest could come around and see it. It was a proposition that seemed irresistible to Earnest and so, that evening, he accompanied Raymond home in order to see the kit and discuss computers, something that Raymond was latterly always ready to do. The computer was a BBC Micro and Raymond had various devices that he was able to connect via the serial and parallel ports. Earnest watched in wonder as Raymond eventually managed to print out a few lines of text on an attached printer, which described a complex calculation. At that moment, he realised that Raymond was probably quite right and, for the first time, a seed of ambition was sown in the wastelands of Earnest's mind.

However, Ernie, as he now liked to call himself, was cognisant of the fact that few computer scientists were likely to be produced by the Academy of Young Gentlemen and that it was likely that he would need a more robust academic background. As he was, in any event, under his last year of Dr Parfit-Twist's guidance, he started to inquire as to the availability of higher education within the Crinkington area. His diligent enquiries quickly revealed that there wasn't any. However, there was a newly formed College of Technology at Fudmill Green, around twelve miles away which, Ernie considered, he could reasonably reach by bicycle. After a few arguments with the more senior branch of the Trubshaw family, who had anticipated that Ernie would soon be earning a wage and thus contributing to the family finances, it was agreed that, if a place was offered, Ernie could accept it. A hasty letter was dispatched to the head of the Computing Department, requesting an interview and, two weeks later, a leisurely reply was received from the secretary advising young Mr Trubshaw that, if he would like to present himself at the College on such and such a date, an interview could no doubt be arranged.

The day finally arrived, ushered in with dark skies and high winds, and Ernie set off on his bicycle for Fudmill Green. It was a tortuous journey, interspersed with difficult moments as Ernie came to appreciate the desirability of proper bicycle maintenance, including to his brakes, as he sped down the hill towards Fudmill. Nevertheless, he arrived safely and was more or less on time as he presented himself at reception. A rather disorientated receptionist discovered, after one or two internal phone calls, where the Computing Department actually was and directed Ernie accordingly. Mr Frederick Bottom was an amiable character, a little oversized and with rather less hair than would have suited him. In addition, each of his inquisitive eyes pointed in different directions, as though surveying distant corners of whatever room he found himself in. "Come in, come in" he gestured jovially to Ernie, waving his arm towards a seat on one side of a desk whose surface was adorned with a few loosely scattered magazines and an oversized ash tray. Ernie sat down and Mr Bottom fell loosely into the chair on the other side of the desk before leaning over it and, clasping his hands together, he surveyed Ernie most intently. At least, that was what Ernie thought he was doing, although one could never be quite sure what Mr Bottom was actually surveying, intently or otherwise. After a few seconds elapsed, Mr Bottom sat back abruptly in his chair. "Well lad. Tell me all about yourself" he exclaimed enthusiastically. Ernie explained his tenure at Dr Parfit-Twist's Academy for Young Gentlemen and indicated that he was particularly interested in computers. "Computers!" boomed Mr Bottom as though taken by surprise, his eyebrows raised and his eyes darting around. "Well, that's interesting. That's what we teach here you know?" Ernie continued with his overview of achievements to date and then sat patiently, awaiting further questions. After a few seconds of silence, Mr Bottom, realising that the applicant had stopped talking, shuffled a few magazines on the desk, cleared his throat and then announced with a smile, "Well Mr Trubshaw, you must come and join us, we are, after all, most keen to take in students who are interested in computers". After the further exchange of a few pleasantries, Ernie was directed back to the reception area where he was requested to fill in an application form. And that was that. Ernie was now officially enrolled in the next course on computing, due to start the first week in September. In the meantime, he would search the library at Crinkington for whatever information he could find on the subject which, it tuned out, was very little indeed.

And so, just as the autumn leaves started to turn, Ernie set off for Fudmill Green once again on his bicycle, filled with anticipation of all the wonderful things he was going to learn. The College of Technology was a fairly modern, beige coloured three storey building of no particular distinction. The Computer Department was tucked away at the farthest corner of the third floor. There were no lifts and the staircase was at the other end of the building, necessitating quite a walk from the reception area. Up until now, Ernie had only seen Mr Bottom's rather cramped office and had imagined the main study area as large rooms filled with computers of all shapes and sizes. The reality was subtly different. There were two other rooms; a storeroom where spare equipment and consumables such as paper and printer ribbons were stored, and a main study area which was by no means extensive. There were six tables, four of which had BBC Micro computers on them, just like Raymond's model, and a collection of randomly distributed chairs, around and between these tables, with some nestling up against the rear wall. On the front wall was a large, double blackboard of the scrolling type, that looked as if it had been hardly used. Upon entering the main room, Ernie was greeted by the senior tutor, a tall, angular man in ill-fitting tweeds who went by the name of Felix Shaw. "Ah, joining us for the new term are you?" he suggested while looking rather quizzically at Ernie. "Yes sir" responded Ernie, looking around in an air of slight disbelief. "Well, this is the main study room, although you may also use the library on the ground floor, where you will of course also find the canteen". Ernie quietly considered that, if nothing else, he would get plenty of exercise at the College of Technology. "How many other students are there?" asked Ernie. "What?, Oh... I think there are six this term" replied Mr Shaw, somewhat absent-mindedly. In fact there were five, including Ernie. He had been the first to arrive that day, followed later by Richard Thorogood, a confident looking chap with thick set brown hair, Mark Pendlebury, who looked perpetually absent minded, as though deep in thought about matters of universal importance, Trevor Lawson, who, with his sticking out ginger hair, protruding ears and permanent grin was clearly was going to be the wit of the group, and Joyce Barrow, who seemed to come from an altogether different background, with a cut-glass English accent and adorned in bright coloured mohair pullovers and tight fitting slacks. They looked, at first sight, an unlikely assemblage of future computer scientists, although it was difficult to suggest exactly what a computer scientist should look like. Ernie had imagined them as studious looking fellows in white overalls with pencils in the top pocket, peering out from behind circular glasses. However, no one in the

College of Technology looked like this, especially not in the Computer Department. After some initial introductions, Felix Shaw explained that they would be learning all about the history of computing which, coincidentally, was his special subject, as well as the rudiments of computer programming. The latter was the preserve of the other tutor, Mr William Flitwick, a strange creature whose upper reaches seemed to consist of a mass of hair and beard, between which it was hard to distinguish, punctuated by two small, manically peering eyes. He was not a great conversationalist and seemed to have few, if any, interests outside of computing. Students, tutors and Mr Bottom soon settled into a fairly harmonious routine as the term set off upon its wondrous path of discovery.

The term began with a series of lectures and discussions around the history of computing, where Felix Shaw was in his element, gesticulating and pacing up and down as he relived the detail of those pioneering days, from Charles Babbage to the advent of Colossus. Much time was spent discussing Turing Machines although Ernie was a little perplexed as to how the conceptual translated to applications for modern computing. Mr Shaw particularly liked to discuss Colossus and the code breaking activities at Bletchley Park and, indeed, there were many enjoyable and extended discussions covering the design of the machine, the number of valves employed, the programming technique and the ingenuity of the team involved, especially Alan Turing and Tommy Flowers. These discussions were enjoyable and, in the first part of term, many a happy hour was spent, tucked away in the top corner of the College of Technology, away from the gaze of the majority. However, Mr Shaw, after a few weeks, had more or less exhausted his supply of anecdotes and observations, falling into a somewhat repetitive mode of continually going over the same ground. The students started to feel like they had embarked on a cruise on The Flying Dutchman and wondered if there would ever be an end to it. Joyce Barrow in particular was becoming rather critical of their esteemed tutor. However, the history of computing was but a part of the curriculum and there was plenty of time to engage in the other major activity, that of learning to programme computers.

Bill Flitwick was a completely different character. In contrast to Felix Shaw, he was quiet, studios and did not readily volunteer information, a characteristic which might have been viewed as curious for a tutor. Nevertheless, the students learned a good deal from him in the early days, while experimenting with the BBC Micro computers within the department. These were model B machines with 32k of memory, running the Acorn MOS operating system and featuring the BBC Basic ll programming language. The department had invested in a few peripherals including serial printers and 5.25" floppy disk drives. One of the machines had also been modified to additionally run the ISO Pascal programming language. And so, the team quickly learned how to write code with loops and 'If Then Else' statements in order to undertake various calculations and represent different scenarios. Initially, this was very exciting and the students readily fell into a programming mode, with a little help from Mr Flitwick. However, just as they had experienced with the history of computing, their lectures and activities became repetitive and seemed to have got into their own endless loop. Bill Flitwick would pose problems for them to solve via programming, but the problems were naturally aligned with the capabilities of the machines being used. There was a certain amount of experimentation, leading to some occasional bright moments when the unexpected occurred, but generally, things seemed to settle into a routine of perpetual regurgitation. Ernie was beginning to wonder what all this had to do with practical computing in the modern world. Surely, the studious men in white coats that he had read about were doing something more exciting, and more valuable than this. The students started to discuss this among themselves and attendance at the lectures started to become a little patchy.

During this period, Ernie, who was a little clumsy at the best of times and had a talent for falling over things, literally bumped into one or two interesting characters. One of these was Father Donovon, the local vicar based at St. Peter's, the little church in Fudmill Green which had undoubtedly seen better times. Father Donovon believed in mingling with the parishioners and did so frequently, at least during opening hours at The Pony and Trap where he typically had a wider audience than he did during his sermons at the church. Early one morning, as Ernie was taking a short cut through the church yard on his way to the college, Father Donovon suddenly appeared out of nowhere and the two of them quickly became entangled with Ernie's bicycle, the whole assemblage ending up sprawled over an adjacent grave. "Are you the fella from the stonemasons?" asked a slightly befuddled Donovon. "No, I am a student at the college" answered a slightly confused Trubshaw. "Then what are you doing in my church yard?" "I'm on my way to the college" "Well, there's no college around here" answered the Donovon as he staggered to his feet, adjusted his spectacles and staggered on towards the church gates where a mysterious looking dark coloured van was waiting. As Ernie followed on and reached the gates, he observed that the still slightly unsteady Donovon was conducting a business transaction with the mysterious visitor to sell off a certain number of gravestones, in order to make way for a fresh intake of those wishing to rest peacefully in the hallowed ground of St. Peter's. Indeed, the leafy environs of Fudmill Green seemed to be full of characters like Father Donovon, some of whom seemed to be living in an altogether different world. It was a similar story with

Mr Griffiths, the baker who seemed to spend most of his waking hours standing outside his baker's shop watching the world go by. He always surveyed Ernie most attentively as he cycled by, as if he had never seen him before. And then, when Ernie visited the shop to buy his rolls for lunch, Mr Griffiths would greet him as though he were a lifelong friend. But then he greeted everyone in the same way, often confusing their names. Ernie was variously addressed as Bertie, Ronald, Richard, Freddie and a few other variants, but it was all delivered in an air of good humour. However, as Ernie quickly learned, it was best to watch your change carefully at the bakery as Mr Griffiths' absent mindedness extended to his calculations of price and given change. The native Fudmillians were of course conversant with each other's little idiosyncrasies and made allowances accordingly, but outsiders often required a little time to settle in to the particular rhythm of life that characterised this picturesque corner of Sussex.

There was another acquaintance made by Ernie which proved to be most interesting and, in a way, influential to his studies. Often, while climbing the stairs to the third floor, he would cross paths with a colourful young man named Matthew Bloggett who was studying engineering on the second floor. After a while, Matthew started to ask about the Computing Department and what they were studying there. Their casual meetings increasingly became punctuated with a few minutes of friendly discussion wherein they would compare notes as to what they were learning and the methodologies being introduced to them. On one such occasion, Matthew casually mentioned that he was sure that he could do anything that a computer could do with his slide rule. Intrigued by the notion, Ernie mentioned this to Bill Flitwick. "Poppycock" announced the latter in an unusually animated outburst. "Computers can process information faster than any human and the results obtained will be much more consistent and reliable". Ernie repeated Mr Flitwick's assessment of the situation to young Bloggett who, after a derisory huff, suggested that they undertake a test whereby the computer will be pitted against the slide rule in a contest to undertake a series of everyday calculations. The gauntlet had been thrown down and, feeling obliged to respond in like manner, Bill Flitwick organised an event to establish the supremacy of the computer over any other means of calculation. The Mathematics Department were engaged to put together a range of straightforward calculations, of varying length, the details of which would be provided in a sealed envelope. Of course, news of the challenge spread throughout the college and, on the allotted day, the Computer Department was full to overflowing as students from both the Engineering and Mathematics Departments crowded in to witness the great event.

Mark Pendlebury was chosen to represent the

Computer Department, partly because of his studious appearance, and Matthew Bloggett was given the honour to represent the Engineering Department as it was, after all, his idea. A tutor from the Mathematics Department, Heather Brownlow, was to act as referee and generally officiate at the event. With everyone in anxious anticipation, Miss Brownlow opened the sealed envelope and recited the first sequence of calculations, while an assistant simultaneously wrote them on the blackboard. Mark Pendlebury hastily started to enter the code into the computer while Matthew Bloggett manipulated his slide rule. Mark was around two thirds of the way through inputting the instructions into the BBC Micro, aided by Bill Flitwick who was reciting from the blackboard, when Matthew casually announced the answer to the posed problem. "Correct" announced Miss Brownlow cheerfully. Pendlebury was stunned. Flitwick was not amused at all and Ernie remained puzzled. The next, slightly longer sequence of calculation was announced and written to the blackboard. Mark Pendlebury, determined to redress the situation, started to frantically enter his lines of code into the computer, urged on enthusiastically by Flitwick. About half way through the process, Matthew, once again, casually announced the answer. "Correct again" announced Miss Brownlow. And so it continued, each time the slide rule in the capable hands of young Bloggett, easily outperformed the computer. As the sequences of calculations became longer, the advantage to the slide rule became more pronounced. The issue was that, while the computer could undertake the calculation more quickly once it had all the relevant information, the time taken to enter the information in a format acceptable to the machine, rendered this advantage as null. Furthermore, if an error were to be introduced into the code, the whole process needed to be repeated, with line by line checking to find out what had gone wrong. The conclusion to the event was a resounding victory for the slide rule which, as Matthew Bloggett was pleased to point out, cost a tiny fraction of the cost of even a basic computer. The Engineering team were delighted with the result. Bill Flitwick was not amused and complained bitterly that it was an unfair contest. Clearly, there were tasks at which a properly programmed computer would excel but these were not among them. The Computer Department shrugged off their defeat as best they could, but Ernie had learned a valuable lesson; that much of the hype around computers was more to do with theoretical promise than actual delivery. It was a realisation that would come to serve him well in his later career.

And so, life continued in much the same way as the venerable Computer Department weaved its way along the path of its chosen course. There was a great deal of repetition which rankled with some of the students. Trevor Lawson emitted an endless stream of jokes upon the matter while, sadly, Joyce Barrow became disenchanted with the whole thing and quietly left half way through the second term. Ernie plodded on through the haze, disregarding the fact that he had learned nothing new after the first term, content with the realisation that it was an approved course with an associated qualification. The seasons rolled on as autumn leaves turned to the bleakness of a Fudmill Green winter, and then again to the blue skies of spring when robins cheerfully hopped among the rambling thorn bushes and crooked gravestones of St. Peter's and crows gathered around the rooftops of the College of Technology. The summer sun would burn brightly for a while and then the picture would repeat itself, as it had done for generations. The days at the Computer Department moved by in a slow procession until one day, a few weeks after the students had taken their examination, Frederick Bottom was delighted to present each remaining student with their Diploma in Computer Studies and, amid much hand shaking and congratulatory remarks, the term, and the course were over. Looking back, it seemed to Ernie that it had all been something of a blur, but here he was, at last, a qualified computer expert. The sky was now the limit and the great world of commerce beckoned.

2 THE BIG CITY

Ernie now had his diploma in Computer Studies and, after consulting various magazines and journals, picked out what he perceived to be the twenty leading organisations in computer technology. He diligently wrote to all of them, with a synopsis of his background, requesting an interview at their earliest convenience. He sat back and waited, confident that he would receive twenty offers of employment, from which he could pick and choose those that he wished to pursue. It was a longer wait than he had anticipated and, actually, not all twenty of them replied. In fact, not even half of them replied. Indeed, after three weeks of waiting, the one and only reply fell quietly on the doormat at the Trubshaw home. It was from Roderick Kington-Smythe of Brinkley Associates, the leading computer consultancy in Europe, at least, that is how they described themselves on their letterhead. Kington-Smythe explained that, as a fast expanding concern at the leading edge of the computer and systems consultancy business, they were always on the look out for unusually gifted computer scientists and that, consequently, they would be pleased to grant Mr. Trubshaw an interview. "Unusually gifted computer scientist. Well, that's me!" Ernie announced triumphantly to his parents. Mr. Trubshaw senior expressed a little surprise that the headquarters of the leading European computer consultancy should be situated off the Old Kent Road in Peckham, but Ernie explained that all the big financial concerns and leading edge technology organisations were moving south of the river in London. In any event, 3a Devon Street sounded like a fairly exclusive address, no doubt one of those new, modern, high tech office blocks.

On the allotted day, Ernie travelled up on the train to Charing Cross main line station and then took the Underground to the Elephant and Castle. After a brief altercation with a bus driver over pedestrian rights of way, Ernie crossed over the roundabout on to the New Kent Road and walked the half mile or so to the next roundabout from where the Old Kent Road branched off towards the south. Ernie felt sure that Devon Street must be towards the top end of the road. However, he walked and walked and there was no sign of Devon Street. He asked a few passers by and they gave him various, conflicting directions, indicating to Ernie that they clearly hadn't a clue where Devon Street actually was. He kept walking. Past the junction with Albany Road, past Trafalgar Avenue and right down to the

Rotherhithe New Road. "It couldn't possibly be down here", he was thinking to himself when, with the gas works suddenly looming into the skyline on his left, there was Devon Street, curving round right in front of the main storage tank. Devon Street is a short, half crescent which joins Devonshire Road which, in turn, leads to the Council rubbish tip. Along its northern edge was a short terrace of houses whose lower stories had been converted into shops. Ernie walked up and down the road, and then up and down again. There was nothing that looked like an office. He counted the houses from the end and reasoned that number three must be the Fish and Chip shop. Stepping inside, he encountered Mr. Kaimakli as he was preparing his equipment for the day ahead. On enquiring the whereabouts of Europe's largest computer consultancy, the latter looked a little puzzled, as if he didn't understand what Ernie was saying at all. "Brinkley Associates" Ernie annunciated as slowly and clearly as he could. "Ah! nei, nei" exclaimed Mr. Kaimakli, "Upstairs parakalo, parakalo, upstairs". He took Ernie to the door and, gesticulating wildly, directed him to the little alley between numbers two and three, just inside of which was a rather scruffy looking green door which bore the number 3A. Ernie turned around to thank Mr. Kaimakli, who was now hurrying back to his fryers. "Kaleemeerah!" he shouted gaily as he disappeared back into the Fish and Chip shop. "Yes, indeed" replied Ernie, his voice trailing away on the last syllable. A little apprehensive at this stage, Ernie pushed open the door and, observing a sign which said 'Brinkley Associates – First Floor' he climbed the stairs.

To Ernie's surprise, upon opening the upstairs door, he found a pleasant, cleanly decorated and quite spacious reception area, from which a corridor led towards the rear of the building. "Mr Trubshaw?" announced a bespectacled lady of middle years and efficient countenance. Upon confirmation Miss Davies, for that was her name, continued, "We have been expecting you, take a seat please". Ernie, by now much relived to find that Brinkley Associates really did exist and, in fact, seemed to be quite business like, sat down and continued to soak up the scene around him. Miss Davies, who had temporarily disappeared into the corridor, quickly returned. "Mr. Kington-Smythe will see you now" she announced coolly. As Ernie ventured into the corridor, a tall, rather elegant looking gentlemen in a pin-stripe suit and bow tie held open one of the adjoining doors. "Come in, come in" he said, as he held open the door, "My name is Kington-Smythe and you, I presume are Mr. Trubshaw?" They shook hands and exchanged pleasantries before sitting down, either side of a plain, but well made desk with a green beige insert, upon which sat two telephones and a rather nice carriage clock. "Did you have a long journey?" asked Kington-Smythe. "yes, rather" replied Ernie. "Well you found us, anyway. We are a little tucked away down here but, actually, this office is very convenient for travel within London and within the southern home counties, where many of our clients are situated". They went on to discuss Ernie's course at the College of Technology and what he knew about the world of business which, of course, was not a great deal at this stage. Nevertheless, Kington-Smythe was sympathetic and explained to Ernie who their clients were and the services that were provided to them. "The first priority is to gain a foothold, usually with the sale of one or two computers, and then to develop the relationship with the sale of additional software, consultancy services and further systems". "I see" exclaimed an enthusiastic Ernie, although, actually, he didn't really understand at all, especially when Kington-Smythe talked of service agreements and ongoing license costs. The operational structure of Brinkley Associates was discussed. Kington-Smythe ran the operation, with Miss Davies providing secretarial support. There were two existing 'business development' consultants, William Button and Joseph Dill, and Ernie, if accepted, was to be the third, with a special responsibility for Government agencies. Kington-Smythe seemed to take a liking to Ernie and the latter relaxed a little when the boss picked up the internal phone; "Priscilla, bring in some tea will you?" he asked cheerfully, and the interview continued along more detailed lines as they discussed computer systems, business software and costs. After around an hour had passed, Kington-Smythe stood up from the desk and went over to the window, with its panoramic view of the gas works. After gazing nonchalantly at the scene for a few moments, he turned around abruptly. "Well, Ernest, I think we can offer you a position at Brinkley Associates". "Oh, thank you Mr. Kington-Smythe, I would like that very much". They shook hands again. "We will put a formal offer together and post it to you this afternoon. Oh, by the way, I take it that you have a drivers licence?" "Yes, I do" replied Ernie. "Good. You will have the use of a shared car for occasions when you need to visit out of town clients". Further pleasantries were exchanged between one and all, before Ernie retraced his steps down to Devon Street.

Walking back up the Old Kent Road, a thousand thoughts entered Ernie's mind as he considered the brilliant future which surely lay ahead as a Business Development Consultant for Europe's leading computer specialists. He pictured himself hob-knobbing with senior Government officials as he helped them shape their future operations. He day-dreamed of how he would quickly become recognised as one of the country's leading computer scientists. He would be quoted in trade journals and leading magazines, his opinion would be sought on matters of high importance. He would be a celebrity back in Crinkington. The world suddenly looked a much brighter place as Ernie walked briskly back up the Old Kent Road. As he reached the roundabout and headed along the New Kent Road, it suddenly occurred to him that he should really move to London in order to be close to his place of work. By chance, on the corner of Balfour Street, he came across Blumdart's Accommodation Agency, a rather bleak looking corner shop with a number of dog-eared cards attached to a board in the window. After a brief perusal of the cards, he decided to make enquiries and pushed open the slightly sticking door, to which was attached a bell on a spring. Inside was a counter, behind which there was a doorway with a hanging streamer style blind. After a few moments Mrs Blumdart appeared. A rotund looking, middle aged lady with short brown hair, thick glass spectacles and a cigarette drooping from one side of her mouth. "Can I help you?" she said rather curtly. Ernie explained that he would be interested in finding an inexpensive flat somewhere in the vicinity. "Well, there's not much around at the moment Ducks" replied Mrs Blumdart. "You see, this is such a popular area, what with all the trade and all". She shuffled through a few cards in a little draw on the counter. "Still, we might be able to find something for you". After a little more shuffling, the ash dropped off the end of her cigarette as she lifted a card out of the draw and held it up as if to get a better view of it. Squinting through her thick spectacles she continued, "Ah! You might be in luck after all Ducks, there's a vacancy at Mrs Isaacs' in Amelia Street, just off the Walworth Road, do you know it?" "Not really" replied Ernie. "Just down from the Elephant and Castle. She's a nice lady, Mrs Isaacs" Mrs Blumdart tapped the card by its edge on the counter, "Shall I make you an appointment Ducks?". Ernie thought for a moment and, flushed with a new found confidence that he would soon be at Brinkley Associates, replied "Yes please, if you would be so kind". Mrs Blumdart stubbed out her cigarette which, by now, was almost expended anyway and picked up the phone. While she made contact with Mrs Isaacs, Ernie gazed around the little shop. The single wooden chair on his side of the counter was old and bore the scars of several generations. The half net curtains in the window were rather grubby and the linoleum on the floor was cracked in places, all of which served to establish an air of systematic neglect and decay. His thoughts on the subject were suddenly interrupted by Mrs Blumdart's raised voice. "Thursday morning all right for you Ducks?" "What?, oh yes, that should be all right" replied Ernie. A few telephonic salutations to Mrs Isaacs later, Mrs Blumdart replaced the receiver and pulled out a blank card from another draw and proceeded to write down the address. "You will need to pay two weeks in advance and one week to me as a fee" she suggested while continuing to write on the card. "Well, I haven't seen it yet" exclaimed a rather startled Ernie. "That's all right Ducks, pop along on Thursday and, if you decide to go ahead, come in and see me afterwards" suggested Mrs Blumdart as she handed Ernie the card. He thanked her for her assistance and promised to come back on Thursday, whatever he decided. Outside the little shop, he looked at the card. 23 Amelia Street, Mrs Isaacs, 10.30. The address had a nice ring to it, thought Ernie as he headed on towards the Elephant and Castle underground station. Events were starting to take a most interesting turn in the life and affairs of Ernest Trubshaw.

Coincidently, on the Thursday morning, Ernie's job offer from Brinkley Associates arrived by the early post. He was to be a Business Development Consultant with special responsibilities for Government agencies and was to present himself on Monday 13th October at the Devon Street headquarters for further instructions. The remuneration wasn't extensive to start, but there was a generous commission scheme and Ernie was confident that he would do very well. It was with a sense of destiny and a spring in his step that Ernie set off for Amelia Street on that rather bleak autumn day. Back on the main line to Charing Cross, he hardly noticed the minutes fly by. Down the stairs and on the underground to the Elephant and Castle and then, just a few minutes walk down the Walworth Road and there, on the right, was Amelia Street, a pleasant enough little road of Victorian terraced houses with the occasional little shop. No. 23 was down on the left, with a red door and brass door knocker and letterbox. Above the door was a half moon shaped coloured glass window with the number 23 depicted clearly upon it. Ernie knocked twice and waited. A few moments later, the door was pulled open and a slightly built, stern looking lady with greying hair beckoned him inside. "You must be Mr Trubshaw" she suggested coolly as she looked him up and down. "Yes, that's right" replied Ernie, "Mrs Blumdart sent me from the agency" "Well, I have a very nice flat on the first floor which should suit you nicely. If you follow me I will show it to you". As they climbed the stairs she continued, "This is a respectable house mind, no coming and going after ten o'clock and no drinking on the premises". Ernie assured her as to his compliance with the stipulated conditions as she unlocked one of two doors which opened on to the first floor landing and pushed open the door. Inside was a sparsely furnished bed-sitting room with a separate, rather small bathroom and a little cooking area behind a folding screen door, which also housed a coin operated electric meter. The window curtains and the carpet had both seen better days, and the floral wallpaper was distinctly faded. Ernie looked around and considered that, while not exactly his ideal in living accommodation, it would serve his purpose while he worked his way up the executive ladder at Brinkley Associates. Furthermore, it was conveniently situated as he could cut through the residential streets, back to the Old Kent Road and down to Devon Street, which was within a reasonable walking distance. After a little negotiation and a few more assertions from Mrs Isaacs as to the respectability of 23 Amelia Street, it was agreed that Ernie would move in on Monday next, whereupon he would pay Mrs Isaacs two weeks rent in advance and then pay weekly in advance from then on.

Ernie returned home to Crinkington where he would start planning his future. He bought a new suit and a couple of new shirts from the discount tailor in town and some new shoes from the shoe shop. He perused the local bookshop to see if there were any books on computing but, of course, there wasn't really a demand for such literature in Crinkington. However, he did buy a couple of business magazines in order to familiarise himself with the terminology of the commercial world. He assured his parents that this would be the start of a glistening career in which he would surely excel and quickly make a name for himself as a leading light in the computer industry. The senior Trubshaws seemed a little bemused at this revelation, but Ernie's mind was made up and he would not be swayed from the course of destiny, the wheels of which were starting to turn on his behalf. Within a few days, he had taken up residence at 23 Amelia Street and was ready to start work at Brinkley Associates on October 13th as planned.

Enterprise House

3 DISILLUSIONMENT

Debate is a wonderful thing. From ancient times to the present, the intellectual exchange of ideas within a natural philosophical framework has been a hallmark of civilisation. From the Roman amphitheatres to the Royal Society, like minded individuals have striven to advance the cause of humanity and science. On the morning upon which Ernie first arrived at Brinkley Associates, there was a lively debate under way between his two colleagues, William Button and Joseph Dill, as to who would have the company car for the day. Apparently, it was customary for them to have the car on alternate days but, on this particular day, Bill Button wanted it when it was really Joe's turn. Various arguments were put forward as to why each had the strongest claim on the vehicle while Miss Davies quietly prepared the office for the coming day. The debate was interrupted by Roderick Kington-Smythe who introduced Ernie and pointed out that there were now three claims upon the custody of the aforementioned company vehicle. The countenance of Ernie's new colleagues was somewhat dimmed by this new revelation and they looked upon him with an undisguised air of suspicion. It was quickly agreed that they would share the car on that day and they departed after a brief handshake and acknowledgement of their new colleague. Kington-Smythe then spent the morning educating Ernie as to the way they conducted their affairs at Brinkley Associates and what was expected of him in his new job.

"The main thing is to get something on the client's premises, even if it is a single computer" explained the boss. "After that, we can sell them a plethora of consultancy services as we systematically complicate the situation by putting in more computers and more software". Ernie thought for a moment. "What about support?" he asked. "Support!" beamed Kington-Smythe, "That's just another word for further sales opportunities. If they want support, you explain to them that they have the wrong systems and need to upgrade to the enterprise level, fully supported plan". "What happens then?" asked Ernie. "Then we make sure that the software they have bought will never actually achieve what they wanted and they will be forced to constantly upgrade and reconfigure their systems". "But they may not be competent to undertake such a task" suggested Ernie. "Exactly" responded the boss, "So they will need more consultancy and more products". Ernie thought again.

"Is that really fair though?" he asked. Kington-Smythe's features darkened a little. "Who said anything about being fair? I am trying to run a business here". He scrutinized Ernie closely. "Look Trubshaw, you are in the real world now. If you want to get paid at the end of the month, we need to maintain a steady flow of sales. We are not a charitable organisation". Ernie took the point and assured Kington-Smythe that he would do his utmost to ensure a continued healthy flow of the aforementioned sales. "Good!" replied the boss, "Now let's get down to who your clients will be". Miss Davies brought in some directories and public sector magazines and Ernie was directed to wade through them and make a short list of 20 prospects for the week ahead. When complete, he was to discuss this list with the boss, explaining why he had chosen those on the list and what his approach to them was going to be. After a little discussion and further instruction from the experienced Mr. Kington-Smythe, Ernie worked with Miss Davies to set up some appointments and start to manage his calendar. All of his initial list of prospects could be reached by public transport and so there was no need for him to engage in battle with his colleagues over the car. The reason for only having one car, the boss explained, was that there was only one spare parking space, once the Kington-Smythe conveyance, a shiny blue Jaguar, had been safely docked at 3A Devon Street. This sounded plausible, although it didn't explain why the car had to be an ageing Vauxhall with faded red paintwork and missing wheel trims. No doubt that particular model was economical to run and well suited to London streets, reasoned Ernie. He returned to Amelia Street that evening, satisfied with his first day at the office and confident that he would soon make his mark as a valued contributor to the fortunes of Brinkley Associates. The world was fast adopting the appearance of Ernie's oyster.

The next morning was rather bleak, with a constant drizzle from a uniform grey sky which hung over London like a malignant overcoat. Nevertheless, Ernie was in good spirits as he finished his corn flakes and prepared for the day ahead. He had four prospects for the day, all of them Government agencies, scattered around the south western corner of the city. A last slurp of tea, a little straightening of his tie and he was ready to exchange the dreary cosiness of Mrs Isaac's establishment for the bustling life of the city. He hurried across to the Old Kent Road where he jumped on the 453 bus to take him to Trafalgar Square. His first port of call was a ministerial building in Whitehall Place, adjacent to Scotland Yard, which housed various functions associated with the Cabinet Office. He was to meet with a Mr Sykes, the office manager. Ernie found the correct address in good time and paused for a moment outside the nicely painted door with its big brass door-knob. He took a deep breath and pushed open the door to reveal a small reception area, wherein was seated an efficient looking young lady behind an enormous typewriter. Ernie explained his mission and was invited to take a seat while he awaited the office manager. Presently, Sykes appeared and ushered Ernie into a large, sparsely furnished room with a large wooden desk, right in the middle. Against the main wall were a row of filing cabinets, with carefully annotated drawers. Sykes, a studious looking man in a well worn pin-striped suit, invited Ernie to tell him all about computers and how they would revolutionise his department.

Ernie entered upon a grand evangelising talk about the future world and the importance of computers to all endeavours, especially those in the public sector domain. After a few minutes, Mr Sykes waved his hand somewhat dismissively; "That's all very well, but what are we actually supposed to do with them. Give me some practical examples". Ernie was unprepared for such a direct question and, after a moments hesitation, glanced at the filing cabinets and announced triumphantly, "You could transfer all your filing system and records on to the computer". "Why?" asked Mr. Sykes. "Well, it is much easier to have them all on the computer, you can find things more easily" suggested Ernie in a slightly less confident tone. Mr Sykes shook his head gently. "We have an excellent filing system in which Miss Timmins and I can find anything within seconds. Why should we want to go to all the trouble of transferring this to a computer? We would then have to start up the computer and wait while it finds what we are looking for". Ernie could see that some quick thinking and positive assertions were needed. "Ah!" he smiled benignly, "But you could also store all your documents on the computer, sort through them and, when required print them out on the printer". Sykes look puzzled. "Why would I want to do that?" he asked. "Well, that's the beauty of computers, you can get them to organise things in whatever manner you wish" responded Ernie. Sykes rose from his seat, went over to the filing cabinet and opened a drawer. "I have all my documents ready to hand right here and, when appropriate, we archive them to a secure store where they are all filed and cross referenced. I know exactly where I can find any document that this office has ever issued. They are all kept safely and I don't have to rely on a computer or any other electronic wizardry to access them". Ernie decided to take a different tack. "Computers are also excellent at calculations and maintaining numerical data. You could have all your accounts on the computer and ready to hand at all times" he smiled, his spirits lifting a little with this important revelation. "Our accounts *are* ready to hand at all times. We keep comprehensive books, which our accountant maintains meticulously" replied Sykes. After a little more duelling along similar lines, Ernie realised that he was not going to get very far with Mr. Sykes. The latter, starting to feel a little sorry for Ernie, suggested that he send him a brochure outlining the computer and its capabilities, which he would be pleased to read, and then file in his filing system.

Leaving Whitehall Place, just a little crest-fallen, Ernie convinced himself that Sykes must be an exception and that his next prospective client would, no doubt, be very different and would readily appreciate the value of computers and what they could do for the department. He made his way back up Whitehall towards Cockspur Street, where another Government agency was situated, with another nicely painted door and brass door knocker. Inside was another nicely manicured young lady, not dissimilar to Miss Timmins, who similarly invited Ernie to take a seat. This time he was meeting with Mr. Brough. After a while, the latter appeared and beckoned Ernie into another large room with a large wooden desk right in the centre and an adjacent wall bedecked with the same grey filing cabinets. "Now son, what can I do for you?" asked Mr. Brough in a strong northern accent. Ernie suggested that, no doubt, the department had been wondering about computers and how they could help them in their daily endeavours. "Can't say that I have lad" responded Brough. Ernie then launched into his evangelising talk once again, but was interrupted in mid stream by an impatient, but good natured Brough. "Yes, yes lad, that's all very well and good, but what do these computer things actually do?" Ernie was now better prepared for such a question and, nodding towards the filing cabinets, explained how Mr.

Brough's department could revolutionise their entire filing system and have everything on a single computer. "And what happens when it breaks down?" asked Brough innocently. Ernie's eyes lit up as he remembered Kington-Smythe's advice. "Ah!" he said triumphantly, "You can take out a separate service contract and we will guarantee a next day response within the working week". Brough stood up and walked over to the filing cabinets. Tapping one of them affectionately he said, "See this cabinet here lad, I can find any document I ever want within seconds. They are all beautifully annotated and cross referenced by Miss Wilkins. After a while, we archive them to a secure store, where they are also labelled and cross referenced. I know exactly where to find any document or communication that this office has ever issued". "Ah, but what about all your accounts. The computer can also store all of those" responded Ernie in desperation. "Young Wetherall keeps books" responded Brough, "and he can tell me anything I need to know in that department". Brough came back and patted Ernie on the back. "Sorry to disappoint you lad, but you see we don't need any computers here, we have everything under control and it all runs like clockwork. Why don't you send in a brochure and we will keep it on file". Ernie thanked him for his time and exited back out onto Cockspur Street. It was almost lunchtime and he decided to call in at Antonio's sandwich bar for a cup of tea and, one of the specialities of the house, a toasted cheese sandwich.

Antonio's friendly banter and good fare lifted Ernie's spirits and, after a while, he was ready to go and meet his next prospects.

Up the road to Pall Mall, a little further along and he found himself in St. James' Square, where there was another nicely painted door and brass door knob. It was Mr. Jenkins this time, with an almost identical dialogue around filing cabinets, archives and accounts. Then Ernie made his way up Lower Regent Street, into Piccadilly and across to Sackville Street, to another nicely painted door and brass door knob, behind which resided Mr. Dowling, who had the patter about filing cabinets, archives and book-keeping down to a fine art. Exiting in as dignified a manner as he was able to maintain under the circumstances, Ernie walked back to Trafalgar Square and caught the 453 bus back to Peckham. His first day as a leading computer consultant had not been quite the resounding success that he had hoped for, but it was a start and he was beginning to get a feel for client meetings. He would just have to find another line of approach. A form of logical reasoning that his clients would find irresistible, but what could this reasoning be? He looked casually out of the bus window at the various shops and businesses and all the people busily going about their particular endeavours. Then it struck him. Computers could do *anything*. He would reverse his approach and simply ask his clients what they wanted to do and then whatever they answered, he would explain that a computer system would be absolutely perfect for them and that he could help them achieve their goals accordingly. He congratulated himself on his reasoning and looked forward to another day at the cutting edge of the computer business.

The next morning dawned bright, with clear skies and a gentle, cool breeze. Ernie renewed his acquaintance with the corn flakes before pulling the door of 23 Amelia Street closed behind him and heading off for the bus stop on the Old Kent Road. Sitting on the upper deck of the 453, he rehearsed his sales patter and was becoming increasingly confident that his propositions would prove irresistible. There were four nicely painted doors with brass door knobs awaiting Ernie's pleasure, at Savoy Place, William IV Street, Exeter Street and King Charles Street. Behind the doors, Messrs Hinkle, Todding, Richards and Cummins were eagerly preparing to lock swords with young Trubshaw. The familiar patter included phrases such as; "Yes, but we don't want anything" and "Why would we want to do that?" and "We already have a perfectly good system" with the equally familiar closing line of "Send us a brochure and we will keep it on file". Clearly, these Government types were ignorant of the wonders that computers could bring to them. Why couldn't they see the benefits of paying over the odds for complicated computer systems, service contracts, incessant software upgrades and the need to retrain all their staff? It all seemed so obvious. At least, it did to

Kington-Smythe and Ernie. He decided that, the next day, he would call in at the office and discuss the matter with the boss. Perhaps they should have some explanatory brochures that Ernie could leave with his clients or, even better, send in ahead of his meetings. In any event, he needed to find a different approach.

The next morning, arriving early at Devon Street, he bumped into Bill Button. "How are you getting on Ernie?", asked the latter with a slight sneer in his voice. Ernie explained that he was not quite there yet and Bill emitted a loud guffaw. Drawing Ernie to one side he spoke quietly, "They tried to get me to take on the Government side of things, but I quickly realised I was flogging a dead horse. There is no incentive for them to buy anything much, whereas the commercial folk are much easier to influence. That's why I concentrate on small businesses, they are mostly dead stupid and will buy anything if you tell them it will help their business to prosper. Accountants and Estate Agents are the best, they like to buy a computer just so they can sit it on the office desk, just to show that they have one. Most of the time it isn't even plugged in, ha!". Bill rather cheerfully patted Ernie on the back and made his way out of the office. Miss Davies eyed Ernie up and down rather suspiciously until the boss arrived. Kington-Smythe breezed into the office waving a copy of the Financial Times towards Ernie. "Ah!, I'm glad you've come in this morning Trubshaw, it's time we had a chat to see how you are progressing". The two of them disappeared into Kington-Smythe's office, closing the door behind them and Miss Davies continued to open the morning mail and attend to her nails. "Well Trubshaw, tell me how you have been getting on" asked the boss. Ernie explained that there seemed to be no real need for computers in Government offices, at least not in those that he had visited so far. "You have to be persistent" insisted Kington-Smythe. "Don't let them fool around with you and don't take no for an answer. They need computers, whether they like it or not. It's just a question of how many". "But they don't seem to see it that way" rejoined Ernie. "Then they're a bunch of ignorant blighters" insisted Kington-Smythe. "The thing is..." started Ernie, but he was interrupted most bluntly by the sound of the boss's fist coming down on the desk. "No ifs or buts Trubshaw, as I have said before, we are not a charitable organisation, you just have to get out there and make them understand that they need computers. And software. And consultancy services to help them get started. So be a good fellow and go and sell them something". A rather puzzled Ernie left the European office of Brinkley Associates and, as he was just about to exit from the alleyway, bumped into Mr. Kaimakli. "Please, this way" said the latter, gesticulating towards the door of the Fish and Chip shop. "I give you some free chips, nei?". Ernie went inside where Mr. Kaimakli gave him a rather small bag of chips and handed him the vinegar bottle. Ernie sat and nibbled at the chips as he stared at the world outside the shop window. "You new here?" asked Mr. Kaimakli with a smile. "Yes" replied Ernie, "I just started this week". "Ah, then you come here at lunch time and I get you nice fish and chips" suggested the ebullient Mr. Kaimakli. Ernie thanked him for his free chips and headed towards the door. "Kaleemeerah!" shouted the proprietor gaily. "Kaleemeerah" responded Ernie cheerfully, reasonably assured that this represented some sort of friendly greeting.

Ernie headed out once more into the hostile world of Government agencies and their various offices dotted around south west London. The driver and conductor of the 453 from Peckham got to know him quite well as he daily went about his business. He was working hard at his job and felt sure that a breakthrough would come at any moment. Unfortunately, his basic salary was barely enough to meet his living expenses and, occasionally, he got a little behind with his rent at 23 Amelia Street. Mrs Isaacs was not overly impressed with the situation. "We are not a charitable organisation Mr Trubshaw" she would say emphatically. "I know Mrs Isaacs and I shall have the rent for you on Friday, I promise" would be Ernie's standard response. The days ran into weeks in a blur of nicely painted doors, brass door knockers, requests for brochures and the occasional bag of fish and chips and then, on a cold, grey December morning, the sun suddenly burst through the skies and, as if by divine intervention, Ernie's breakthrough arrived.

It was at the Ministry of Agriculture and Fisheries where Ernie met with Mr. Desmond Pyle, a wiry man of medium height with sandy hair and bulging eyes who seemed perfectly suited to his position at the Ministry of Ag and Fish as it was popularly known. Ernie proceeded through his usual line of patter, slightly bewildered by the fact that Mr Pyle didn't interrupt him, not even once, but sat quietly at his desk with a quizzical smile on his face, as though deep in some pleasant thought. Ernie wondered if he was perhaps remembering his holidays or some other more pleasurable occasion. Nevertheless, Ernie ploughed on stoically and even gave a special flourish at the end with the conviction that computers were the future of civilisation. There was a pause, and then Mr Pyle suddenly sat bolt upright in his chair, his hands clasped tightly together. "I say, how absolutely marvellous" he exclaimed joyfully. "And I could really have all my files and records on that wonderful little computer?" he asked innocently. After his previous experiences, Ernie was wondering if this was some sort of joke on Mr Pyle's part, but nevertheless decided to give him the benefit of the doubt. "Yes, of course" he assured the office manager of the Ministry of Ag and Fish. "And how much would one of these computer thingies cost?" asked Pyle. Ernie, slightly taken off guard, thought for a moment, took the recommended price and added around a third on top. "Somewhere around a thousand pounds" he suggested. "Is that all!" exclaimed Pyle somewhat incredulously. Ernie thought quickly, his pulse accelerating; "Of course, there will be an installation and commissioning charge, the cost of the associated software and you will probably want a printer, let's say around three thousand pounds". Pyle eased back in his chair with his fingertips together and his bulging eyes raised to the ceiling, looking a little like a frog. "How soon can you deliver?" he suddenly blurted out. The shock was almost too much for Ernie, but he quickly composed himself. "I will have to check stock levels, they are of course very much in demand. But if you give me the order now, I might be able to get something to you next week". They continued to thrash out the details and Mr Pyle gave instructions to Miss Boltrope to type out the order then and there. Ernie left the office and walked through the streets on his way to the bus stop in a state of grace. He didn't hear his own footsteps and had no recollection of his pedestrian route before arriving at the bus stop, just as the 453 came along the road. He hopped on joyously and scrambled up the stairs to take his usual seat by the rearmost window. George, the conductor came up after him; "The Old Kent Road is it sir?" he asked with a smile. "Yes please", replied Ernie. "Turned out nice again!" suggested George as he cranked the handle of his ticket machine and handed Ernie his ticket. "Yes, it is indeed a beautiful day" confirmed Ernie as he paid his fare and then sat back to relive his triumphant activities of that glorious morning.

Kington-Smythe was suitably impressed. "Good man,

Trubshaw. Now make sure that they have just enough to whet their appetite, but not enough to be able to do anything useful. Then you can go back in and sell them some more software". He thought for a moment. "The Ministry of Agriculture and Fisheries, you say? They should be able to accommodate a good few computers. Find out where their other offices are and start hitting them as well". Ernie was so pleased with his success that he even offered to stand Miss Davies a bag of fish and chips downstairs at Mr Kaimakli's emporium. "No thank you" she replied rather haughtily, with her nose pointing distinctly skyward. Ernie shrugged his shoulders and went downstairs to order one of Mr Kaimakli's finest, with salt, vinegar and all the trimmings. They enjoyed some innocuous banter while Ernie tucked in to his chips, before parting again, against a background duet of "Kaleemeerah!" as Ernie pulled shut the door and headed back upstairs to attend to the detail of his order. It was straightforward enough, one of the new fangled 'personal computers' with some word processing software, a printer, keyboard and one of those new pointing devices which Miss Davies thought was ridiculously named, after all they don't squeak, they are not cuddly and don't seem to do very much at all when you stand and watch them. In order to make a good impression with his new client, Ernie thought it would be a good idea to borrow the car the next morning and deliver the new computer personally. That would surely impress the Ministry of Ag and Fish who would certainly not be used to such efficiency. Kington-Smythe agreed. "Good idea Trubshaw, after all we have everything in stock and it will be a good opportunity to tell them about the other software which they shall need". It was all agreed. "Just one thing though Trubshaw" he ventured, just as Ernie was leaving the room, "You can't have the car tomorrow as Bill Button is taking it down to Slough to visit one of our most important clients. Better take the bus instead". Ernie spent the rest of the afternoon packaging everything up into two big parcels, tied up with string and with a makeshift string handle on each one. They were heavy, but Ernie reasoned that he should just about be able to mange them. In any event, the 453 passed quite close to the Ministry of Ag and Fish. Ernie duly took the parcels home with him, in order that he might make an early start the next morning. However, with every step towards Amelia Street the parcels became heavier and heavier, the string cutting into Ernie's hands and leaving big ridges imprinted on the underside of his fingers. He decided that he would have to improvise some better handles for the morning.

The next day dawned slowly and mischievously, with dark clouds on the horizon which seemed to making directly for Amelia Street. Ernie bid adieu to his cornflake bowl and, with some old magazines wrapped around the string handles of his parcels, pulled the door closed behind him. He had taken no more than twenty paces and was congratulating himself on his ingenuity when a frighteningly loud thunderclap seemed to shake the very pavement he was walking on. He hurried towards the bus stop as quickly as he could. There was no shelter there, but he might be lucky and catch the earlier bus. As he hurried along, the magazines wrapped around the string handles started to disintegrate and fall in little soggy patches to the ground, leaving an identifying trail of Ernie's journey. The cardboard boxes housing the equipment started to become equally soggy and the string cut into them, rendering them a little unstable. Ernie rushed even faster until he came to the bus stop. There was no bus in sight and no-one at the stop, suggesting to Ernie that he had just missed the earlier bus. He tried to duck into the doorway of an adjoining shop, but the rain was blowing in almost horizontally and Ernie continued to get soaked. He tried his best however to protect the cardboard boxes, lest they should fall apart completely. Eventually, the 453 appeared on the horizon and Ernie stumbled to the bus stop to meet it. George, the conductor who, by now, knew Ernie well, laughed out aloud. "Gordon Bennet Ernie, what have you got there! Looks like you've run off with the office safe". "Very funny!" replied a dripping and dishevelled Trubshaw as he struggle to fit himself and his parcels into a single bench seat. George rattled his ticket machine and Ernie retrieved a half crown from his sodden wet pocket. "Look, its turning out beautiful now" quipped George. And indeed it was; all the way up the Old Kent Road and round the bottom half of

Trafalgar Square, the sun shone down joyfully upon London Town. It was only after Ernie had alighted and adjusted his parcels that the heavens opened up once again and continued what Ernie was now taking as a personal affront upon his dignity. Pushing open the door at the Ministry of Ag and Fish, he was greeted by a shriek from Miss Gloria Boltrope, who was not used to such apparitions, certainly not at that time in the morning. "I've brought your order" explained Ernie, as the rain continued to trickle from his face, his clothes, his parcels and on to the Ministerial carpet. Miss Boltrope looked horrified and quickly picked up the internal telephone in order to warn Mr. Pyle. "It's that man again" she blurted into the receiver, "He has come with the computer – I think". A minute or two later, Desmond Pyle appeared from the corridor, beaming happily. "My dear boy, you shouldn't have troubled, not in this weather". "Well, we always strive to give prompt service" replied Ernie. "What are those!" cried a horrified Pyle as his eyes suddenly beheld two jumbled piles of soggy cardboard with coils of wet string dangling from them. "This is your new computer" replied Ernie proudly. "I am afraid the boxes may have become a little damp" Mr Pyle's jaw dropped, his eyes bulged and he started to stammer a little. "Don't worry" Ernie reassured him, "Everything will be fine. The computer is protected with a plastic wrapping. Where would you like it set up?". Pyle regained his composure as best he could, and led Ernie back into his office. "I will get a table brought in" he suggested, while Ernie started to peel off layers of wet cardboard as if he was peeling an orange. Actually, the computer, which was an ex-demonstration model, hadn't been protected by a plastic wrapper after all, but it didn't look too bad and Ernie borrowed some tissues from Miss Boltrope in order to dry it off a little. By the time Pyle returned with the table, both computer and printer were looking in their prime and ready for action. Amazingly, after connecting everything up, Ernie was astonished to find that the computer actually worked and that he was able to demonstrate it to a very happy Desmond Pyle, who was becoming more pleased with his purchase with every passing minute. Ernie made some recommendations for some additional software which Mr Pyle said he would consider most carefully.

And so, against all the odds, Ernie had found a Government Sector customer and managed to deliver a working computer into the Ministerial office. It was no small achievement. But some people are never satisfied, and Kington-Smythe, just like Rocco in the film Key Largo, wanted more. "That's all very well Trubshaw" he insisted, "But you will need a couple of those every week, plus follow on orders, in order to keep things on an even keel". And so Ernie went out once more into the cold hard world of Government agencies in order to repeat his success with the Ministry of Ag and Fish. He knocked on every nicely painted door and spoke to every Miss Boltrope look-alike, and was even introduced to some senior managers, but all to no avail. However, at least once a week, he would call in on Desmond Pyle, under the pretence of seeing how things were going, and usually walked out with another order for one thing or another. This kept a steady flow of orders coming through, even if the value was rather lower than Ernie would have liked, given his paltry commission payments. This was particularly relevant as Mrs Isaacs was becoming a bit touchy about the tardiness of Ernie's rent payments. Even though she frequently reminded him that she was not a charitable organisation, Ernie was rarely forthcoming on the due date and was becoming increasingly behind on his payments. He had economised on his other outgoings as best he could, but things remained rather difficult. Still, with luck, he might find another client soon and this would double his chance of selling additional peripherals. After all, Desmond Pyle now had three computers, a network router and associated network software, three sets of word processing software, three spreadsheet programs, a database and a few other bits and pieces. Ernie just needed two or three additional clients like the Ministry of Ag and Fish and he would be able to make it all work nicely enough. Such were his thoughts as he entered his third month with Brinkley Associates.

Fate works in strange ways and, on a dreary February morning, it decided to deal Ernie Trubshaw a particularly cruel blow. It seems that the hard disk on Desmond Pyle's main computer crashed. This was the one where he kept all his files and all the records that had, very laboriously, been entered into the database. This event also seemed to corrupt the network and it was found that the two remaining machines would not only fail to communicate with each other, but would also fail to start properly at all. A distraught Mr Pyle rang Brinkley Associates and managed to get through to Kington-Smythe. "Have you got a maintenance agreement with us?" asked the latter. "What maintenance agreement? Nobody said anything about a maintenance agreement" replied Pyle. Kington-Smythe explained that, without a maintenance agreement to charge against, regrettably, there was nothing he could do. Upon receiving this pearl of commercial wisdom, Desmond Pyle found a few words which were not often heard at the Ministry and indicated, in round about terms, that Brinkley Associates could have all their computer equipment back forthwith. The next morning when Ernie happened to call in at the office, he was instructed to hot foot it to the Ministry of Ag and Fish and sort out their problems, without delay. He was soon on the 453 and turning over in his mind how he would quickly solve all their difficulties and, perhaps, might even be able to sell some more software. Pushing open the nicely painted front door, he was met by a particularly cool Miss Boltrope who advised him to take a seat. After a few minutes he was ushered in to Desmond

Pyle's office. Ernie quickly noticed that the main computer was not on Pyle's desk where it belonged. "Have you relocated the computer" he asked innocently. "Yes" answered Pyle sharply, "We have relocated it back to your office and shall be demanding a full refund accordingly" "But if there is a fault with the computer, it can soon be fixed" advised Ernie, "Indeed, that is why I have called in". "And how are you going to replace all the data we have lost, and how are you going to compensate us for all the wasted hours inputting it in the first place?" enquired Pyle. "Ah" replied Ernie, his agile brain racing to find a satisfactory explanation. "Well, that is always a risk with computers of course, although we do have a very good data backup system that you might be interested in". Pyle assured him that he was not interested and that he did not expect to see Ernie at the Ministry of Ag and Fish ever again. "It was a bad idea" he concluded, "We shall return to our tried and tested system". With that announcement, he wished Ernie a good day and gesticulated towards the door. Realising that the probability of getting any further with Mr. Pyle at this juncture was minimal, Ernie decided to return to the office in order to consider his next move.

Back at 3A Devon Street, Ernie's arrival was preceded by the arrival of all the Ministry's computer equipment, roughly wrapped in ministerial brown paper. Kington-Smythe was not amused. "Well Trubshaw", he announced, "You had better ensure that this stuff is checked over and returned to the client immediately". Ernie explained that such a course of action might prove a little difficult, given Pyle's earlier directive. "I hope not for your sake" replied Kington-Smythe as he disappeared into his office. Ernie checked the equipment and replaced the hard disk in the main computer. He also connected everything together again and confirmed that the network equipment was also working. He then telephoned the Ministry. Upon eventually getting through to Desmond Pyle, he announced in a cheery voice; "I have good news for you Mr. Pyle, all the equipment has been checked over and we have replaced the hard disk in the main computer at no charge. When shall I deliver it back to you". "You can keep it. I don't want any of it back". "But it was only a minor glitch" assured Ernie, "Everything should be fine from now on". "I don't care whether it was minor or not. I am not having that equipment back in the office. It has wasted an enormous amount of everyone's time". Ernie explained that they do not usually accept equipment back once it has been sold. "That is your problem" replied Pyle. He added that he would expect a full refund before the end of the week. Ernie relayed this information back to Kington-Smythe. "Well, they can't have a refund. They bought the equipment and it now belongs to them. Besides, they have lost the original packaging". Ernie sidestepped the issue of the packaging and suggested that they might perhaps retain some goodwill if they were to make a refund on this occasion. After all, there are other ministries and, no doubt, new orders would soon be flooding in. But Kington-Smythe was adamant. So was Desmond Pyle.

A week or two passed by and the computers sat, gathering dust, in a corner at Devon Street. Ernie continued canvassing new clients, but no new orders were coming in. And then, one morning when he called into the office, he was summoned to Kington-Smythe's office. "Have you seen this?" bellowed the boss. "Your friend at the Ministry is claiming compensation for lost time, on top of demanding a full refund". "Well, I did suggest that we should have refunded him immediately" suggested Ernie. "And where would we be if every computer we sold had to be refunded?" asked Kington-Smythe angrily. Ernie was temporarily lost for an answer. "Trubshaw, we cannot have this sort of thing happening at Brinkley Associates. We are terminating your employment forthwith" bellowed Kington-Smythe before adding "Oh, and by the way, you shall have to pay back the commission you earned on the Ministry sale". Ernie was devastated. This was not the trajectory he had in mind for his career as one of the country's leading computer scientists. He retuned to 23 Amelia Street where he was greeted by Mrs. Isaacs who immediately asked him for the rent. "I shall have it at the end of the week" he assured her. He had wondered whether he might ask Mrs Isaacs for a small loan in order to pay back his commission to Brinkley Associates, but, observing the tone of her expression, he considered that this might not be a particularly good idea. That evening, he sat in his apartment and considered his options. The process didn't take very long as there were really not many of them to consider. The next morning, he hurried round to all the local employment agencies in order to get a feel for available vacancies in the computer industry. That didn't take long either. There weren't any. He returned to Amelia Street, somewhat dejected. There was only one thing for it. That evening, he packed his suitcase and, when everyone was safely in bed, he quietly let himself out of the front door and posted the key back in the letterbox. He had left a short note for Mrs. Isaacs, regretting any inconvenience and assuring her of his best intentions.

Ernie wandered around for the rest of the night, wondering where he might go where he would be safe from both Mrs. Isaacs and Kington-Smythe. After much deliberation, he remembered that he had an auntie Freda who lived in the quiet little hamlet of Boggle-on-Sea, somewhere down on the Thames estuary. She would surely put him up while he readjusted his career. He might even start his own little business. After all, he had learned much at Brinkley Associates as to how the computer business operated and it didn't seem that difficult. He made his way over to Fenchurch Street station, where everything was closed for the night, and, choosing a nearby bench, he sat and rested his eyes for a while. At six the next morning, the station was open and Ernie presented himself at the ticket window as porters swept the pavement around him. "Second class, one way to Boggle please" he asked a bemused ticket officer. "Where?" the latter replied in astonishment. "Boggle-on Sea" Ernie affirmed. The ticket officer perused a faded list of stations on the adjacent wall. "Ah, Boggle" he announced triumphantly. "Yes, I remember now, leaves from platform four on the old line". Ernie just about had enough loose change for the fare and a ticket was duly procured. He made his way over to platform four, sat on one of the slatted benches and patiently awaited the next train to Boggle-on-Sea.

Enterprise House

4 THE MOVE TO BOGGLE

It was eight o clock on a dreary Thursday morning when Ernie arrived at the quaint little station at Boggle-on-Sea, which hadn't changed much since Victorian times. He roughly remembered where auntie Freda lived and, after asking directions, made his way over to Westminster Drive and knocked on the door of number nine, a semi-detached 1930s built house with a nice little front lawn and hanging flower baskets by the front door. "Hello auntie Freda" announced Ernie cheerfully. "Hello, eh.." she replied, not having a clue who Ernie was. "I am your nephew, Ernie" "Oh, I see" replied Freda, still not absolutely sure who she was speaking with. "Well, you had better come in" she continued, looking a little suspiciously at Ernie's suitcase. Freda made some tea and brought out some scones which had been made previously, and Ernie recounted recent events to her, explaining that he intended to start his own computer consultancy in Boggle-on-Sea and wondered whether she might be able to put him up for a while, just while he was getting started. Freda, who had been living alone since her husband Arnold had passed away some years back, was intrigued by the thought of having a lodger and agreed to let Ernie stay. "Of course, I won't be able to pay any rent for a while" he explained, "but I will make it up to you later, when I have established the business". Freda looked a little bemused for a moment or two, wondering whether this was a good idea after all, but then, on balance she concluded that it would be nice to have some company in the house. "Oh, I see" she smiled, "Well, I suppose that would be all-right. I will set up the spare room for you". Ernie was truly grateful for auntie Freda's support at this awkward time and resolved that, when he was a millionaire, which probably wouldn't take very long, he would remember her kindness towards him.

Having settled in at 9, Westminster Drive, Ernie set about looking for some low rent office accommodation. Freda had suggested that he tried the local Council as they seemed always to be either selling off or renting out property, as Boggle wasn't exactly booming at that time. Ernie duly went around to the Council offices where he met with a Mr. Pembroke who was in charge of properties and commercial lettings. Actually, Mr. Pembroke very rarely had any visitors as, strangely, not many first rate, successful organisations chose Boggle-on-Sea as their home location. When Ernie enquired at reception, the young lady thought for a few moments, as if trying to remember something. "Ah..." she said at last, "That will be Mr. Pembroke's office". After consulting an internal list, she directed Ernie to a first floor rearward facing office where Pembroke was enjoying a quiet cup of tea, his third that morning. After Ernie had explained what he was looking for and how much he thought he could afford to pay in rental, Mr. Pembroke stroked his chin and looked nonchalantly at the wall for a moment. "Well" he finally exclaimed, "There is not much available at that sort of cost. However, I think I might have something for you". He rummaged around in his desk drawer and brought out a memorandum that described a certain property. "There is a new development called Enterprise House, situated in a lovely, quiet location at Estuary Gardens. I believe that it might suit you perfectly and, by chance, there is just one unit left". The address, No.1, Estuary Gardens sounded very upmarket to Ernie and he was keen to view the property right away. Mr. Pembroke's memorandum had perhaps embellished the description of Enterprise house, just a little. In fact, it was a prefabricated, single storey block left over from the War years where it had been a Home Guard store. Situated on the corner of North Lane, which led directly to the Council refuse tip, Enterprise House was in fact the only property in the recently named Estuary Gardens, and backed on to the gas storage tanks which the council had not been able to afford to demolish, even though the gasworks had ceased operating a few years back. The block had been divided into three units and repainted inside and out in a creamy, off-white colour, chosen, as Mr. Pembroke explained, to give a modern, contemporary, business-like feel. In fact, it was chosen because that was all the Works Department happened to have in stock at the time. "The other two units sold like hot cakes" enthused Pembroke as he pushed open the sticking door, letting out a dozen or so bluebottles that had become trapped. "You will be lucky to snap this one up". Ernie realised that he hadn't many options at that juncture and so decided to accept the 'once in a lifetime' offer that Pembroke was making as, the latter explained, he thought it important to encourage the high-tech industries to Boggle and was therefore prepared to make a special, advantageous exception for Ernie. Back at the Council offices, the deal was done and Ernie agreed to move in the following Monday.

Having collected the keys, Ernie took a box of various papers and text books on computing and pushed open the sticking door to Enterprise House. Inside, a little hallway connected with the interior doors to the three units and, as Ernie unlocked his own, he heard voices from the adjacent unit, although he didn't like to enquire about his business neighbours at that stage. He turned the waste basket upside down and sat for a few moments perusing his new office and thinking that he really must find a second hand desk from somewhere and, perhaps, a filing cabinet and some chairs. After a few minutes, there was a knock on the door, followed immediately by its part opening, upon which two smiling heads protruded into the office. "Good Morning" one of them announced, "We are Proudfoot and Jingle, legal advisors, and, it seems, your next door neighbours". "Oh, good morning" Ernie replied, "I am Earnest Trubshaw, computer consultant and here to establish a new business in the area". The neighbours now entered completely and Ernie rose and shook hands with them. Percy Proudfoot was tall and slim with a large nose and close set eyes hiding under a mop of greying hair. Herbert Jingle was a more robust, jovial fellow with ruddy cheeks and round wire spectacles. The two explained that, after a particularly successful career in the heart of London's legal community, they had decided to adopt a quieter life in suburbia, in order to bring the benefit of their wide experience to the good residents of Boggle. Ernie rejoined with a similar tale of outstanding success as a London based computer consultant and, as a result, now wishing to establish a brand new venture in his preferred location of Boggle-on-Sea. Both parties viewed each other's claims with a tinge of cynicism, however, they were now neighbours and so might as well get along together. After all, there was little point in raking over the past, it was the future that was important. After a nice little chat, Proudfoot suggested that Ernie probably wanted to un-pack and so they would take their leave and, no doubt, bump into him later in the week. "Of course, if you ever need any legal advice, we would be delighted to be of service" he offered. "Similarly, if you need any help with computers and software" Ernie replied, and they nodded to each other briefly before the faces returned into the adjacent unit.

The occupier of the third unit was something of a mystery. Proudfoot and Jingle explained that they could see some boxes in there through the outside window but, as yet, they had no idea who their other neighbour was. The mystery was solved later in the week when a taxi pulled up outside Enterprise House. An argument ensued between the taxi driver and the occupant, the latter insisting that the driver had deliberately taken the long way around to Estuary Gardens in order to increase the fare. The exasperated taxi driver asked how he was supposed to know where the accursed Estuary Gardens was, when it wasn't even on the map. "That's no excuse" claimed the occupant, "I shall give you half the fare and no more as you have taken twice as long to get here as you needed to". A few more words were exchanged, some of which were quite new to the ears of the established occupants of Enterprise House, before the occupant's bags were unceremoniously dumped on the un-made road and a disgruntled taxi driver took his half fare and sped off back towards the centre of Boggle. As the occupant, a distinguished looking and rather elegant lady, looked around her, the three intrepid occupiers of Enterprise House rushed out and offered to help her with her luggage. "Oh that really is so kind of you" she announced in a majestic tone. Her name was Natasha Seminovsky and she was, as she later enlightened them, from an aristocratic Russian family of high repute who had emigrated to England following the revolution. She intended to establish an art studio where she would focus upon embroidery, avant-garde imagery and raffia mats. The boys carried Natasha's various bags to the end unit before wishing her well and returning to their own offices. After a little while, just when all seemed peaceful, there was a blood-curdling scream, and then another even worse, louder and more horrifying, emanating from the far unit, "You brute, you brute, keep away from me" the cacophony continued. Percy, suspecting murder most fowl, ran bravely to the rescue, hotly pursued by Ernie, while Herbert looked on from the open door of the middle unit, ready to call the authorities if and as required. "Oh, it's awful, awful" blurted Natasha who was now standing on one of her boxes. "Over there, quickly" she screamed, pointing towards the corner. "Oh, I cannot bear it, I shall die" she announced dramatically, a hand held to her forehead. Percy could not find anything untoward and was a little puzzled, until Ernie noticed, sitting peacefully in the corner, a large, slightly bemused spider. "Come on old chap" he said quietly, "Let's find you a new home". Ernie went outside with the intruder and Natasha, one hand still on her forehead, climbed off the box and shivered a few times, before thanking her rescuers profusely.

"Only too pleased to help" ventured Percy. "Indeed" confirmed Herbert who had now joined them. "It was nothing, really" suggested Ernie modestly.

And so, all the occupants of the newly established Enterprise House were now acquainted and it seemed, almost serendipitous, that they had much in common. They all seemed to be individuals who, for one reason or another, had not been wholly accepted into the main-stream of their chosen professions and yet, they all clearly had aspirations for better things. Every morning, they would greet each other cheerfully and enquire as to the progress of the other party and their respective endeavours. "All going to plan" would assure Percy and Herbert. "Progressing beautifully" would assure Natasha and Ernie equally would give the impression that his consultancy was beginning to pick up although, in reality, all of their various endeavours had not progressed beyond the aspirational stage. One day, as Ernie was unlocking the front door with Natasha just coming in behind him, a large black crow settled on the flat roof immediately above the door and looked down at them. "Caw" said the crow. "Its all right for you" replied Ernie, as he pushed open the sticking door. "No, no" cried Natasha, "It's an omen. The crow is telling us that today is going to be a magical day". Ernie brought in the milk and Natasha put the kettle on, just as Percy and Herbert were arriving. "Morning all!" announced Herbert joyfully. Natasha explained the good omen of the crow and suggested that they should all get together for a deep thinking, spiritual meeting over their morning tea. "Now you come to mention it" suggested Percy, "There was a red sky last night". "Yes!" rejoined Herbert enthusiastically, "And a black cat ran in front of me as I was coming out of my lodgings this morning". "There you are, that settles it" affirmed Natasha, "You can't argue with facts like that. We are all destined to have a most meaningful, spiritual meeting. It's written in the stars". Ernie was not entirely convinced. However, in the absence of any other planned activity, he thought that he might as well go along with the idea, although he suggested that it should, in fact, be a strategy meeting, rather than a purely spiritual one. Percy and Herbert agreed and Natasha simply smiled sweetly as she stirred the teapot and resigned fate to the wind. But of course, fate works in strange ways and who would have thought that that single black crow would actually change forever the lives of the intrepid occupiers of Enterprise House.

They all assembled in Ernie's office as the crow looked in through the window from his vantage point on the broken fence outside. Ernie sipped his Darjeeling and started off the conversation. "Well, my idea was for a computer consultancy to educate people as to the potential for using computers and then sell them the necessary goods and ongoing services". Percy thought for a moment. "Of course, they will need a contract and it will all need to be drawn up properly and legally". Herbert stroked his chin. "And someone will need to manage the accounts and take care of the financial planning". Natasha put her cup down with a jolt on Ernie's second hand desk. "But what about marketing?" she blurted out. "No business will thrive without proper marketing and well considered sales campaigns". "You are right" exclaimed Ernie as he thought it over. "And an image" continued Natasha, "The business must have an image, and a name which conjures up reliability and steadfastness in the face of competition and changing times". The four remained silent, locked in deep thought for a few moments, each of them pursuing their own particular thread of creative thinking. Herbert was thinking of his landlady. Suddenly, he jumped up from his chair, spilling the remainder of his tea down his trousers. "I've got it" he cried out enthusiastically. Taking a deep breath, he lifted his chin and announced in a measured, stentorian tone; "Dreadnought Consultants". There was a silence for a few moments and, just as Ernie was wondering whether Herbert had really said 'Dreadnought Consultants' or whether he had been dreaming momentarily, Natasha let out a shriek; "It's absolutely wonderful!" she shouted as she leaped from her chair and proceeded to jump up and down, her hands clasped in front of her. "Crikey" exclaimed a startled Percy. "Caw" said the crow. "Indeed" whispered Ernie in quiet disbelief. Herbert, by now highly excited and carried away with enthusiasm clapped his own hands together. "And we shall call this place Dreadnought Laboratories". Another silence ensued and, as they all looked out of the window, the crow lifted his gaze towards the heavens, the clouds overhead started to clear and a beam of sunshine shone down directly upon Enterprise House. "I told you" said Natasha emphatically. "This day was destined to draw us all together under a single purpose and shape the course of our future". Ernie had to admit that this was certainly no ordinary morning at Enterprise House. Boggle-on-Sea started, all of a sudden, to seem like an interesting place after all. Perhaps they really could make a go of it if they joined forces as had been suggested. Memories of the Old Kent Road started to fade into the distance as the dawning of a new beginning was starting to reveal itself. But they would require a proper plan, with roles and responsibilities clearly defined. They all set to work accordingly, in order to draft the future of what they were convinced would quickly become the leading computer organisation in the country, if not the civilised world. Natasha brought in some brown wrapping paper from one of her boxes and they stretched it out across Ernie's desk, whereupon they plotted a crude timeline and noted down all the things they would need to do in order to properly launch Dreadnought Consultants. It was exhausting work which required several more cups of tea, but our intrepid heroes were undaunted and continued well into the afternoon. Finally, Ernie stood back and folded his arms. "Well!" he said stoically, "I think we have accomplished all that we can do today.

Tomorrow, we shall start buying in what we need to get started". "And we shall launch our great marketing plan" insisted Natasha. "Yes, of course we shall, and we shall get the accounts firmly established" suggested Percy. They had another cup of tea before deciding to call it a day and return to their respective lodgings. As they gathered outside the entrance to Enterprise House, Ernie pulled the sticking door closed and turned the key in the lock. "Caw" said the crow. "I know" said Ernie. "Indubitably" agreed Herbert. "Bless you" added Natasha. They strolled back up the unmade road towards down-town Boggle as the sun started to settle over the mud flats and the full moon rose slowly in the sky, casting distinctive new shadows across the deserted gasworks. A new era was about to begin.

Back at Westminster Drive, Ernie explained these wondrous developments to auntie Freda as she prepared his dinner. "It won't be long now before the business really starts to take off" he assured her. "Oh" she said politely, "But didn't you say that three or four weeks ago when you first moved in?". "Yes, but these things do take a little time" Ernie assured her, "and, of course it will mean that I won't be able to pay you any rent for a little while longer" he added timidly. But, by now, Freda was already resigned to the fact that she was now supporting two individuals at number 9 and that she might be doing so for some considerable time. "Oh, that's all right dear" she said quietly, "I expect it will all come good in the end". Ernie wolfed up his scrambled eggs, beans and toast with a new enthusiasm as he thought of all the exciting times that lay ahead. Back at the Sea View Guest House, Percy and Herbert continued to discuss the detail of the financial plan over their scrambled eggs, beans and toast. On the far side of Boggle-on-Sea, high on the hill overlooking the estuary lay the dusky, grey stones of Boggleton Hall, where Liliya Seminovsky, Natasha's mother, continued to hold court, even though the building was in a rather dilapidated condition. Over the fireplace in the main room, in thick wooden frames hung portraits of Valerij and Anastasia Seminovsky, Natasha's grandparents, with a smaller portrait of Sergey, her late father between them. These portraits and a few pieces of silver cutlery were all that remained of their once proud heritage. Natasha also had a sister, whose name was Fenella and who was married to a local Boggle man, although she frequently spent evenings back at Boggleton Hall. Fenella had a daughter, named Violet, who Natasha doted on and often spent time with. The two sisters always exchanged notes about their respective experiences in Boggle and Natasha couldn't wait to tell Fenella all about the wonderful day she had had at Enterprise House. "It sounds absolutely wonderful", exclaimed Fenella excitedly, "I am very happy for you dear and I do hope that it all goes well". Liliya Seminovsky was rather more doubtful as she considered the local Boggle men to be pale shadows of the likes of Grandpa Valerij and unlikely to come to any good. "It's time you settled down with a real man" she frequently told Natasha. "Someone like a doctor or lawyer, a man of some substance". "Yes Mama" was Natasha's standard answer. But men of such substance were not easy to find in Boggle-on-Sea. Most of them left town as soon as they were able and those that were left didn't really measure up to Mama's expectations. Nevertheless, things were looking up in the Seminovsky household as Natasha's infectious enthusiasm spread slowly through the musty hallways and rooms. Perhaps she alone would restore the Seminovsky pride.

5 REBIRTH

Throughout the week, the newly formed Dreadnought Consultants team worked hard to establish the base from which they would launch their business venture. Computers were sourced from a wholesale supplier that Ernie had become aware of in London. One for Natasha with which to manage marketing, sales, clients and general activities. One for Percy and Herbert with which to manage the sales ledger and general finances, and one for Ernie which would also function as a development machine. Natasha swapped offices with Ernie so that she could be sited by the front door and they all agreed their various roles and responsibilities. After arranging the fundamentals, they sat down to plan and agree their marketing approach. "Precisely what services will we be offering?" asked Herbert. "Everything" suggested Ernie. "Everything?" echoed a startled Percy. "Yes" responded Ernie. "We shall offer business consultancy and planning services, followed by systems design and implementation and backed up by support and maintenance contracts". Natasha thought for a moment or two and then suggested, "It's simple really. Every time someone phones and asks us if we provide a certain service or product, we say yes and then add it to the list of offered services". "That's it exactly" confirmed Ernie. "Yes, but who is actually going to provide the service?" asked Herbert. "We will worry about that when the time comes" rejoined Ernie. "The first thing is to attract some clients and assure them that we can supply anything at all, at a lower cost than anyone else and with better support". "But we can't" protested Herbert. "Yes, but they don't know that" confirmed Ernie. The discussion continued along similar lines and it was agreed that they would let their strategy be driven by client requirements. "But we ought to specialise in something" suggested Natasha, "after all, every organisation should have specialist skills". "Very well" replied Ernie, "We shall specialise in identity management and large scale systems". Natasha diligently wrote everything down as the boys produced various ideas and suggestions for approaching prospective clients. They would start with Boggle-on-Sea and then work their way up the estuary to Limewell, Greycliff and Sodleigh as their influence and good name spread. However, to achieve that end they needed clients and, consequently, a focused marketing campaign needed to be designed and entered into with some relish.

That night, among the dark and dusky corridors and rooms of Boggleton Hall, a pale yellow light shone out from one of the smaller upstairs windows, contrasting with the soft light from the moon as it rose high in the sky above Boggle, bathing the occupants of that town with its benevolent rays. Inside the room, on an old but not very distinguished little desk, Natasha was teasing out the details of what would become the great Dreadnought Consultants marketing plan. The next morning, she hurried to Enterprise House, just as Ernie was leaning his newly acquired, second hand Raleigh bicycle against the wall and removing his bicycle clips. "I've got it all worked out" She exclaimed joyfully. "The marketing plan" she added, in case Ernie was in any doubt. "Fantastic!" cried Ernie. "Caw" said the crow. And they made their way into the newly configured Dreadnought offices. As soon as Percy and Herbert arrived, they all brought their morning tea and biscuits into the front office in order to discuss the plan. "Its very simple really" explained Natasha. "First, we print out a few hundred of these little leaflets that I have designed and, while we are delivering those to every business in the area, we also send a press release to The Boggle Examiner, explaining the new business venture and offering to write a feature for them". "But will they publish it?" Asked Percy. "Of course they will" replied a confident Natasha. "Nothing ever happens in Boggle and they will be glad of a news-worthy item to break the monotony". "That's right!" added Ernie. "And we can invite them here to take a photograph or two of the team". "Is that wise?" asked a concerned Herbert. "After all, this place isn't exactly the last word in modern executive offices". "But they can give any impression they like with carefully chosen camera shots" explained Ernie. "Furthermore, we will invite the Mayor along to share in this outstanding Boggle success story, springing, as it does, from council rented offices". "Exactly" agreed Natasha. "I saw the Mayor in the last edition of the paper, his name is Claude Bonking, a nasty looking little man, who, I am quite sure will relish the opportunity". "There is one thing though" explained Herbert. "Where are we going to get the money to print the leaflets? Our combined finances are looking a little weak at present". "How much?" asked Ernie. "About seven pounds ten" replied Herbert. There was a pause for a few moments as the team considered their dilemma. "I know!" exclaimed Percy in a jubilant tone. "We shall get a bank loan". Ernie looked at Herbert. Herbert looked at Natasha and Natasha looked at Percy. "It's easy" he continued. "The main bank in Boggle will be only too pleased to oblige as they get very few opportunities to make loans to anyone". "You may have something there" agreed Ernie. Natasha immediately telephoned the Boggle Mutual Bank and, putting on her very best posh voice, arranged an appointment with the manager, Mr. Stephen Spindlebrook for the Wednesday morning. It was agreed that Ernie and Natasha would attend the meeting with the bank manager while Percy and Herbert manned the offices. In preparation, Percy would prepare a business projection and cash flow statement for them to take along with them. Finishing touches were put to the marketing plan and, based upon Natasha's design, the leaflets were ordered from the local printers, Peter Bloggs and Son, not knowing, at this stage, whether they would be able to pay for them. Mr. Bloggs, who rarely saw new orders these days, suggested, as a special offer, a complete set of matching stationery, which Natasha readily agreed to. After all, they would need stationery.

Wednesday came around and Ernie and Natasha duly presented themselves at the Boggle Mutual Bank, a badly maintained mock Georgian building with a large, faded wooden door. Inside, a small corridor led from beside the two teller windows, at the end of which was Mr. Spindlebrook's office. The latter was a fairly squat, serious looking man with a small moustache and horn rimmed glasses. After the customary pleasantries, Ernie explained their requirements, with occasional interjections from Natasha to emphasise the salient points. Ernie then sat back in the hard wooden chair, feeling quite confident that he had put forward a very good case. Mr. Spindlebrook took a deep breath and leaned back in his luxurious, high backed leather chair. "So, what you are proposing" he started, "Is that I lend you £10,000 in support of a business venture which has no track record, no customers, no sales to date and nothing at all to offer in way of security. Furthermore, you are new to the area and have no references from local trades people that can be verified. You are wasting the bank's time Mr. Trubshaw". Ernie was somewhat taken aback by this surprise rebuttal and was momentarily speechless, but Natasha quickly rejoined the conversation. "All good businesses have to start somewhere Mr. Spindlebrook, and Dreadnought Consultants have a unique business model, with absolutely no competition in the area. It can't possibly fail". "They all say that" replied Spindlebrook with an air of impatience creeping into his tone. "Computers are the future" suggested Ernie as he recovered his composure. "Dreadnought Consultants will be the only local business with competence in this area and will undoubtedly go from strength to strength as the industry matures. We just need a little help to get started". Spindlebrook was still looking unconvinced and a little impatient, when Natasha suddenly had an idea. She edged her hard wooden chair closer to the desk and, smiling sweetly, looked straight into Spindlebrook's eyes. "We chose your bank especially Mr. Spindlebrook, because we had heard what a good business manager you were and how everybody in town looked up to you. Even Mr. Bonking, the Mayor, said that he was looking forwards to having his photo taken with you at our press launch next week". "You are having a press launch?" Interjected Spindlebrook. "Of course" replied Natasha. "All good businesses have a press launch. Everybody will be there and the event will be covered by the Boggle Examiner. It will be a celebration of the inspiration that Boggle-on-Sea brings to the technological world, with the Boggle Mutual Bank being a cornerstone of that initiative" Even Ernie was blushing a little at this stage, but he noticed that Spindlebrook had relaxed a little and swore that, for a moment, there was the flickering of something akin to a smile on the latter's features. "The Boggle Examiner?" he asked quizzically. "Indeed" replied Natasha, "They recommended you most strongly". Spindlebrook rose from his luxurious chair and paced up and down for a moment or two. "Well, maybe I could provide you with an agreed overdraft, along the lines of the sum you suggested, in order to help get the business going. After all, the Boggle Mutual is a progressive institution and an important player in the affairs of this town". "Isn't that curious?" responded Natasha, "That's exactly what the Mayor was saying". "He was?" replied Spindlebrook. "Oh yes, he thinks of the bank as being central to the future direction and prosperity of the town" replied Natasha, still smiling sweetly. Spindlebrook sat back in his chair and discussion continued around the finer details of the arrangement. Twenty minutes later, Ernie and Natasha emerged from the crumbling building with a proper bank account and an agreed overdraft. "Thank goodness for that" exclaimed Ernie. "Now we can pay the printers and the computer wholesalers and maybe even bring in a little stock" "Yes, but we have to organise the press launch and make a good impression" replied Natasha, half to herself as she walked along, deep in thought. They arrived back at

Enterprise House and Ernie pushed open the sticking door. Percy and Herbert came running out of the front office. "Success?" asked Percy with a slightly worried expression. "Of course" replied Natasha dismissively, "We got exactly what we wanted". "Wonderful" exclaimed Herbert. "Excellent" agreed Percy. "Caw" said the crow. And they all settled down with a nice cup of tea as the late afternoon sun made its way over the mud flats towards the Boggle-on-Sea horizon. It had been a most beautiful day.

All things must pass however and, over the next few days, the team were busy organising the press launch. They started off with a brainstorm session, fuelled by tea and biscuits and focused via a damaged flip chart that Ernie had bought cheaply at the local stationers. "The first thing" explained Natasha, "is the invitation list". "Well that's easy" replied Percy jovially, "there's the Mayor, Claude Bonking, the Bank Manager, Stephen Spindlebrook, and, er...". "The Boggle Examiner" interjected Herbert, trying to be helpful. "Yes, but we can't have a press launch with just two people and a reporter" explained Natasha, "we shall have to invite everybody we know to come along and pretend to be interested clients". This idea presented something of a challenge as, actually, they didn't really know that many people, let alone any prospective clients. Nevertheless, undaunted, they started putting together a list of VIP invitees. There was Auntie Freda of course, and Natasha's sister Fenella, her cousin

Charlie Higgins who worked at the Council refuse site, Mrs. Cravat, the landlady at Percy's boarding house and Peter Bloggs from the printers (if he wanted to get paid, that is). However, even after adding all their friends and acquaintances, the list was not looking overly impressive. "There's nothing else for it" exclaimed Ernie, "we shall just have to go to every small business and retail establishment in Boggle and personally invite them to the press launch". "We'll lay on some orange juice and sandwiches" suggested Natasha. "Yes, but what shall we say to everyone?" asked Herbert. "We shall simply tell them, in no uncertain terms, that we are the country's leading experts in computer science" explained Ernie, "and that no situation is too small or too large for us to tackle". "Is that true?" asked Herbert incredulously. "Well, it's close enough" reassured Ernie. And so they set off into the bustling streets and dynamic business world of downtown Boggle, Ernie and Natasha taking the High Street, and Percy and Herbert tackling the Station Approach and adjoining industrial area. In truth, in didn't take too long as there are relatively few businesses in Boggle. Nevertheless, they managed to enlist Ivor Williams from the fish and chip shop, Mrs. Didley from the newsagent, Ronald Carrion from the solicitors office, Miss Felicity Trinklebaum from the children's outfitters, Glenda Pugh from the library and one or two others. They were all invited to the official, grand launch of Dreadnought Consultants, the new inspiration for the future of Boggle-on-Sea. Natasha put together a welcoming speech and Ernie set up a working computer in the front office in order to demonstrate some of the inherent capabilities. Percy and Herbert made some notes and would respond to any enquiries about the company's trading position with a lot of nonsense about funding, capitalisation and future projections. Confident that all which could be done had been done in terms of preparation, the team decided, after the exhaustion of their mental efforts, to leave early that afternoon. "It should be a great event" commented Percy as he tripped over the ledge of the open door. "Indeed" said Herbert. "Of course" said Natasha. "Caw" said the crow. And Ernie pulled closed the sticking door and turned the key on another exciting day at Enterprise House.

The day of the press launch arrived and everyone was excited as a succession of colourful people started to arrive outside Enterprise House. Ernie had taken the precaution of wedging open the front door with a brick and Natasha had prepared some buffet sandwiches with the help of a couple of cheap cut loaves and a few jars of special offer fish paste. Percy had prepared a couple of jugs of orange squash with a few ice cubes floating on the top in order to complete the refreshments. The Mayor's official limousine arrived bang on time, as he was always receptive to the idea of free refreshments and associated photo opportunities. Natasha welcomed him with a smile. "Ah! Mr. Bonking, how nice of you to come". "It's my pleasure" he replied, "I always like to support local business initiatives" he continued, somewhat absent mindedly, while stretching his neck in search of the refreshments. Natasha steered him towards the buffet as the other guests started to arrive. Auntie Freda looked resplendent in her 1940s style gown. Actually, it wasn't so much 1940s style as genuine 1940s apparel, but she carried it off gracefully. Fenella charmed everyone with her social chit chat and, by the time Spindlebrook the Bank Manager arrived, things were in full swing, with Percy and Herbert talking interminable nonsense to anyone within earshot and Ernie showing everyone the computer in the front office and explaining how it was going to change the civilised world. The only invitee conspicuous by their absence was the reporter from the Boggle Examiner, Juliette Slinkbottom. Natasha was becoming a little concerned at the non-appearance of Miss Slinkbottom when a hastily driven, dusty old Ford pulled up abruptly, just an inch or two from the bumper of the shining Mayoral Daimler. "Come along, quickly, quickly" cried a flustered Miss Slinkbottom to a hapless driver and photographer whose name was Joss Finkle. Natasha rushed out to meet them, as Juliette smiled cheerfully. "I am afraid we are running a little late this morning. The editor wanted us to cover the main story of the day before coming over to join you". "Oh I see, what was it?" asked a curious Natasha. "A cat got stuck on the pull out awning above the greengrocers and had to be rescued" replied the senior Boggle Examiner reporter.

After a few introductions and pleasantries, the guests lined up outside Enterprise House, with His Worshipful the Mayor, Claude Bonking, shaking hands with Earnest Trubshaw Esq. while Spindlebrook, the Bank Manager, looked on approvingly through his thick glasses. Behind them stood a motley assortment of relatives, small shopkeepers and a couple of men from the refuse site. Joss Finkle waved his hands about and herded them more or less into position and then, instructing them to say 'cheese' and hold it for the camera, took his first shot. They then moved inside, where Ernie, Spindlebrook and Bonking crowded around the computer while holding their Cheshire cat expressions long enough for Joss to crank his camera and take another shot. He gestured for a few of the other guests to move in behind the computer and, Auntie Freda, always ready to oblige, moved swiftly into the scene. Unfortunately, her stiletto met with the mains electricity lead to the computer, jerking it from the wall with a flash as she stumbled over the table, spilling her orange juice over both the Mayor and the computer keyboard. In a desperate attempt to stabilise the table, Herbert lurched forwards, tripped and displaced the computer completely, which then fell on to the floor, dragging with it an assortment of wires and leaflets. Joss Finkle, being an experienced Pro, simply continued to crank and fire his camera without comment. The others all crowded around as Ernie and Herbert man-handled the computer back on to the table while Mayor Bonking, with a look of pained astonishment, stepped backwards as if to disassociate himself from the ensuing fiasco. He stepped back a little further, hoping to make a discreet exit, when the official polished shoe slipped on one of Natasha's glossy leaflets and launched him sideways into the wall, from where he stumbled over the potted plant that Fenella had brought down from Boggleton Hall, in order to lend a little class to the proceedings. Joss continued to crank and shoot. Auntie Freda, in a state of confused shock, gathered together with Mrs Cravat, Miss Trinklebaum and Glenda Pugh to commiserate, effectively blocking the path of Stephen Spindlebrook who was also desirous of a discreet exit. "Ladies, please" he begged as he jostled from side to side. Joss continued to crank and shoot. Cousin Charlie and his colleagues from the refuse site, after finishing off the sandwiches, joined the melee as they made their way towards the door in their council tabards. Joss continued to crank and shoot. Soon, they were all outside again and Natasha was assuring Miss Slinkbottom that the event had been an entire success and that Dreadnought Consultants would no doubt soon be gracing the front pages of the national dailies and specialist glossy magazines as the new wave business inspiration that they undoubtedly were. "I see" said Miss Slinkbottom in a not altogether convincing tone. "We are the pioneers of 20th century computer science, you know" continued Natasha triumphantly as the guests started to drift away, back towards Boggle. "Oh!, wasn't that the Mayor's car" exclaimed Slinkbottom as the Daimler spun its rear tyres in desperation to get away. "Oh yes, so it is" replied Natasha. "He has such a busy schedule, but was so insistent on joining us for the press launch, we just couldn't keep him away". By then, Ernie, Percy and Herbert had got Miss Slinkbottom surrounded and Ernie, after clearing his throat, recited his carefully rehearsed press speech. Joss continued to crank and shoot. The remaining stragglers dispersed, apart from Fenella and Auntie Freda who were determined to see the occasion through at all costs. Eventually, Juliette Slinkbottom and Joss Finkle managed to break free and reach their car. With a confused smile and a brief wave, they sped away from the scene. Ernie breathed out deeply. "Well, that seemed to go off all right" he suggested. "Wonderful" suggested Freda. "Fantastic" agreed Fenella. "Excellent" exclaimed Percy. "Remarkable" said Herbert. "Caw" said the crow. Ernie took away the brick and pulled the sticking door closed behind them as they re-entered Enterprise House. An important milestone had been reached in the annals of computer science.

The next day, on the last page but one, the Boggle Examiner ran the story of the official opening of Dreadnought Consultants, together with a selection of small photographs which seemed to capture the spirit of the occasion quite nicely. Filling the front page, was the story of the stranded cat, whose name was Stanley, complete with a full colour photograph of the aforementioned feline in the arms of its grateful owner, Mrs. Wilberforce, decked out in her best apron and matching turban. In the background, the entire Boggle Fire Brigade, consisting of Jack Paddings and his two sons, smiled cheerfully as they held the ladder. That day, the Examiner's switchboard was jammed with calls enquiring about Stanley's health and hoping that the ordeal had not been too much for his poor little nerves. Mrs Wilberforce received a plethora of well wishing letters and gifts of cat food and bright coloured little fluffy toys for Stanley, who apparently expressed his sincere gratitude to all his well wishers. Later that evening, over on Albert Street, Mr Robin Figget, the Headmaster of Boggle Comprehensive was kneeling down in the hall, cleaning his shoes over the Boggle Examiner, when he noticed the brief editorial appertaining to Dreadnought Consultants. He wiped away the smudges of shoe polish and peered at the text. He had often wondered whether a computer might be useful in order to log the names of all the pupils and keep records of their academic progress. He tore off the corner of the page and resolved that he would contact Enterprise House the next day. It looked as though fate was about to take a hand in procuring Dreadnought Consultants their very first customer.

Julian Ashbourn

6 THE CONFERENCE

The team at Enterprise House had finished their first cup of tea and were gazing nonchalantly out of the rear windows as the sun peeked through the clouds behind the gasworks storage tanks. Suddenly there was a knock at the door, an occurrence to which they were not especially accustomed. "That was a knock, wasn't it?" exclaimed Herbert. "No. Couldn't be. It was probably just the pipes playing up" suggested Percy. "There it is again!" said Natasha incredulously. Ernie sprang forward and forced open the sticking door, just as Robin Figget was walking away. "Ah! There you are" he shouted after him. "I thought you were out" replied Figget as he turned around". "No, I was just on an international call" "At 9.30 in the morning?" enquired Figget. "Yes, er.. Singapore" suggested Ernie nervously. "Oh, I see", replied Figget as he re-approached the nerve centre of global computing. Natasha had by this time come to the door and was peering inquisitively at the approaching apparition, her tea cup still in hand.

"My secretary, Miss Seminovsky" suggested Ernie as he motioned her away and held open the sticking door for Mr. Figget. Once inside, Ernie showed him the main computer and started to wax lyrical about the fate of the civilised world but, to his surprise, Figget interrupted him. "Yes, yes, I know all that" he said impatiently, "but can I maintain a list of all our students, their details and their progress?" "Er.. yes of course" replied a slightly bemused Ernie. "And all the exam results?". "Indeed you can" confirmed Ernie, starting to warm to the situation. "And can I produce reports?" "Very easily" replied Ernie nonchalantly. By this time, slightly surprised at the lack of any obvious agitation or histrionics, the other members of the team started to gather around this strange manifestation of what looked suspiciously like a potential customer. A few minutes more of questions and answers and Mr. Figget was convinced. "Right. How much would all this cost?" he asked, standing slightly aback with his hands on his hips. Ernie had to think quickly. "Well, you will need two computers, to ensure that everything is backed up, plus the necessary network components, a printer, some consumables and leads, and of course the custom built software which we shall provide" he suggested. Figget eyed him steadily while Ernie made some mental calculations. He reasoned that the whole lot should cost him about £1200 wholesale. He pretended to scribble in a pad, and then announced in his best business like voice; "Three thousand seven hundred and ninety pounds should cover it". "Is that all?" rejoined Figget. "Plus of course the software development costs and an initial service contract, say six thousand pounds all in" suggested Ernie. "Right, I will have the order sent over this afternoon" replied Figget as he made for the door. Natasha, smiling sweetly, rushed forward to open the sticking door for him and the others, still in a state of shock, congregated outside to watch the esteemed Mr. Figget as he disappeared back towards the metropolis that was Boggle-on-Sea. "A customer" whispered Herbert in hushed tones as he looked incredulously at Ernie. "A customer" agreed Ernie, almost in disbelief. "Of course" exclaimed Natasha jubilantly. "Indeed" said Percy. "Caw" said the crow. And they returned inside for another cup of tea.

All that day, there was an air of subdued reverence within Enterprise House as Ernie wrote down what was needed to fulfil such an order and the others looked on. The custom software posed an initial issue until Ernie remembered that he had a free copy of dBase which had come with one of the computers. "We can use that" he claimed. "Will it work though?" asked Percy, somewhat hesitatingly. "Of course it will work" interjected Natasha confidently. Later that day, just as Mr. Figget had promised, a messenger came round with the order from Boggle Comprehensive, which Percy immediately scrutinized most carefully under a magnifying glass. "It all looks in order" he exclaimed, as though such an occurrence was most unlikely.

"Right" said Ernie joyfully, "Natasha, you order the computers and I will start developing the database". Dreadnought Consultants had their first customer. Slowly, the word got around and other customers appeared, albeit with slightly varying requirements. Some of them clearly had no idea at all what they were going to do with their new computer, but it would at least provide a talking point and would lend an air of high-tech sophistication to their particular operation, something which, in the main, Boggle sorely needed. And it wasn't just Boggle. Orders drifted in from nearby Limewell and Sodleigh. Even the dilapidated hotel at Greycliff ordered one for their reception. It seemed that Dreadnought's star was at last in the ascendency and then, as suddenly as they had began, the orders seemed to dry up. After three weeks of absolutely no interest from anyone, not even a solitary phone call, Ernie decided to hold an emergency summit meeting in order to discuss strategy. Natasha brewed up a large pot of tea, Percy broke open the last of the biscuits and Ernie arranged the chairs in a semi circle in the office, with the last page of his flip chart sellotaped to the wall. "Right, let's have some ideas" he asked positively. There was a long silence, punctuated occasionally by Herbert slurping his tea. "Stop doing that!" barked Natasha, "I'm trying to think". "Sorry" replied Herbert nervously. A few moments later, all chaos ensued as Percy leapt from his chair, overturning it in the process, and proceeded to jump up at down. "I've got it! I've got it!" he bellowed.

"What?" asked Ernie excitedly. Percy took a deep breath and, steadying himself with one hand on the desk, he announced, in his best Gilbert and Sullivan voice, "We will hold a conference". "A conference?" repeated Ernie, almost to himself. "A conference?" repeated Herbert. "Of course, a conference!" cried Natasha as she jumped up from her chair. "It's a wonderful idea, we'll ask all our friends and advertise it in the Boggle Examiner" "Bother the Examiner" rejoined Percy, "we will advertise it nationally and in all the best glossy magazines". "But that will cost money" interjected Herbert. "Not necessarily" replied Percy, "we will send out a series of press releases, announcing the Dreadnought Computer Science Symposium". "The Dreadnought *International* Computer Science Symposium" suggested Ernie. "Of course" agreed Natasha, "we will also send press releases to the International press. The Americans will love it". "Americans!" cried Herbert in a state of agitated alarm, his eyes almost escaping their sockets. "I don't like the sound of that. Dreadful fellows. My father told me about them, always chewing gum and leaning on lamp-posts. They're an absolute shower. Most of them can't even speak English properly". "You can't expect too much" protested Natasha indignantly, "after all, they've only been at it for a couple of hundred years or so. In any case, one or two of them are quite nice really. There's Clark Gable, Jimmy Stewart...". "Even so..." complained Herbert. "Not to worry" said Ernie, "we shall have a special price for

Americans. We will call it the 'early bird' discount and add on forty percent. They'll never notice it, what with the currency conversion and all". "Ah!" exclaimed Herbert, somewhat reassured as he scribbled the details down in his notebook. "And they will come from all over Europe, won't they?" suggested Percy. "Exactly, that's the whole idea" confirmed Ernie, "we shall meet a whole gamut of new prospective customers, and they will pay us for the privilege". Herbert took it all down in his notebook as they discussed costs and duration. They decided that the Dreadnought International Computer Science Symposium should be a three day event, for which delegates would each pay two hundred and fifty pounds (three hundred and fifty pounds for Americans).

The discussion continued excitedly and then, just as they were starting on their third cup of tea, Natasha suddenly stood up with a concerned look upon her features. "Wait a minute. What about a venue? There are no conference facilities in Boggle". The team were temporarily taken aback as the realisation that Boggle-on-Sea was not renowned for hosting international conferences sunk in. "What about the Civic Centre?" suggested Percy. "No, nobody ever goes near there and, in any case its very cramped, I visited it when I was speaking with the property department" replied Ernie. "The British Legion Club?" suggested Herbert helpfully. "No, you can't get near the place for regulars" explained Ernie, "and they get quite touchy if you encroach upon their favourite positions at the bar. Reverend Clancy in particular always stands at the same spot in the corner. Bert has had the counter raised three inches at that point in order that the Reverend can rest his elbow comfortably, with a pint in one hand and a cigar in the other. If anyone else stands there, he becomes most indignant". A few other likely locations were considered, including the Quaker Meeting House, as the Quakers had long since abandoned Boggle as a lost cause, but nothing really seemed quite suitable, and then, in a flash of pure inspiration, Natasha suggested the old Sea Scouts hut which had fallen into disrepair since the last Boggle Sea Scout lost interest more than twenty years ago. "You know" she exclaimed enthusiastically, "just past the pier, on that scrap of ground over-looking the mud flats. Fenella used to go there with her boyfriend before they were married. It's a large hall and could easily be converted into a conference centre". The others looked dumbfounded for a while. "I know where you mean, but there are no facilities, surely" complained Percy. "There are the public toilets just over the road and two or three small café's along the sea front. They would be glad of a little additional business". Ernie thought hard for a moment or two. "It could work" he suggested. "We could do a deal with the Council to get them to help refurbish it while we turn it into a proper conference centre, bringing badly needed new visitors to Boggle. In return for rent-free usage, we will guarantee to run at least one conference a year". "But where will the delegates stay?" asked Natasha. "Well, if we put two to a room and reopen the basement, Mrs. Cravat's boarding house could accommodate quite a few" suggested Percy. "Exactly, and there's the Sea View Hotel, up on the hill. They always have vacancies, even in the height of the summer season" confirmed Herbert. "And there's that guest house by the pier" added Natasha. "They would all be glad of the extra business. Indeed, it may be the only bookings they get all year" suggested Ernie. "We will speak with all of them and, for a small fee, include them on our conference brochure and on the new web site we are putting together". Natasha subsequently worked on the brochure which proudly announced; 'The Dreadnought International Computer Science Symposium, held in the delightful coastal setting of historic Boggle, with its quaint listed buildings, Market Town centre and attractive, world class facilities'. It went on to stress how Boggle-on-Sea remained at the cutting edge of technology and how Dreadnought Consultants spearheaded that initiative. However, she appreciated that an exciting agenda should really be an integral part of the brochure and was struggling a little to put this together. "What are we going to say to them?" she asked Ernie. "We will just mention a few topical concepts and dress them up a bit" he replied. "How about; 'New Dimensions in Quasi-Concentric Networking' followed by 'Adaptive Strategies for Maximising the Cloud' and then, 'Biometrics and

Informatics in The New Age', that sort of thing". "And how about, 'Balanced Algorithms for Automated Compliance'?" suggested Percy. A few other suggestions and they had enough topics for a full three day conference.

Another cup of tea and some digestive biscuits served to fuel the ongoing brain storming as the rain beat against the windows of Enterprise House. "There is one snag though" suggested Herbert. "Who are we going to get as speakers and will they know anything about these subjects?" "We will take it in turns to speak" Suggested Ernie. "But we don't know anything either" protested Herbert. "That's all right" replied Ernie "Most speakers at conferences haven't a clue what they are talking about. Its expected". "Then why do they come?" asked Percy. "Because it is a day or two out of the office and a chance to go out to the local pubs in the evenings" replied Ernie. "I still think that we need more speakers" insisted Herbert. "Don't they usually have something called a key fob speaker to start the day?". "You mean a key *note* speaker" replied Ernie. "That's it!. A key notes speaker. We ought to have one or two of those, surely" suggested Herbert enthusiastically. Natasha, who had been quietly listening while she finished her tea, suddenly had an idea. "Herbert is right" she said, "and I think I know the perfect candidate". The boys all looked at her expectantly. "Cousin Charlie" she explained. "He would be glad to help out if there are some free refreshments on offer". Percy looked horrified. "But he knows even less than us and, in any case, he couldn't very well turn up in his council overalls". Ernie jumped up from his chair. "Of course he could" he insisted. "Just look at the scruff bags that turn up for the big IT conferences in the city. Charlie would be perfect, and the fact that he knows absolutely nothing will simply add to his appeal. We will write him a brief script and he can ad-lib his way around it to fill in the time". "Exactly!" agreed Natasha, "and I will see that he has a reasonably clean set of overalls for the occasion. We shall bill him as Professor Charles Higgins HRD, BSA, AJS". "What do those letters stand for?" asked Herbert. "It doesn't matter" replied Natasha, "the audience will be suitably impressed and Charlie will carry it off with aplomb". The discussion progressed along similar lines as the fine details of the conference were hammered out, including the concept of an evening drinks reception in Enterprise House for a few select delegates, at an additional cost. In due course, Ernie arranged to get the Sea Scouts hut refurbished and a ' Boggle-on-Sea Conference Centre' sign painted to put above the door. They removed the seats from the Quaker Meeting House and, complemented by a few more from the Civic Centre, managed to gather together enough to fill the new facility. In parallel, Natasha designed a very nice brochure and talked Peter Bloggs, the printer, into printing a few hundred for nothing in return for having his name on the bottom of the back page. She also set up a special conference page on the new Dreadnought Consultants Internet site. Percy and Herbert helped by sending the press release to every single publication that they could find, as well as contacting the regional radio and TV stations to explain how Boggle-on-Sea was at the forefront of the computer age and how the conference, as the most important event of the year for the industry, should really be covered by the broadcast media. With all preparations made, it was just a matter now of sitting back and taking the registration requests which would undoubtedly come flooding in. At least, this is what Ernie suggested one dark Friday afternoon as they were leaving the premises. "It will be a resounding success" he said as he pulled closed the sticking door. "Of course it will" agreed Natasha. "Indubitably" said Percy. "Indeed" said Herbert. "Caw" said the crow. They wandered back up the un-made road towards town, as the clouds passed in front of the full moon, still discussing the conference as they went. The crow sat patiently on the roof of Enterprise House and watched them grow smaller and smaller until, eventually, they disappeared over the horizon. He then closed his keen eyes on another Boggle day and dozed off.

The next week passed quietly enough until the Friday when, all of a sudden, enquiries and registrations started to come in for the conference. The week after, more registrations followed and, by the Wednesday, they were being flooded with enquiries. "We already have more than we can fit into the Scouts hut" complained Natasha, but the registrations continued to flood in. By the end of the week, Dreadnought Consultants had made more money than their entire career to date, without doing anything at all. However, the team were starting to get a little concerned at the sheer numbers of visitors that were going to descend upon Boggle-on-Sea and whether the town would be able to cope with this sudden influx. As for fitting them into the new 'Conference Centre' it was decided that, if need be, they would have to run a shift system with morning and afternoon sessions, although Ernie felt sure that they would manage as many of the delegates would simply want to enjoy their day or two by the seaside. Indeed, some of them would probably not actually attend the conference at all, as was often the case with business conferences. Further arrangements were made and Ernie struck a franchise arrangement with Luigi's Ice Cream and Bert Scarlett's Fish and Chips, both of whom would be allowed to park their Dormobiles outside the Scouts hut for the duration of the conference. All of the available accommodation in Boggle was quickly spoken for, even though it was charged at double the usual rate, and emergency discussions were made with the Council who kindly made available a row of derelict Council properties on Queen Mary Terrace, a short walk from the venue. Ernie bought a few tubs of whitewash from the local suppliers and, with help from Percy and Herbert, quickly redecorated the small terraced houses and, describing them as Senior Executive Penthouses, let them out to small groups of delegates at exorbitant rates. However, there remained a number of delegates who had paid their subscription and yet clearly would find no accommodation in Boggle. "They might be lucky at Limewell or Greycliff" suggested Natasha, "there are a few guesthouses there after all, and its only a few miles walk". "Well, they will just have to take pot luck" affirmed Ernie as he was totting up their earnings to date. Mr. Spindlebrook at the Boggle Mutual was going to be very pleased indeed. Herbert suggested that, if need be, some of them could sleep on the beach if the weather was nice. He was overlooking the fact that the beach was actually a series of mud flats with intertwining little creeks which, at high tide, would swamp the lower lying areas. There was though the Boggle Pier which, as Natasha pointed out, although a little windy, did represent dry ground – unless of course it rained, which it often did at Boggle-on-Sea. There was also a slight issue with seagulls. Nevertheless, the team felt that, overall, the delegates would be reasonably well catered for during their visit to this historic town.

In due course, the first day of the conference arrived. Delegates had been arriving during the previous day and Boggle was bustling with activity, in spite of the rain teaming down in near horizontal sheets as it blew in from the sea. The Conference Centre started to fill up as the queue stretched away across the muddy lane.

A few delegates had to leap out of the way as the Mayor's official limousine arrived with lights ablaze and the Boggle-on-Sea crest flying from the radio aerial on the roof. The Daimler was dutifully parked next to the fish and chip van and his worship, Mr Claude Bonking, complete with his chain of office and pin-striped trousers was ushered past the queuing delegates and into the Conference Centre. There was a brief moment of concern as the chain of office became entangled with the galvanised door latch of what was the original Scouts hut door, but, after a minute or two, they had his worship free and implanted upon the makeshift stage, ready for the official opening. Bonking stood erect, with his chain of office, newly pressed trousers and muddy boots, his bosom swelling with pride as he announced the Great Boggle-on-Sea Computer Science Symposium, hosted by Dreadnought Consultants – a slight variation on what he had been instructed to say, but it was close enough. He went on to welcome citizens of all nations, hoping that they would enjoy their stay in this delightful, cultural centre of the Western World. The delegates squeezed the rain from their sodden clothes as Bonking retired to the back of the hall for a well earned mug of hot tea and a bag of chips, courtesy of the conference organisers. Ernie was acting as the master of ceremonies for the day, thanking the Mayor and outlining the exciting agenda to follow, starting with the keynote presentation from the renowned Professor Charles Higgins, HRD, BSA, AJS. As a nervous Charlie mounted the stage in his Council overalls, the sound of the official Daimler, honking its horn and spinning its tyres in order to put as much distance as possible between itself and what would follow, could be heard through the half open skylights. Ernie had provided Charlie with a brief script, which was really just a selection of prompts, the idea being that Charlie would create a story around them as he went. Its possible that Ernie and Natasha had slightly overestimated Charlie's ability to rise to such a situation. Once on stage, he shuffled about a bit, hands deep in the pockets of his overalls, before, to Ernie's horror, he pulled out the 'script' and started to read from it verbatim. "The importance of cloud technology and third party infrastructures" he announced proudly. The audience looked straight ahead in an impression-less stare as if mesmerised. "Data security might become an issue" he continued. The audience continued to look blank. After one or two more pronouncements, Charlie remembered that he was supposed to adlib a little, with some relevant anecdotes from the real world. Unfortunately, Charlie's real world was slightly different from that of the delegates and the only anecdotes he knew were those he picked up on the dustcart round. He threw in what he supposed were a few gems, including the story of how he had to fish Mrs Wainwright's cat out of the back of the dustcart, seconds before it was due to be crushed by the compressor. Then there was the one about Fred Crumple forgetting his belt and having to hold up the trousers of his overalls with one hand while he dragged the bins with the other. Ernie peeked out apprehensively from the wings, but the delegates continued to look straight ahead with blank expressions as Charlie moved on to explain why federated identity was important and also why it was important not to over-inflate the front tyres of the dustcart in the winter months. Accompanying these pearls of wisdom, was a backdrop of colourful slides provided from a 35mm carousel projector that Natasha was operating. They were mostly views of impressive looking buildings in the city, interspersed with pictures of computers, making the point about the necessity of computers in the modern world. Unfortunately, after the fourth slide, the mechanism jammed, leaving a picture of one of the leading banks skewed sideways across the screen with a large black bar across the top. To complement the dulcet tones of Charlie's engaging voice, a backdrop of clicking and clunking from the projector as it struggled to right itself, completed the scene nicely. The audience continued to stare straight ahead with no sign of any emotion or acknowledgement. Eventually, Charlie's thirty minutes were up and, to Ernie's utter astonishment, the audience applauded loudly as Charlie gave a friendly wave and headed off for his tea and chips.

Next up was Percy, who had prepared a well rehearsed speech about financing IT projects and the importance of proper planning, including the choice of the right consultants with which to realise the corporate objectives. He threw in lots of phrases around 'enterprise level technology' 'corporate budgets' 'return on investment' and other such nonsense, interspersed with a lot of figures and pretend calculations which proved irrevocably the importance of consultancy and how Dreadnought Consultants had consistently outperformed the world's top 500 organisations in its exciting, groundbreaking endeavours. A flip chart had been erected on stage and Percy flipped the pages back and forth, showing a variety of completely meaningless graphs and charts. The audience continued to doggedly look straight ahead with blank expressions as Percy went through his routine. They were beginning to dry out now and settle into a bemused stupor, one or two of them looking at their watches in eager anticipation of the forthcoming coffee break. Unfortunately, one chap in the second from back row started to snore rather loudly and Natasha was quickly dispatched to go and poke him in the ribs with her umbrella in order to restore the status quo. Eventually, Percy's font of interminable nonsense dried up and the hapless delegates were released to go and fight for a tea and some light refreshments. Two kind ladies from the Salvation Army had established a tea urn under a makeshift awning at the side of the hut and this quickly came under siege, as did Bert Scarlett's fish and chip van, while others rushed across the road to the public conveniences. The entire area around the old Scouts hut was awash with confused looking individuals, tumbling over each other in the drizzling rain as they struggled to get in a luke-warm cup of tea and, for the lucky ones, a small bag of chips, before the next session. And so the conference continued, with Herbert's presentation bringing a welcome break in the weather as a beam of sunshine broke through the clouds and illuminated the area, steam rising from the felt roof of the Conference Centre as the delegates were treated to another two hours of complete nonsense while they sat dutifully on the hard wooden chairs and tried to look as interested as possible under the circumstances. Some of them thumbed through their dog-eared conference brochures, while others simply stared straight ahead and Natasha kept a careful watch on those in the second from back row, ready to intervene if necessary. When the lunch break came, the delegates suddenly came alive and pressed their way eagerly to the door and out into the sunshine. For a few minutes, Luigi's Ice Cream and Bert Scarlett's fish and chip vans were inundated, as was the Salvation Army tea urn, but, after a while, the delegates dispersed randomly, some going to stare at the mud flats while others made their way into the High Street in order to explore the historic Boggle that they had heard so much about. Many of the shopkeepers were asked for directions to the town centre. When it was explained that this *was* the town centre, the bemused delegates took to wandering up and down the same stretch, crossing each others paths repeatedly, as if hoping to discover some hidden little gem of cultural interest.

However, little gems of cultural interest were quite hard to find in Boggle-on-Sea, in spite of the Mayor's pronouncements. Nevertheless, such endeavours did make a welcome break from the conference. Those on the mudflats were systematically attacked by seagulls, who, with a particularly well organised campaign, managed to steal all the chips which, just a few minutes before had been warming in the pans of Bert Scarlett's Dormobile. The witless delegates didn't stand a chance against this high precision military operation as staged by Boggle's most industrious and capable residents. An hour and a half later, the still hungry delegates returned to the Conference Centre as the seagulls sat, looking quite pleased with themselves, on the edge of the pier and looked on with interest. They knew that they would have another chance when the afternoon break came.

And so the pattern continued on that seminal first day of the conference. The delegates squeezed back into the former Scouts hut and took their places on the hard wooden chairs, ready to be assaulted with the most bizarre, interminable nonsense that the English language could be contorted into delivering. They stared ahead dutifully as Ernie, Percy, Herbert and Natasha went through their various routines, all of which were simply variations on the same theme; a few popular buzzwords and phrases, interspersed with the blatant promotion of Dreadnought Consultants and their extensive capabilities which, apparently, were able to meet any challenge that the civilised world was capable of producing, all at a most reasonable cost and with service second to none. It was a reasonably polished performance, but not half as polished as that of the seagulls who, flush with their earlier success, attacked the delegates with a new vigour during the afternoon break, parting them from their fish and chips with a style and efficiency that was simply breathtaking. During the last sessions, some of the delegates started to look a little weary and, unfortunately, Natasha's services with the umbrella were required once or twice among the rearward ranks. Nevertheless, it all seemed to go off OK and, eventually, the closing speech from Ernie rounded off what had been a milestone in the annals of both Boggle-on-Sea and the computer industry at large. The hitherto blank faces of the delegates were beaming with joyous relief as they filed out of the Scouts hut. They had made it to the end of the first day of the conference and dispersed happily to their various lodgings. Mrs. Cravat welcomed several of them back to the guesthouse and took orders for their evening meal. There was no choice of menu, simply what ever she could come up with to meet the demand. Those on Queen Mary Terrace returned to empty rooms where they sat for a while in dismay, wondering where they might get a meal in Boggle as they hadn't noticed too many restaurants in the town centre. A fortunate few, those who had opted for the 'premium' delegates package at additional cost, were invited back to the drinks reception at Enterprise House.

In preparation for the drinks reception, Ernie and Natasha went to the local store and bought six bottles of cheap Riesling, a few cartons of orange juice, some giant size bulk packets of crisps and a few packets of chocolate digestive biscuits. Upon careful consideration, they decided it would be better to decant the wine into some glass jugs, watering it down in the process in order to make it go further. A couple of decorators tables were hired, cloaked in old bed sheets, and the office furniture rearranged in order to accommodate a reasonable number of standing guests. Charlie was retained to check the delegates tickets as they arrived and Natasha changed into one of her posh frocks for the occasion. A stack of Dreadnought Consultants brochures had been liberally distributed and some enquiry forms were placed on the drinks tables. Ernie had brought in his radio / cassette player and some tapes of innocuous background music to complete the scene. At eight o'clock precisely, the sticking door was wedged open with a brick, the cassette player started and the Dreadnought team stood by in eager anticipation of their guests arrival. They didn't have long to wait, as most of the 'premium' delegates had hardly eaten that day and were keen to get to the refreshments, such as they were. They descended on Enterprise House like a swarm of locusts and, within minutes, the crisp bowls were empty and the plates where the chocolate digestives had been showed not even a crumb. Realising that there was nothing more to come, they fell in to some half hearted conversation with the Dreadnought team about computer systems, networks and other such topics. Ernie got stuck with Dr Roderick Grimping from the GCHQ, who insisted on talking about the relative efficacy of encryption algorithms, while Percy entertained a couple of Dutchmen who were keen to collaborate with Dreadnought, providing they could supply systems in Dutch. Natasha entertained the various media representatives who consisted of Juliet Slinkbottom from the Boggle Examiner, and a young lady from the Colchester Gazette who had no interest whatsoever in computers but fancied a day or two at the seaside. Herbert however was, for a moment or two, in a state of deep shock as a loud, brash and highly animated woman made a bee-line for him, having seen his performance at the Conference Centre. "Aw, there you are!" she exclaimed loudly while giving him a pat on the back that nearly knocked him off his feet. "What a cute little place this is" The realisation that this was an American seeped into Herbert like an intravenous injection. Not only an American, but a lady American, an eventually for which poor Herbert was totally unprepared. However, with the initial shock slowly subsiding, he joined into the conversation as best he could while nervously looking around him in the hope that he might be rescued by one of his colleagues. The lady in question, Bethany Bugalberg, poured herself another glass of watered down wine from the nearest jug. "Curious taste this" she opined, "is it vintage?" "Oh yes. 1946 I believe, quite a good year" suggested Herbert. "Oh! You're such a dear" she continued. "By the way, down in the town today, one of the shopkeepers told me that Henry the eighth used to regularly come to Boggle on his vacations" "His what?" asked Herbert. "Vacations" she repeated. "Oh, those" Herbert looked a little perplexed. "It's such a historic little place" she suggested with a sense of wonder. "Oh yes" replied Herbert, "if you look at the end of the pier tomorrow, you can still see the rope marks where Nelson used to moor HMS Victory". "Lord Nelson!" exclaimed Bethany with a gasp. "Oh yes, he used to like to come and see Nell Gwynn when she was acting in one of Shakespeare's new plays down at the Boggle open air theatre". "William Shakespeare!" she gasped, "did he used to come to Boggle-on-Sea?". "Oh yes, we couldn't keep him away" suggested Herbert, "if you pop in to the saloon bar at the Rabbit and Trap, you can see the little bench by the fireside where he used to sit, a pint in one hand and his notebook in the other". "Really!" exclaimed Miss Bugalberg, her eyes growing wider. "Samuel Pepys used to sit opposite, unless of course Charles II was down for the day, in which case he would take the chair nearer the fireplace as his gout used to play up something dreadful in the autumn months" explained Herbert. "Of course, the railway wasn't electrified then, and Boggle was something of a haven for the upper crust celebrities from London" he continued. "Well, I'll be blowed" exclaimed Bethany, "just wait till I tell the folks at home". She smiled and moved closer. "You know, you're really quite a cute little fellow" she said, tapping Herbert affectionately on the shoulder, just as he was taking a slurp from his wine glass. "We should stay in touch. Who knows, perhaps we can do business together" she purred. Herbert looked a little panic-stricken at such a suggestion, but quickly regained his composure, as he wiped the spilt drink from his jacket and smiled back at his new found companion. Meanwhile, the other guests had started to slowly disappear until, around ten o'clock, only the Dreadnought team were left. They quickly cleared away the glasses, grabbed their coats and made for the door. After all, it had been a long day. "What a great success!" suggested Natasha as Ernie pulled closed the sticking door. "Wasn't it just" agreed Percy, "Of course it was" said Ernie, "Indeed" said Herbert, "Caw" said the crow, and they headed off into the darkness of a still Boggle night, as an owl hooted somewhere in the distance.

The next day, the conference continued in the same vein, with a mixture of wonderful presentations, interspersed with periodic breaks when the delegates could network among their peers, although most of the networking was undertaken by the seagulls who were determined to make the most of the rare opportunity afforded by the conference. Bert Scarlett and Luigi were struggling to keep up with demand and the Salvation Army ladies, Miss Sims and Miss Huckles were particularly enjoying the event as they doled out endless mugs of stewed tea from the urn, which was replenished shortly before each break. The highlight of the day was inadvertently caused by the bad weather of the previous day, which had damaged the fence on the adjoining piece of land to where the Conference Centre sat. This allowed the goats who were grazing there to get loose and, being of a curious disposition, some of them wandered into the Conference Centre and up the central aisle towards the stage, just as Percy was entering upon his afternoon presentation on data mining. Natasha and Ernie quickly came to the rescue by herding the goats gently back towards the rear of the hall and back out of the door, although one or two of them were particularly difficult and proved adept and running back in among the delegates at the last moment. "Shoo, shoo you beastly creatures" hissed Natasha under her breath, at which invocation the lead goat bleated back loudly in defiance. Nevertheless, by the time Percy had started on his concluding remarks, they had all been escorted safely back outside. The audience sat looking straight ahead throughout the whole episode, as if determined not to acknowledge the reality of what was occurring. After Percy's presentation, Ernie continued with the last item of the day and, in due course, the delegates were released, much to their relief, back on to the streets of beautiful Boggle-on-Sea. Not a word was said about the goats. In the evening, the drinks reception at Enterprise House proved as successful as the that of the day before and everything went according to plan.

The final day dawned brightly over the Scouts hut and Ernie noticed that attendance had fallen off somewhat. Presumably some of the delegates had taken the early train back to London, possibly over-stimulated by the wonderful events of the past two days. However, there were still quite a few left and the hall was about half full as Ernie gave the opening address. Those remaining stared blankly ahead, as was their fashion, as Charlie, Percy and Herbert worked through their inspiring revelations from the world of computers. After the morning break, less returned than went out and numbers were further reduced. At the lunch break, several delegates could be seen heading for the station and the seagulls were a little disappointed at such a display of weakened constitution, although they continued their interaction with those that were left. The remaining delegates were getting a little demob happy and becoming rather more chatty than they had been over the previous two days. Bethany Bugalberg, who now insisted absolutely that Herbert call her Beth, was in top form as she pinned Herbert against the side of Luigi's ice cream van while she told him all about her home town of Lompoc in California and suggested that he really must come out for a visit, as soon as possible, a prospect that chilled Herbert to the bone. In due course, they filed back inside for the start of the afternoon session. By now there were around ten delegates left, dotted sparsely around the hall, as the

Dreadnought team embarked upon their remaining presentations. After the afternoon break, there were just four left. Even the redoubtable Miss Bugalberg had thrown in the towel and headed for the station. Nevertheless, the remaining presentations were unleashed upon the audience and, to round things off nicely, Ernie gave a round up speech of conclusions to the conference, emphasising the various ways that interested parties could contact Dreadnought Consultants for all their IT related needs. Finally, after explaining to the remaining delegates that the conference really had ended, there was a spatter of applause and everyone filed back out of the Conference Centre, Ernie padlocking the door behind them. Luigi and Bert Scarlett had already driven their Dormobiles away and the Salvation Army ladies were nowhere to be seen. Even the seagulls had gone. The Dreadnought team, exhausted by their efforts, made their way back to Enterprise House as the sun started to cast long shadows across the mud flats. After a nice cup of tea, they reflected upon the great success that the Dreadnought Consultants Computer Science Symposium had undoubtedly been. "Wasn't it just marvellous?" opined Natasha. "It was indeed, and very profitable" agreed Ernie. "I should say so, we did wonderfully well" said Percy as he was totting up the receipts. Herbert remained quietly sipping his tea. "And I see you made a new friend Herbert" suggested Natasha enthusiastically. "Oh no" replied Herbert, "I was just being professionally courteous". "But she seemed to like you" rejoined Ernie. Herbert shuddered and turned a little pale. They continued to chat about the various aspects of the conference and how, next year, they would make it even bigger and better. Eventually, the time came to go home and the stalwart team gathered outside as Ernie pulled closed the sticking door. It was a Friday and they had the whole weekend before them. "Well, I shall sleep well tonight" suggested Natasha. "Me too" agreed Ernie. "Indeed" said Percy. "Certainly" said Herbert. "Caw" said the crow. The pale Boggle moon was in the ascendancy and the leaves were blowing around the unmade road as the gas tanks were silhouetted against a darkening sky. All was well with the world.

7 MEETING VIOLET

Things had settled into something akin to a rhythm at Enterprise House. New customers had been found and Ernie had created a raft of fairly useless applications with which to separate them from their available funds. In addition, they all had equally useless service contracts which, if called upon, would often result in a visit from Charlie, moonlighting from the Council depot, simply to explain to them that whatever issue they were experiencing was, unfortunately, outside the terms of the contract. After questioning Charlie for a few minutes on the small print, they invariably gave up the endeavour as a lost cause and simply bought some more software and hardware from Ernie. Percy and Herbert looked after the books and Natasha attended to marketing and the maintenance of the Dreadnought Consultants web site which, naturally, billed them as the world's leading systems integrator and computer science consultants. A picture of a large modern office block was shown on the front page and there were pages with profiles of the Executive Board (Ernie, Percy, Herbert and Natasha), a list of competencies, pictures of racks of computers and of course a contacts page. Indeed, things were bubbling along quite nicely.

One sunny morning in June, the boys were a little perturbed that Natasha hadn't arrived at the usual time. This was most disconcerting as it meant that they had to make their own morning tea and Percy's skills in the kitchen were, unfortunately, a little lacking. As they sat back in their chairs to contemplate the exciting day ahead of them, Ernie reading the morning newspaper, Percy looking out of the window and Herbert gently dozing off, they heard voices approaching the front door. One of them was Natasha's as she said, "now wait their darling while I explain things to the boys". The front door juddered open and Natasha breezed in smiling sweetly. "You'll never guess" she exclaimed cheerfully, "I have a lovely surprise for you". The boys looked a little worried. "You see" she continued, "Fenella has some private business to attend to this morning and, it being half term, I agreed that Violet could came and stay with us for an hour or two". With that, and notwithstanding the panic stricken expressions turned her way, she motioned Violet in. "Isn't she a little dear?" suggested Natasha. "Er, oh yes, quite" stuttered Ernie. "Hello dear" volunteered Percy a little nervously. Herbert simply looked dumbfounded as he sat quietly in the corner. Violet marched in sharply, in her lovely little blue dress with big yellow flowers upon it, her chestnut brown hair arranged in a neat pony tail. "Uncle Ernie will show you the nice computers while I organise some orange juice and biscuits" said Natasha, disappearing into the utility area, oblivious to Ernie's protestations that, actually, he *was* quite busy. "Well?" exclaimed Violet expectantly. There was nothing for it, Ernie would have to explain the Dreadnought computer systems to little Miss Violet, although, he was quite sure that it would all pass over her head. "This is our new, Dreadnought branded email client" he explained, clicking a few buttons and showing how it worked. "You sell it to people, do you?" asked Violet. Ernie proudly confirmed that that was indeed the case, to which Violet rejoined, "but why should they pay for that when there are a number of others available for free, and which look much nicer?" "But they don't perform as well as this one" replied Ernie, in a somewhat patronising tone. Violet looked at him sharply. "Of course they do" she said, "all they have to do is make a connection and pass a stream of text". Ernie, temporarily lost for words fumbled with the computer and Herbert, who had been listening attentively suddenly exclaimed, "she's right you know" as he looked on with ever widening eyes. As Ernie continued to fumble, Violet interjected. "What's that?" "Oh, you wouldn't understand, it's our new cloud offering" replied Ernie. "How does it work?" insisted Violet. Ernie took a deep breath and explained the concept of the cloud and how Dreadnought had established a couple of servers at Enterprise House in order to provide this exciting new capability. Violet thought for a moment. "That's just plain silly" she suggested confidently, "why would people pay for a third party infrastructure, outside of their control, when they already have their own infrastructure which they can support themselves?". Ernie looked pained and was wondering how much longer Natasha would be with the orange juice. Herbert moved a little closer. "She's right you know" he said again. Much to Ernie's relief, the orange juice and biscuits finally made an appearance. "How are you getting on darling?" asked Natasha. "Fine thank you" replied Violet as she took hold of the orange juice. Ernie gave a sigh of relief, but his optimism was premature. "Tell me how you support all these systems" Violet blurted out between slurps of orange juice. "Oh, isn't she a treasure?" suggested Natasha. Ernie winced and explained how they charged extra for support contracts, according to the complexity of what had been provided. "But that's dishonest" rejoined Violet, "you should support everything that you supply as a matter of course, without charge and indefinitely, as a matter of courtesy and goodwill towards your customers". Herbert gasped. "She's right you know" he repeated. "Nonsense" blurted Ernie, by now becoming a little impatient, "we would be bankrupt within a month". "No you wouldn't" insisted Violet, "the increased volumes and economies of scale would ensure that you realise a more consistent revenue stream, making it easier to plan ahead. Furthermore, the perception of the company within the marketplace would steadily increase". "She's right you know" insisted Herbert once again. "Of course she is, she's a little darling" affirmed Natasha. Ernie looked at Percy in desperation. Percy looked back at Ernie and Violet took another slurp of orange juice and selected a biscuit from the plate. The dialogue continued in a similar vein until it was time for Natasha to escort Violet back to the welcoming arms of Fenella and Boggleton Hall. Violet made her goodbyes, with a special farewell handshake to 'uncle Herbert' who, she suggested, she looked forward to meeting again. Natasha pulled closed the sticking front door and the boys gave a sigh of relief. Except for Herbert, who had clearly become smitten with little Violet and was hoping that he would indeed see her again.

Fate works in strange ways, especially in Boggle-on-Sea where what will be, will undoubtedly be. And so it was that, by invitation from Fenella, Herbert found himself walking up the gravel path and swinging the lion's head door-knocker of Boggleton Hall one windy evening as the summer sun started on its descent towards better climes. Unaccustomed to visitors at the Hall, Liliya Seminovsky had been primed for Herbert's arrival, while Fenella and Violet sat reading quietly in the library. The old oak door creaked open slowly to reveal the lady of the house, standing in the shadows in her long dress and pince-nez spectacles. Herbert announced himself. "Ah, yes, I believe we were expecting you" drooled Liliya as she looked him up and down with an air of thinly disguised distaste. She would have preferred someone in a military uniform, or perhaps dressed like an international diplomat, but Herbert was at least presentable, in a downtown Boggle sort of way. As he entered the hallway, Fenella came waltzing out from the library. "You came, how sweet of you, dear Herbert" she smiled, holding out her hand, an appendage which Herbert was not quite sure what to do with. Should he kiss it? Shake it? He held it limply for a while and indicated that he was pleased to be there. Herbert had never really been a ladies man and felt a little unsure when in feminine company. The visit had been arranged by Natasha and Fenella, upon the pretence that Herbert had never been to Boggleton Hall and would appreciate its classic architecture and assorted, if somewhat faded, works of art. The real reason was that Violet had requested a meeting with Herbert on her own ground. Fenella showed Herbert into the library. "You're late" exclaimed Violet as her bright eyes drilled into Herbert. "It was a longer walk than I expected" replied Herbert apologetically. "Well, in future you must be on time" suggested Violet in an authoritative voice, "come and sit here". Herbert, a little puzzled by this development, looked anxiously towards Fenella. "Oh, she has been so looking forward to your visit" smiled Fenella. "Why don't you have a little chat while I prepare some tea". Fenella disappeared and closed the library door behind her, leaving Herbert alone with Violet. "Right" announced the latter, "I want you to tell me everything about the computers and software being sold by Dreadnought

Consultants". "But I can't do that" protested Herbert, "that is confidential company information". "Don't be silly" responded Violet, "how can it be confidential if people are buying them? Now, do as you are told, or you won't be invited here again". Poor Herbert was in a quandary. He considered it not quite right to discuss company business outside of Enterprise House, but he was also fascinated, if not bewitched, by the Seminovsky household and, in particular, by young Violet. While turning it over in his mind, Violet offered some gentle encouragement. "Come on, come on. What are you waiting for? I've got other things to do this evening. Now, sit down and tell me everything". Herbert sat down nervously while Violet picked up her notebook and pencil. It was a full half hour before Fenella returned with some tea, by which time Violet had dragged almost all the relevant information out of Herbert and noted in down in her little book. "I thought you were going to show me around the house" suggested Herbert meekly. "Oh, it's a little dark now, maybe another day" Fenella smiled, "In any case, I am sure that you and Violet have lots to talk about. She is such an inquisitive child". Inquisitive isn't the word, thought Herbert to himself while he sipped his tea. He had barely drained half the cup when Violet, after consulting her notes, insisted that he go over the whole thing again, so that she could check the details for accuracy. Eventually, Herbert was released back into the wild and made his way back to Mrs Cravat's boarding house.

Over the ensuing weeks, such visits to Boggleton Hall became more frequent. Herbert developed a genuine affection for Violet and, interestingly, so did she for him. They were completely comfortable in each other's company and developed an understanding between each other that required few spoken words. Violet systematically extracted information from Herbert while simultaneously developing her own IT skills. And then, one overcast evening as the wind was howling around Boggleton Hall, she casually announced to Herbert her plan. It was a bold plan which required complete and absolute loyalty from Herbert, together with secrecy in its initial execution. Herbert was not at all sure that he should go along with it, but Violet persuaded him. "If you do not do exactly as I ask, you will not be invited back and I shall never speak to you again" she announced in a matter of fact manner. Herbert realised that he had no choice in the matter, as Violet already held quite a spell over him. He reluctantly, agreed that he would play his part in the plan. The details were gone over once more and Herbert was given his explicit instructions, in fine detail, with the reassertion that he must not, on any account, fail. Violet was very clear on that point as she escorted him to the door. As the big oak door closed behind him, Herbert felt his heart jump a couple of times in anticipation of what was coming. He walked slowly down the gravel path but dud not hear his own footsteps and then, at the corner with the flickering street lamp, two black cats crossed his trail, one from each side, meowing hysterically as they went. He looked up, it was a full moon, with dark clouds rapidly crossing its face as a lone bat fluttered silently around Herbert's head for a moment or two before moving on and disappearing into the night. Herbert drew a deep breath. Fate was calling and what would be, would be. He marched forward resolutely and thought of the charge of the Light Brigade as he made his way towards Estuary Gardens. Before long, he was at his destination and, as he turned the key in the lock of Enterprise House, he looked up instinctively towards the flat roof. "Caw" said the crow. "Its all right for you" replied Herbert as he pushed open the sticking door and nervously turned on the light. Thirty minutes later, he was to exit through the same portal, clutching a supermarket plastic bag in one hand and looking around anxiously before turning the key in the lock once again. This time it seemed to make a very loud and final sounding clunk and Herbert swallowed hard as he withdrew the key and looked up toward the flat roof again. The crow said nothing but seemed to look at Herbert with a knowing stare as he cocked his head to one side and fixed his beady eye firmly upon the shadowy figure standing before him. Nevertheless, the deed had been accomplished and there was no turning back now, so Herbert quietly made his way home and tried his best to grab a little sleep before the rigours of the new day ahead.

As Ernie leaned his bicycle up against the side of

Enterprise House, a peal of thunder rolled across the sky and the heavens opened, delivering sheets of rain upon that little piece of Boggle known as Estuary Gardens. The gas tank behind Enterprise House could hardly be discerned in the mist and the unmade road was quickly becoming a quagmire. He pushed open the sticking door and rushed inside to revel in the comparative cosiness of the Dreadnought offices. Heaving a sigh of relief as he shook the rain off his jacket and headed to the utility area to fill the kettle, his mind was dancing happily, thinking of what he would sell to the hapless Dreadnought client base that day. He heard the front door judder open again and the happy voices of Natasha and Percy as they joked about the weather and shook the rain from their respective garments. "Kettles on" he shouted as Natasha made her way to the utility area. "Oh good" she exclaimed enthusiastically, "I do so need a nice cup of tea. I will see to it". Ernie returned to the main office area to find Percy looking, with some curiosity, at a blank screen. "What's up Percy" he asked. "Doesn't seem to want to boot up this morning" replied a confused Mr. Proudfoot. While they were trying to breathe life into Percy's computer, Herbert arrived and quietly made his way to the utility area. Natasha had by that time sat down at her computer and suddenly cried out in dismay, "Something's wrong. My computer won't boot up, the stupid thing". Ernie went over to have a look and then, suddenly thinking of his own computer, the one with all the development work and source code for all of the Dreadnought applications, rushed back to his desk and pushed the power button. The computer whirled and bleeped and then came up with a message that informed Ernie that no operating system was found. Herbert sat quietly in the corner with his tea. "There must have been a freak power surge or some other catastrophic event" suggested Ernie as he went from computer to computer, all of which were effectively dead, "we had better dig out the backup disks and reinstall everything". "Oh what a nuisance" exclaimed Natasha, "I was going to work on a new brochure today". Herbert sat quietly in the corner with his tea. Ernie unlocked the filing cabinet where all the backups were stored, and stepped back in astonishment. "Its empty!" he cried. "It can't be" exclaimed Percy. "It is, look for yourself" replied Ernie. "But wasn't that where you held all of our back up files, customer records and service contracts, in case anything went wrong with the computers?" asked Natasha. "Exactly" cried Ernie. Herbert sat quietly in the corner with his tea. After some more exclamations and worried expressions, Ernie turned his gaze towards Herbert. "Wait a minute" he blurted out, "how come you haven't tried to fire up your computer. You know something about this" "I don't know what you mean" replied Herbert with mock indignation. "Yes you do. It's that damn girl isn't it, she put you up to this". The others all turned towards Herbert and he felt three pairs of eyes burning into him. Suddenly, he stood up abruptly from his chair. "Well, what if I do know something. Violet is right, I told you so all along" "Oh no" cried Ernie, his head in his hands, "I should have expected something like this. We shall be ruined". "Not at all" replied Herbert enthusiastically, "If we follow Violet's plan, we shall be more successful than ever". "Violet's plan!" exclaimed Ernie in horror. "Of course" cried Natasha, "that must be what the little dear has been working on these past weeks of her school holiday, how wonderful". "Indeed" continued Herbert, and he went on to explain how Violet was producing a new range of software for them that would be sold exclusively on line, each application costing £50 and with free support for life. The first couple of examples of which would be ready the next day. Ernie flew into a rage and, accusing Herbert of lapsing into lunacy, demanded that he return all the backup discs immediately. "I can't, they've been destroyed" claimed Herbert. "What do you mean, destroyed?" rejoined Ernie. "Incinerated, on Violet's orders" confirmed Herbert. A stunned silence ensued for a few moments. "It's brilliant!" Natasha suddenly blurted out. "Of course, we shall make a fortune" she continued, "people will be buying our software hand over fist, don't you see?" Percy thought for a moment. "And there will be no competition, because none of the big companies would ever dare to follow such a model" he suggested as he slowly warmed to the idea. "It's crazy" insisted Ernie, "we shall be bankrupt in a month".

As the clouds dispersed and the sun climbed high in

the sky above Boggle-on-Sea the occupants of Enterprise House continued to discuss the momentous events of the day. It was evident that they could not continue to run the business in the way they had been doing to date, as they had lost all of the relevant information. They would simply have to start all over again and support their existing customers as best they could. Furthermore, in the absence of any other business plan, they might as well give Violet's idea a chance. At least, that is what Natasha and Percy thought and, naturally, Herbert was very happy about the prospect. "You should see what Violet is developing for us" he enthused. "Probably software with little pink lambs and bright coloured flowers all over it" suggested Ernie sarcastically. "Oh, how wonderful, I do hope so" replied Natasha. Percy, meanwhile, had been making a few calculations and was quickly coming around to Violet's way of thinking. "You know, such a model could actually work quite well" he suggested, "after all, we would have very few costs and, if we can find the necessary economies of scale, it might prove quite profitable". "Economies of scale? In Boggle?" countered Ernie. "Not just Boggle, but the whole world" suggested Natasha. "We will construct a new Internet site, based around Violet's business model and enable customers to purchase and download the software directly". "With free lifetime support" added Herbert. "Of course" replied Natasha, "we will include an on-line forum where users can share their experiences and offer help to each other. It can't fail".

And so the discussion continued, with suggestion and counter-suggestion, argument and counter-argument until, after their fourth cup of tea, the milk had run out and, in any event, they were all quite exhausted with their intellectual efforts and so decided that they would finish early. Gathering outside the entrance to Enterprise House, Ernie pulled closed the sticking door. "We are ruined" he sighed. "Not at all" said Herbert. "Of course not" said Natasha. "Never" said Percy. "Caw" said the crow. They slowly dispersed in their various directions and Ernie put on his bicycle clips and headed back towards Westminster Drive where he could commiserate with auntie Freda. It was all a very long way from dear old Crinkington and Ernie's original aspirations to be a computer scientist.

The next day, as the boys were gathering at Enterprise House, they heard Natasha approaching while chatting with someone else. Upon recognising the other voice, Herbert's face lit up with undisguised joy, Percy looked a little perplexed and Ernie's expression betrayed a look of impending doom. "Look who's come to join us this morning" Natasha announced cheerfully. Before the boys could acknowledge their visitor, Violet explained, "I have come to establish the first two applications on your web site and explain the business model to you. I will work with auntie Natasha to set everything up and then we will have a meeting to discuss support and ongoing roles and responsibilities". Ernie and Percy looked dumbfounded. Herbert looked calm and collected. "I will help you" he suggested to Violet. "No, you work with uncle Percy to set up the credit card payment account with the acquirers. I've written the instructions for you here" replied Violet, handing Herbert a piece of paper. The morning rushed by in a blur of activity as Violet and Natasha placed details of the first two applications on the web site. These were a personnel directory and badge printing system, and a file backup system. Both were presented in an attractive blue and grey design with an attractive new Dreadnought Consultants logo which Violet had designed, the words highlighted with a little flower symbol. Ernie looked on in anguish as the deed was done, wondering if he would ever be able to show his face again in the rarefied circles of the IT fraternity. "There, its simple" announced Violet presently. "Every Dreadnought Consultants application will have a standard, one off price of £50, payable by credit card on the website. Users may then download the application and use it however they wish, with free lifetime support via phone or email". "Its ludicrous" exclaimed Ernie, "no-one will take us seriously". "Quiet!" said Violet sharply, "I've already told you how it will work. People will be delighted and you will have more customers than ever before, and more sales. Furthermore, customers will remain loyal to Dreadnought Consultants, buying every piece of software that we announce". "Oh, how wonderful" exclaimed Natasha, "isn't it exciting?". "Its brilliant" confirmed Herbert proudly, "Violet has thought of everything" in so saying he looked warmly across at Violet who was turning the pages of her little pink notebook. "I will now explain the ongoing business strategy to you" she announced in confident tones. "Auntie Natasha will manage marketing, uncle Percy will manage the accounts and Herbert and Ernie will provide support as required by our customers. I will develop the technical strategy and produce the applications". "Just a minute" interrupted Ernie impatiently, "this is my company you know, and I will decide who does what and what our strategy is". "Nonsense" cried Natasha indignantly, "we are a partnership and, by a majority decision, we have welcomed Violet to the company as our new technical and business manager". "But she will be going back to school after the holidays" suggested Percy nervously. "Of course, the whole idea is absurd" rejoined Ernie. "Quiet" cried Violet, stamping her little foot. "I will continue to develop the business model and associated applications in my spare time. You will run the day to day activities as suggested". "Exactly" agreed Natasha, "it will all work like clockwork. Violet is such a dear, she has worked everything out for us".

Ernie and Percy remained unconvinced but, in the absence of any other plan and considering that their previous applications and contracts had all been lost, they decided to go along with Violet's idea, at least in the short term. In the background, Ernie would be designing a new business model, with new applications and associated support plans. Two days passed and they had not received a single enquiry from the new web site. "Well, what do you expect?" smirked Ernie, "I told you the whole idea was preposterous. That demented little brat should be locked up somewhere". "Don't you dare speak about poor little Violet like that" protested Natasha sharply. "Indeed" agreed Herbert, "she has come up with a better business model than we ever had". "But we haven't sold anything" continued Ernie, "how long do you think we can go without sales". "We weren't selling anything anyway" suggested Percy. And so the discussion went on in a much subdued Enterprise House, under a dark Boggle-on-Sea sky, the monotony only broken by the odd cup of tea here and there. And then, on the third day, the sun broke through the clouds and, by ten o'clock in the morning, they had received three orders. By twelve o'clock, they had received five. By the end of the working day, they had received eleven orders, all paid for and downloaded by the customers. "Isn't it wonderful" beamed Natasha, "just as Violet had suggested and we haven't had to do a thing". "That's quite right" agreed Percy, "the revenue just comes straight into our account without us having to do anything at all". "Just wait till they all start phoning in with complaints about the software" said Ernie cynically. The next day, more orders came in and, the day after, even more, and not a single phone call for support. Even Ernie was reluctantly agreeing that the idea seemed to be working, at least for now. On the Monday of the next week, Violet visited again, this time with a new application, the Dreadnought Office Manager, a complete system for managing contacts, transactions, invoices, bills and a comprehensive reporting system. It was duly placed upon the web site and, within a couple of hours, orders were being placed for the new application. As the week drew to its close, Dreadnought had sold well over a hundred applications from the web site and the numbers were still climbing strongly. When they came in the following Monday, the total was nearing two hundred and climbing. They had also started to receive email messages via the dedicated support address, but these were not complaints or requests for support. They were all messages of congratulations on providing excellent software at affordable prices. Natasha started to read through them. "These are wonderful" she exclaimed, "every one of them is praising our software. Listen to this; 'I just wanted to let you know how useful your software has been to our small business and how much we appreciate the free support, signed Mrs Teresa Wilson' and they are all essentially saying the same thing. Violet was right". "I said so all along" stated Herbert proudly. That evening, the sun sank low over the mudflats and the wind whirled up around Boggle-on-Sea, as if to blow away the cobwebs of the past and make way for the rising sun of a bright new dawn.

8 A NEW REGIME

Things were starting to change at Enterprise House. There was a new wave of optimism growing around the name of Dreadnought Consultants as more people downloaded and used the genuinely useful software applications that Violet had so painstakingly designed. For the first time in their existence, significant amounts of mail started to arrive at Enterprise House. Trevor, the postman, was a tall gangly man with straw coloured hair poking out at all angles from beneath his cap. A man who was tailor made for bicycle clips and ill-fitting trousers and who was incapable of arriving quietly anywhere. They had never really noticed him before, except by the sound of him noisily forcing the odd bill through the door. But now, even Trevor was remarking on the amount of mail that Enterprise House was receiving, causing him to knock on the door and hand over bundles of letters held together with an elastic band rather than posting them, one by one, through the squeaking letter box. "You will be the death of me" he exclaimed joyfully one morning to

Natasha. "All them letters make my round a lot heavier now". Natasha took pity on the man and invited him in for a cup of tea. It became a regular ritual and the whole team got to know Trevor quite well. From him they learned what was going on in the town, who was doing what and the news of any little scandal, of which Boggle seemed to be an efficient incubator. He knew who subscribed to what magazines, what cars they drove and where they parked them, who lived in which house and most of their family histories. Indeed, Trevor was a hive of information about Boggle and a welcome source of entertainment with which to ease the day along at Enterprise House.

Business was picking up nicely and, on the face of it, all was going well. However, Ernie remained concerned about the direction in which things were going. It was, after all, his company and yet Percy, Herbert and himself seemed increasingly to be becoming little more than office administrators. He decided it was time to straighten things out once and for all and called a summit meeting of the boys at lunchtime down at the Rabbit and Trap. Ernie pushed open the creaking door and headed for the bar where the landlord, George Thorogood, a burly looking character with a handlebar moustache and side whiskers plonked his dishcloth down on the counter. "What will it be gentlemen" he announced, looking at them through piercing black eyes. "Three pints of best please George" said Ernie as he turned towards Herbert, "you got us in to this so you can pay" he suggested as he headed for the snug with Percy in tow. Herbert sighed and rummaged through his pockets for the necessary change. "Right you are" said George after carefully scrutinising the coins proffered to him and Herbert struggled over to the snug, dripping a trail of watered down best bitter as he went. The boys quickly entered into a heated discussion. "Its not right" complained Ernie. "That damned girl acts as if she owns the place, telling us what we are going to sell and for how much. Its time we sorted her out once and for all". "It does seem a little odd" confirmed Percy. "We just seem to be doing the accounts and answering letters, although there is a steady stream of revenue coming in". "Exactly" said Herbert. "We are doing better now than ever before". "That's not the point" continued Ernie, "I didn't start this company to be ruled over by a twelve year old girl". The discussion went on along similar lines, with Herbert occasionally dissenting and trying to defend Violet as best he could until, getting a little frustrated, Ernie banged his first on the table and said; "Look, we are like the Three Musketeers, we must stand all for one and one for all, united in our intention to take back control of the company and run it how we want to run it, not how some precocious little brat wants to amuse herself with it. After all, we must think of the future". Reluctantly, Herbert agreed and, after a little more bravado and another of George Thorogood's finest, the three of them headed back to Enterprise House uttering slurred affirmations of their right to run their own company as they saw fit. Unbeknown to the boys, Violet had popped in as it was half term again at school, and was discussing some enhancements to the web site with Natasha. Coincidentally, they had also been discussing roles and responsibilities and had concurred that the boys were best left to administration and support tasks while they would set the ongoing strategy. As Violet sipped her orange juice and Natasha clicked through the pages of the web site, the sticking door at Enterprise House suddenly juddered and flew open with a bang. The Musketeers stormed inside and stood defiantly in a row, hands on hips while Ernie made his announcement. "Right" he barked. "This nonsense has gone on long enough. From now on, I will decide what we sell and how, what our service contracts will be and how we deal with our customers. Furthermore, I shall be designing a new suite of software for the Dreadnought portfolio. We shall not need your services anymore Violet. You may return to school". With that, Ernie took a step backwards and stood, smiling triumphantly as he glanced towards Percy and Herbert. Violet took a last sip of orange juice and then slowly slipped down from her stool. "Herbert, come here at once" she announced authoritatively. Herbert, starting to feel a little unsure of himself started nervously towards Violet. "Stay where you are man" barked Ernie. Violet simply gazed quietly at Herbert and he settled, a little closer to her than to the other Musketeers. She had effectively broken their solidarity.

"Listen to me" she started. "In the first place, you would not have survived as a company if I had not stepped in and organised things for you" "But that's ridiculous.." interrupted Ernie with a sneer. "Quiet!" said Violet, stamping her little foot. "You do not understand anything about marketing or the software that I have produced. If I leave now, the software that you have will expire as the internal certificates start to run out and you will not have a business". The Musketeers looked at each other in horror. "She's right you know" whispered Herbert nervously. "Nonsense" exclaimed Ernie. "We shall simply build better software and start again". "And what about all our existing customers" interjected Natasha. "They will lose confidence in us completely. They will never deal with us again". "We shall be a laughing stock" muttered Percy, as if to himself. An eerie silence descended upon Enterprise House, as though time itself temporarily stood still. And then, raising herself slowly to her full height, Violet declared "I shall take over forthwith as Chief Executive Officer, and we shall all take an equal share in the profits, providing that you men stick to the tasks allocated to you and leave the running of the business to auntie Natasha and myself" The boys were dumfounded, but their brains, still a little muddled by George Thorogood's concoctions, could not rise to the challenge of defending their position against the unquestionable logic of Violet's proposition. "Right, that's settled then" she declared haughtily. "Furthermore, there will be no more drinking in office hours and you will report for work promptly at eight in the morning, every morning. Now, go about your business and let us here no more of this". She shrugged her little shoulders and threw back her hair before turning her attention back to Natasha and the web site. Percy slinked off back to his computer. Herbert sheepishly fumbled about and then returned to check the support forum and Ernie, after standing for a few seconds in shock, went back to his desk. The rebellion had failed and the status quo had been restored. The Musketeers would have to hang up their swords and knuckle down to the new working regime. No more was said on the matter, although something had undeniably changed in the prevailing atmosphere at Enterprise House. Violet would breeze in occasionally and explain a new piece of software that she had written and how it should be described for marketing purposes. Natasha looked after all the practical marketing and communication issues, just as before, although now she took her lead from Violet. Percy kept an eye on the accounts and, together with Herbert, ensured that all the bills were paid and that everything was in order from a financial perspective. Ernie was left with little to do except check the support forum and answer emails from satisfied customers. It was not what he had envisaged for Dreadnought Consultants. However, business was healthy as Violet's applications continued to sell and, each morning, Trevor the postman struggled up to Estuary Gardens with a bunch of new letters, free magazines and other communications as befitting a thriving organisation at the forefront of industry. After sitting down with his tea, he would provide an update of what was going on in the town and how everyone was talking about the success of Dreadnought Consulting. It was clear that Enterprise House had become an accepted landmark in the town of Boggle-on-Sea.

Violet continued to develop useful applications in the evenings up at Boggleton Hall. Her mother Fenella and Grandma Liliya would sometimes ask her about Herbert and her ongoing relationship with Dreadnaught Consultants. "I am simply helping them out while I develop my own computer skills" she would reply quietly. Herbert would occasionally come to Boggleton Hall, but his visits were less frequent now and he always seemed a little embarrassed when there, although he enjoyed talking with Violet and hearing her plans for the future. Back at Enterprise House, the orders and revenue continued to come rolling in. They now had seven applications in their portfolio, all in the house style and all selling very well. The need for actual support had proved miniscule, just as Violet had predicted. In fact, everything seemed to turn out just as Violet had predicted. It was a constant source of consternation for Ernie, but he had to admit that business was thriving and that Dreadnaught Consultants were now firmly on the map. In that respect, his own dream had been realised, albeit in an unexpected fashion. Percy and Herbert were content and Natasha seemed to revel in her various marketing activities, liaising with the local press and specialist media, further developing the web site and working closely with Violet on new ideas. There were other changes too. After frequent requests to Mayor Bonking and the Town Council, it had been agreed that the unmade road that constituted Estuary Gardens would finally be given a proper surface and that a pavement would be laid down in front of Enterprise House. On the allotted day of the works, early in the morning, a rough looking portly gentlemen in ill-fitting overalls knocked on the door of Enterprise House. Natasha opened the door. "Come to start work on the road Ma'am" announced the gentlemen in question, a cigarette dangling from one side of his mouth. "Only, you won't be able to park outside for a few days" he continued. "Oh that's all right" answered Natasha. "None of us have cars anyway. Would you like a cup of tea before you start?" she added as an afterthought. "Very kind of you Ma'am" replied Bill, as that was his name. "Oi, lads" he called back to the lorry parked outside, "come in for a cuppa before we start". On his bidding two equally rough looking men casually lumbered over and pushed the sticking door wide open. "These are my mates Al and Dick" announced Bill with a sly grin and the three of them piled into the main office and made themselves comfortable. It was not quite what Natasha had in mind but it was too late to argue now. Ernie, Percy and Herbert soon arrived to find the three scruffy, unshaven workmen lounging in their chairs. "Mornin' Guv" beamed Dick as the boys came in. Percy looked with horror at the spectacle before him. "Oh, these gentlemen will be doing the road outside" said Natasha sheepishly. "After we've 'ad our tea of course" smiled Bill. "Oh, I see" said Herbert as he stepped over the outstretched legs of the latter. As they spoke, the resurfacing lorry pulled up rather noisily outside, clanking hissing and emitting a good deal of unsavoury fumes. Another rough, lanky man climbed down, slammed the drivers door shut and, after looking around him, sauntered over to Enterprise House. Before anyone else could say anything, Bill announced "Oh, its OK, its only Wally and the lads". He got up and, pulling open the sticking door, called out, "Oi, Wally, over 'ere mate, we've got time for a cuppa before we start". Wally whistled back towards the lorry and two more rough looking characters named Pete and Reg sauntered over to Enterprise House. They all piled in and Natasha was kept busy providing cups of tea for the entire crew. After about half an hour or so, they sauntered back outside. "Very nice of you Ma'am" said Bill. "We'll see you the same time tomorrow". As they pulled closed the sticking door, Ernie dusted off his chair. "Now look what you've done" he grumbled to Natasha. "They'll be in here every morning now". "Oh I hope not" said Percy in alarm. "Well, what if they are" exclaimed Natasha defiantly. "It's worth it to get the road done. As they argued the point, Herbert came up with something in his arms. "I think one of them has left his cat behind" he said rather sheepishly. "Aw, what a cute little chap" said Natasha stroking the head of the new arrival, a ginger Tom whose coat was of a not dissimilar appearance to the shabby overalls of the work men. Herbert took it outside to enquire whether it belonged to one of the men. "Not ours mate" called Reg as he leaned on his shovel. At that point, the cat leapt from Herbert's arms and darted back inside the office. "He must be a stray" observed Percy. "Perhaps we had better take him down to the vet". "How can you suggest such a thing" barked Natasha. "Of course we wont take him to the vet, he can stay here with us. He will be lucky for us, won't you dear" she said, stroking the feline head once again. After a couple of saucers of milk and some broken biscuits, the new arrival chose the most comfortable looking chair and curled up for a nap. "What shall we call him?" asked Natasha. "Trouble" suggested Ernie. "Felix" suggested Percy. "Tiddles" suggested Herbert. After much deliberation, they settled upon Ginger.

What an eventful morning it had been. Invaded by road workers and then adopted by a stray cat. Boggle was becoming an interesting place. Indeed, Enterprise House was becoming widely known to the residents of the town, some of whom would pop in, simply out of curiosity. Celia Pumblepink of the Women's Institute, after visiting once and having a long chat with Natasha, in which she provided a wealth of good advice about working with men, had become something of a regular and would often pop in for afternoon tea. She was a tall, elegant lady who liked to dress in long skirts and always wore a hat, even indoors. Natasha welcomed her visits as a diversion from the day to day routine, although the boys were less convinced. "We might as well open a café" suggested Ernie sarcastically one day as Miss Pumblepink was leaving. Unfortunately, she heard the remark. There was not much that Celia Pumblepink missed. Returning into the office, she poked Ernie sharply with her umbrella. "Don't you be so rude young man" she snapped. "In any case, opening a café would at least be an honest business, unlike selling people things they don't need". A final poke with the umbrella and Miss Pumblepink, with nose pointing skyward, took her leave. Ernie had been put in his place and Natasha finished the job by informing him that, as he didn't like cafes, she would not be making him any more tea. Such was life at Enterprise House. Due to Violet's business acumen and software authoring skills, revenue flowed in a regular stream and there was relatively little to do other than simple book-keeping and addressing the odd enquiry. Consequently, the office was becoming something of an unofficial community centre as Boggle residents popped in and out at will. Ginger quickly became a further attraction as people brought him in all manner of toys and little treats and he settled in nicely to his new home. Furthermore, Violet had instructed that Ginger should have the best chair by the window and that everyone should say good morning to him upon arrival. A cat flap was installed within the sticking door and Ginger fell naturally into his role of caretaker at Enterprise House.

Workman's tents were erected outside and slowly, very slowly in fact, Estuary Gardens was levelled off ready for resurfacing. The preparatory work had taken two weeks with, every day, the entire team of workmen coming in for their morning tea and explaining, in great detail, how they liked to do a job properly without rushing things. "That's the trouble these days" said Bill as he gazed philosophically above the rim of his mug of tea. "People are too hasty. They rush into everything and don't take the time to do a proper job". "That's right enough" agreed Pete as he slurped his tea. The others nodded in agreement. The conversation ran along similar lines most days and the Enterprise House team learned a great deal about the finer points of public works. After taking a good deal of time to do an excellent job of levelling off the unmade road, everything was cleared ready for the surfacing work. The tar was boiling nicely on the purpose built lorry and, very slowly, it inched its way forwards, laying down a two inch thick road surface which was starting to look very good indeed. Unfortunately, after about five yards the lorry stopped abruptly. Wally turned the starter key but the engine wouldn't start. "What is it Wal?" called Bill. "Out of diesel" shouted Wally from the open window. Bill looked at his watch and drew in a deep breath. "Well, its two thirty, not much more we can do today, we had better come back and finish it off tomorrow" "Right oh mate!" answered Wally and the others threw their shovels in the back of the lorry and, cramming into the Council van, headed off towards the depot. The next day, they all arrived promptly for their tea and had a good chat about how they would finish the job. Of course, it would take longer now as they would have an unsightly ridge where they stopped and re-started, so they would have to level that off before starting on the pavement. "We'll 'ave to bring in the roller" advised Reg as he slurped his tea. "Yeah, that's right" agreed Pete. "It will mean another few days of course". "Of course it will" agreed Bill "You can't just leave a job, 'alf done like, can you?" "No, 'course not" agreed the others in chorus as they shook their heads and looked deep into their mugs. And so it went on. Three weeks later, the job was finished and the crew, after calling in to advise that they had completed the work, and to have a last cup of tea, reluctantly took their leave of Estuary Gardens. In truth, it was far from a perfect job, but at least Enterprise House now had a stretch of paved road outside. It was all starting to look very much better. Ginger inspected the road and pavement carefully and seemed satisfied that it met his requirements. "Isn't it wonderful" said Natasha as they all went outside and looked at the new stretch of road. "Yes it is" agreed Ernie with a smile. The others agreed and, after a peaceful cup of tea on their own, they closed for the day and filed slowly out of Enterprise House. "Everything seems to be falling into place very nicely now" observed Herbert. "It is indeed" agreed Ernie. "Of course it is" said Natasha cheerfully. "Indubitably" said Percy. "Caw" said the crow. They pulled closed the sticking door and, for the first time, walked on a proper pavement as they headed off towards the town. The sky was streaked with red and gold as the sun drifted slowly down beyond the Boggle-on-Sea horizon and the moon rose serenely in the night sky, bathing Boggle in its benevolent pale light. Ginger closed his eyes and drifted off into a deep sleep, snuggled up nicely on the cushions of his favourite chair. What a wonderful world it was.

9 THE BOGGLE FESTIVAL

Celia Pumblepink, in addition to being the leading light at the Boggle Women's Institute, was generally well connected in the town, sitting on many committees and taking a keen interest in all local activities. Indeed, there was very little occurring in Boggle-on-Sea that Miss Pumblepink wasn't aware of. One bright morning, having decided to call in at Enterprise House, she was sitting majestically in the office and chatting with Natasha about the various events and initiatives with which she was involved. "Of course, I have been trying to garner support for a Boggle-on-Sea festival, but those Philistines down at the Civic Centre haven't the vision to understand or support the idea" she announced casually while sipping her tea. It so happened that Violet was also present that morning and, upon hearing Celia Pumblepink's dilemma, a thought occurred to her. "Well Miss Pumblepink" she interrupted, "Dreadnought Consultants would support the idea and would be happy to sponsor the festival. We shall make it the cultural highlight of the calendar and will gladly arrange all the attractions for you". Natasha temporarily choked on her tea, but started to see the possibilities. "Oh, what a wonderful idea" replied the venerable Miss Pumblepink. "I will put it to the committee". "Yes indeed, and we could use the Conference Centre as the main focus of activities" suggested Natasha. "Of course, we shall need a liaison officer at Dreadnought Consultants to manage all matters of finance and support" claimed Miss Pumblepink. Violet called Herbert over. "Mr. Jingle will be your point of liaison" she explained, "and he will be happy to attend your meetings and help with all aspects of the festival". An expression of undiluted panic swept across Herbert's face as Violet fixed him with one of her penetrating eye to eye stares, a device for which he had no defence. "You *will* be happy to offer your full support, won't you Mr. Jingle" she said. "Oh, er, yes of course" replied Herbert meekly. "Good, then that's settled" exclaimed Miss Pumblepink. "I will contact Jessica Clinkworth-Sykes at the Rotary Club and, together, we shall develop a proposal to put before the Boggle Town Council". She rose from her chair and glided towards the door. "Mr. Jingle, we shall be in touch" she announced haughtily as she waited for Herbert to open the door for her. "What was all that about?" asked Ernie as Herbert pushed the sticking door back into its frame. "Well, I don't really know" answered a bewildered Herbert. "Of course you know, you silly man" interjected Violet, "Dreadnought

Consultants are sponsoring the Boggle-on-Sea Festival and uncle Herbert is seconded to the Festival Committee in order to help things along". "What!" exclaimed Ernie in alarm, "it will cost us a fortune". "Not necessarily" interrupted Natasha. "We will use the Conference Centre again and issue press releases to attract entrants. I will get Peter Bloggs to print some programmes for free, in which we shall have advertisements from the local trades-people". "That's right!" offered Percy. "We shall actually make a healthy profit while gaining a great deal of free publicity as the sole official sponsors of the event". Herbert's head was swimming. "But they want me on the committee" he cried in anguish. "What will I do?". "You will do exactly as I tell you" replied Violet calmly. "Oh, yes dear" whispered Herbert, somewhat relieved that he wouldn't be required to make any decisions. With Violet organising things in the background, it was bound to go smoothly. They spent the rest of the day discussing how they would attract the performing arts to the Boggle-on-Sea Festival, making it a rival to Glyndebourne, Edinburgh, Bayreuth and the other great cultural events of the Western World. They were a little short on operatic or symphonic works, on account of Boggle not having an orchestra, or even any musicians, but reasoned that they could compensate with some high brow theatrical content, preceded by local acts. There would be a carnival procession through the town, gala dinners in the evenings and posters placed in all the shops. Dreadnought

Consultants would also promote the festival on their web site, noting that they were the sole sponsors of this important cultural event on the world calendar. The ideas flowed free and fast with Ginger looking on approvingly until, after their last cup of tea and with all the milk gone, it was time to go home. The sticking door juddered into position and Ernie turned the key in the lock. "Well, it might go off OK at that" he said. "Of course it will" said Natasha. "It will be a resounding success" said Percy. "A wonderful success" said Herbert. "Caw" said the crow. And they wandered off into the distance, casting shadows on the new pavement as they continued to chat enthusiastically about the exciting prospect of the Boggle-on-Sea Festival. Ginger curled up on the cushion and closed his eyes. It had been another exciting day at Enterprise House.

Later in the week, Celia Pumblepink telephoned and advised that Mr Jingle's presence would be required at an extraordinary meeting of the Boggle-on-Sea Town Council to be held at the Civic Centre that afternoon. The trouble was that Violet was at school and Herbert had no idea what he was supposed to say. Nevertheless, Natasha assured him that all he had to do was to agree to the proposal and offer some further suggestions along the lines of their previous discussions. They wrote down some rough notes as an aide memoir and, at the appointed time, Herbert left nervously for the Civic Centre. The Council Chamber was a large wood panelled room with a long oval table surrounded by high back chairs. On the wall was the Boggle-on-Sea crest; a shield divided into four segments with a crown in one quadrant and a seagull in the opposing one, supported on crossed swords. There were also portraits of all former Mayors, grinning like maniacs from the walls. Herbert was a minute or two late as Alan the doorman was hesitant to admit him. "Are you a member of Council" he asked Herbert. "No, not exactly" answered the latter. "You have to be a member of council, we don't just let anybody in here you know" explained Alan. "But I have an appointment" replied Herbert. There followed a good deal of shifting papers and looking in notebooks before Alan reluctantly issued Herbert with a temporary paper badge which he was instructed to display prominently at all times. "We can't be too careful you know" he shouted as Herbert hurried up the stairs towards the Council Chamber. Awaiting his arrival were the Council Leader Arthur Appleby, the Community Affairs Councillor Penelope Wilting, Councillor Markus Junklesides from Planning and Finance, Celia Pumblepink representing the Women's Institute and Jessica Clinkworth-Sykes from the Rotary Club. Together, they would constitute the Boggle-on-Sea Festival Working Group. "You're late" Announced Councillor Appleby. "Well, its quite difficult to gain access" replied Herbert in his defence. "Well, let's get on with it then" replied Appleby and Celia Pumblepink, always ready to take the lead in such matters, provided an overview of the festival idea and why it would be such a good thing for the Boggle community, placing them firmly on the map in both Britain and further afield. "But that will cost money" interjected Councillor Junklesides gravely, a worried expression etched into his features. "Nonsense" replied Miss Pumblepink. "In any case, Dreadnought Consultants are sponsoring the whole thing, isn't that right Mr Jingle?" "Er, yes, I suppose so" replied Herbert cautiously. Junklesides expression relaxed a little as Miss Pumblepink continued her presentation. Jessica Clinkworth-Sykes then explained how the event would also help to raise money for the Rotary Club and how Dreadnought Consultants would be helping them in this respect. "Isn't that right Mr Jingle?" she concluded. "Er, well, yes" replied Herbert. The discussion continued, confirming the use of the Conference Centre as the main focus for the festival activities. It was decided that the highlight of the event would be a theatrical production and Jessica Clinkworth-Sykes remembered a play that her cousin Angelica had written. "It was called Look Back in Wonder" she advised. "A beautiful play set in the Australian Outback, with plenty of human interest, it will be absolutely ideal" she insisted. The Councillors looked at each other, a little dumbfounded as they wondered how best to let Clinkworth-Sykes know that this wasn't really what they had in mind. Seeing the hesitation in their eyes, Celia Pumblepink acted swiftly. "Right, that's settled then" she exclaimed authoritatively. "A marvellous idea Jessica, Mr Jingle will help you with the casting and production, won't you Mr Jingle?". "Er... well yes, all right then" replied Herbert. "Are you writing all this down Mr Jingle?" asked Clinkworth-Sykes as she peered intently at him through her designer spectacles. He wasn't, but quickly set to work with the supplied Council pencil. The Working Group continued to outline the proposed activities in some detail, the majority of actions being assigned to Herbert and Dreadnought Consulting, eagerly proposed by Councillor Appleby and seconded by Councillor Junklesides. Councillor Wilting suggested that it was essential that there be special concessions for pensioners and unwed mothers. It was pointed out that all the attractions would be free to everyone. Nevertheless, Councillor Wilting stood her ground and insisted that Boggle was becoming an unfair society and that there was much too much of that sort of thing going on these days. Something really ought to be done about it "Yes dear, quite" interjected Miss Pumblepink as she took back control of the conversation. A minute or two later, the first meeting of the Boggle-on-Sea Festival Working Group (or the BoSFWG as Councillor Appleby insisted on calling it) had concluded and Dreadnought Consultants' generosity in sponsoring the entire event was duly noted in the minutes. As they went back down the stairs, Celia Pumblepink turned towards Herbert. "Well, that all went quite nicely, don't you think Mr Jingle?" "Yes" replied Herbert meekly. "I will be in touch with further instructions as we go" explained Miss Pumblepink and, smiling sweetly, she and Jessica Clinkworth-Sykes exited rapidly from the building, leaving Herbert to negotiate the return of his paper badge with the doorman.

Back at Enterprise House, there was some initial consternation when the team examined Herbert's notes and realised just what they had let themselves in for. However, Natasha reassured everyone that, actually, it would not be too costly an exercise for them and, in any case, they would surely benefit from all the publicity. And so the planning and preparations commenced for what would undoubtedly become an historic occasion in the annals of Boggle-on-Sea. Natasha agreed to organise the carnival procession while the boys would scour the town for suitable acts to be showcased at the Conference Centre. Herbert would assume special responsibility for the theatrical play and would liaise with Jessica Clinkworth-Sykes accordingly. A telephone message from Celia Pumblepink confirmed that, from now until the date of the festival, she would be visiting Enterprise House for regular weekly progress meetings, which she would chair herself, starting on the following Monday. The Town Council would also schedule regular progress meetings to be held every Thursday at the Civic Centre, to which Herbert's attendance would also be required. The wheels of destiny had been set irrevocably in motion and the Boggle-on-Sea Festival was about to enter the international social calendar. It was an exciting time.

Business continued as usual at Enterprise House as customers continued to purchase and download Violet's excellent and genuinely useful applications. Consequently, apart from the obligatory book keeping and the odd enquiry, there was little to distract the team from their festival preparation duties. Percy and Ernie had, mainly through conversations down at the Rabbit and Trap, been able to secure the services of some exciting amateur acts. Landlord George Thorogood, also a keen amateur magician, had himself volunteered to put on a magic act. Their friend Charlie Higgins would do a stand up comedian routine as he had, he assured them, a wealth of jokes and anecdotes that he had picked up on the refuse collection round. Popular local couple Reginald Kane and his wife Priscilla had agreed to give a demonstration of their celebrated balloon bending skills. Dick Dimplesnod had agreed to do some impressions, a skill he was renowned for as the evenings wore on at the Rabbit and Trap and the assembled townsfolk became increasingly inebriated. Aloysius Browning had insisted that he should lift the tone of the occasion with some poetry recitals. The star attraction though, by popular consensus, would undoubtedly be the Corking twins, Daphne and Elisabeth, who would offer the audience some popular arias, accompanied by Fred Smith on violin. The Corking sisters were somewhat reclusive, living in a slightly dilapidated old shuttered house up on Ladysmith Hill, overlooking the Boggle Downs and the mudflats beyond. They were rarely seen around town these days and their appearance at the festival would undoubtedly be a rare treat for all music lovers. With further discussions, aided in no small measure by George Thorogood's best bitter, the Boggle Players started to take shape. They would consist of Pete Barrow and Wally Gammer from the Borough Council's Works Department, Charlie Higgins, Natasha's sister Fenella Seminovsky and Emily Bonking, wife of the Mayor. They would be ably directed by no less than Jessica Clinkworth-Sykes herself. With such a stellar cast, supported by the excellent script of Look Back in Wonder and the direction of Mrs Clinkworth-Sykes, the play would assuredly be a resounding success. In parallel, Natasha had been organising the carnival procession for the first day of the festival which would be headed by Mayor Bonking and the Council Festival Committee. Several of the local trades people had agreed to participate and there would be posters and coloured bunting displayed all along the route. In fact, as Boggle High Street was a little short of two hundred yards in length, the route had been extended along the sea front and up to Estuary Gardens where the participants would be offered refreshments, courtesy of Dreadnought Consultants. Natasha would organise some bulk orange squash and Rich Tea biscuits accordingly. All in all, with the regular meetings and input from all concerned, but especially Celia Pumblepink, preparations for the Boggle-on-Sea Festival were looking very good indeed.

Soon enough, the calendar rolled around and it was time for the great event. A long weekend of celebration and cultural enlightenment to rival anything within the civilised world. At the far end of the High Street, by the war memorial, the carnival procession gathered under darkening Boggle skies, ready for their procession. Mayor Bonking was wearing his chain of office and holding the mace, while Councillors Appleby, Wilting and Junklesides were dressed in their best, ready to lead the procession. Robin Figget, the head of Boggle Comprehensive was in his gown and mortar for the occasion, accompanied by a selection of pupils of varying ages, neatly decked out in their school uniforms. Peter Bloggs had a handcart with a model of a printing press and was distributing leaflets about the theatre programme, and various trades people including the butcher and greengrocer also had little handcarts with placards depicting their name and business activity. Natasha had them all neatly assembled, ready for a group photograph by Joss Finkle from the Boggle Examiner, aided by reporter Juliette Slinkbottom. With perfect timing, the moment Joss pressed the shutter, there was a peal of thunder and the heavens opened, as if to bless this special occasion. The procession squelched on through the High Street, the water running like rivers along the gutters and the crowds who ordinarily would have been pleased to stand at the roadside and cheer them on, retreated swiftly into the adjoining houses and shops. They did look through the windows though, as strands of the colourful bunting became detached and blew on to the procession, adding to their distinctive appearance as they trudged on regardless. As they turned the right angle onto the sea front, the wind blew in fiercely from the estuary, with visible sheets of water, both salt and fresh, bathing the carnival participants as if in a ritualistic baptism. It was an awe inspiring sight, full of symbolism and guaranteed to start the Boggle-on-Sea Festival off on the right foot. The procession finally reached Estuary Gardens where, as if in a preordained miracle, the rain ceased, the howling wind dropped to a pleasant breeze and the dark clouds began to disperse inland. A little later, a hazy sun bathed Enterprise House in its benevolent light as the members of the procession crowded into the main office for their refreshments. The orange squash flowed like wine and the Rich Tea biscuits were quickly cleared as the air filled with animated chatter about the Boggle weather, the procession and the events of the coming day. Mayor Bonking attempted, several times, to launch into a speech, but they were all swept up in the sense of occasion and, much to the Mayor's chagrin, were not really interested in speeches. However, he did manage to corner Juliette Slinkbottom who, he felt sure, would wish to have his views on the festival for the front page of the

Examiner. Joss Finkle's flash gun was popping off repeatedly, capturing the historic occasion for posterity. Eventually, Juliette Slinkbottom was rescued by Natasha and the carnival participants filed back out of Enterprise House and made their way back towards the town centre, still chattering away like demented starlings.

In the early afternoon, with the sun now shining brightly, the visiting community poured out of Mrs Cravat's boarding house and other such establishments, onto the colourful streets, with their window posters and bunting, where they quickly joined into the festival spirit. The Rabbit and Trap was packed with visiting tourists, as was Reg's Pie Shop and the other gourmet centres in the town. Bert Scarlett had his fish and chip Dormobile parked on the sea front, where the seagulls waited in eager anticipation for the first wave of customers and Luigi, the ice cream man, was also expecting a brisk business and was preparing accordingly. They didn't have long to wait as the visitors swarmed like ants around the parked vehicles. chattering away and handing their cash through the Dormobile portals in exchange for their ice creams and fish and chips. The chip packets were small and gaping with warm chips, giving the impression that the portions were large. This ingenious design was welcomed by the seagulls who, swooping on the hapless visitors, emptied the bags with ruthless efficiency before the owners had much of a chance to even taste the chips. It was an excellent example of forward-thinking Boggle business cooperation. A similar situation existed with Luigi's ice cream cones, most of which were reduced to their wafer shells with breathtaking speed, the Boggle seagulls being particularly well practised in the art. Nevertheless, the visitors enjoyed the occasion and, at six o'clock, exhausted from their revelry and enjoyment of this historic town, they were happy to file into the Conference Centre for the start of the evening celebrations. Ernie, as master of ceremonies, explained that Dreadnought Consultants were proud to be the sole sponsors of the great Boggle-on-Sea Festival and welcomed visitors to a jam packed evening of traditional entertainment. A group of visitors from China were eagerly taking snapshots of everything, the walls of the conference centre, the audience, Ernie and, of course, the various acts as systematically announced by the master of ceremonies. At the front, were a group of stern faced German visitors, sitting bolt upright on the hard wooden chairs, who had come for the cultural experience, while most of the remaining audience was composed of Boggle residents and those from the neighbouring towns of Limewell, Greycliff and Sodleigh, interspersed with a few random Americans and Europeans. The evening began with the colourful and intriguing act provided by Reginald and Priscilla Kane with their balloon folding skills. Reg pushed the button on the cassette player which they had brought along to start off the accompanying music,

Tchaikovsky's Nutcracker Suite, and Priscilla launched into the first exercise, with much squeaking and twisting. The Chinese snapped happily away and, after a minute or two, Reg motioned to the audience and to his wife, suggesting that the first creation was complete. Priscilla curtsied while holding her creation aloft. "What is it?" shouted someone from the audience. "A dog" suggested someone else. "No it isn't, its a rabbit" suggested another. Reg, somewhat perturbed, decided to put them out of their misery. "Ladies and gentlemen that, as you can plainly see, is a giraffe". "Nothing like it" shouted someone from the back of the hall. Priscilla started torturing a fresh set of balloons and, this time, Reg joined in, eventually bringing their two creations together and holding them high in the air. "It's a cow" shouted one of the audience. "A pig" suggested another. With most of the animal kingdom enunciated one way or another by the enthusiastic Boggle residents, Reg announced to a dumfounded audience that this was, of course, a race horse. The squeaking and twisting continued as Priscilla, sporting a fixed grin like a Cheshire cat, manipulated the long-suffering balloons into yet another weird and wonderful construction while Reg aided and abetted her. "The Albert Hall" suggested a man in a raincoat and flat cap. "The Empire State Building" called another among peals of laughter from the audience. "No, its the 8.30 from Fenchurch Street" bellowed another. Priscilla, unperturbed by such interruptions continued with her squeaking, bending and stretching until, among energetic applause from Reg, she held her creation proudly aloft. "That, ladies and gentlemen, as you can plainly see, is our old friend the Octopus" announced Reg triumphantly. The local crowd whistled and applauded loudly as Reg and Priscilla took their bows. The Chinese snapped away enthusiastically and the Germans sat rigidly upright, a look of confused horror etched upon their faces. There were one or two American couples sitting just behind. They didn't really understand the act, but thought it was a quaint local custom and so applauded loudly with the others.

"Wasn't that wonderful?" claimed Ernie as he kicked one or two stray balloons from the stage and joined briefly into the applause. "And now it gives me great pleasure to introduce Boggle-on-Sea's resident comedian, Mr Charlie 'turned out nice again' Higgins". The locals whistled and cheered as Charlie, still in his Council overalls, loped onto the stage, grinning widely and waving to the crowd. "There was an Englishman, Irishman and Scotsman on a train" he began, thus launching into a series of jokes he had picked up from a an old music hall book in the local library. These quickly expended, among roars of approval from the local audience, he moved on to anecdotes from the refuse collection round. "There was that time when we ran over Mrs Hodge's guinea pig..." he continued among cheers and whistles. The Americans didn't understand any of it. The Chinese snapped away happily and the Germans sat transfixed, their eyes bulging in disbelief. Charlie continued to expose the embarrassing secrets of Boggles' upper crust community as he rolled with laughter on the stage and the audience roared their approval. All too quickly, his act was over and he exited among much whistling and cheering. Next up was a change in pace and an elevation in content as Aloysius Browning took to the stage, elegantly attired in his tweed suit and clutching a couple of books. "And now ladies and gentlemen" announced Ernie, "Mr Aloysius Browning will recite". The chattering died down as Browning looked down scornfully upon the audience, his eyes roving from side to side as though trying to find a cultured expression among the mob as the flashguns from the Chinese visitors popped of all around him. Eventually, he took a deep breath and, looking towards the rafters embarked upon his first recital. "I cry your mercy—pity—love!—aye, love!

Merciful love that tantalizes not...". The Germans relaxed a little. The Americans sighed and leaned back in their chairs. The locals looked at each other with expressions of consternation. Having exhausted his font of Keats, Browning moved on to his namesake Robert. "If one could have that little head of hers, Painted upon a background of pale gold, Such as the Tuscan's early art prefers!..." The locals continued to look perplexed and silence permeated the former scouts hut such as it had never done before. A little

Shelley, Wordsworth and Shakespeare to finish off with and Aloysius Browning was satisfied that he had raised the tone of the event to a level of which Boggle-on-Sea might justifiably be proud. The locals however were not convinced. He exited the stage to a mixture of catcalls, jeers and whistles to which he was singularly unaccustomed. Nevertheless, the deed had been done and Browning was happy with his contribution, even if the Philistines in the audience did not wholly understand it. He was about to exit the hall when a young girl and an elderly lady approached him. "Thank you Mr Browning, it was a lovely recital" said the little girl. "Oh yes, it was a wonderful recital and so beautifully delivered, thank you so much Mr Browning" expressed the elderly lady. Browning shook their hands gently, a tear in his eye, and thanked them for their compliments. The elderly lady gave him a card and suggested that he pay them a visit one day as they would be delighted to welcome him to tea. Browning produced a card of his own and assured them that he would be in touch, before exiting the hall, his head held high. The young girl was Violet and her companion, her grandmother Lilia Seminovsky.

Next up was Dick Dimplesnod with his impressions. The problem was that none of the audience were familiar with George Arliss, Will Hay, Flanagan and Allen and the other characters within Dick's portfolio of characterisations. The advantage of course, was that no-one knew whether the impressions were in any way lifelike or otherwise. Indeed, the way that Dick portrayed them, they might all have been the same person. Nevertheless, the audience cheered and clapped in good spirit and, to Dick's delight, the Germans laughed loudly, although whether they were laughing at Dick Dimplesnod or his impressions was a matter for conjecture. After a few more facial contortions and funny voices, the ebullient Mr Dimplesnod bowed to the audience and skipped off the stage to loud applause and whistles from his friends in the audience. There was a short intermission while a table and some props were brought onto the stage in preparation for Alonso the Great Magician, otherwise known as George Thorogood from the Rabbit and Trap public house. With much whirling of handkerchiefs and startled expressions, Thorogood bounced onto the stage and, miraculously, produced a deck of cards. He then asked for a volunteer from the audience. He had, in fact arranged for a couple of his chums to be present towards the front in order that they might volunteer and thus ensure a polished performance. Unfortunately, they were beaten to the draw by Mrs Pamela Ponsonby from the Boggle-on-Sea Christian Association, who was generally against any form of card play on principle. She mounted the stage and fixed George with the sort of steely eye that might have stopped a small cavalry charge. "Take a card madam" George began nervously as he proffered a fan of cards towards the good lady. Pamela plucked a card disdainfully from the pack and looked at it sternly as the Chinese flashed away with their cameras. "Now I will read your mind and tell you which card you are looking at" declared George as he looked confidently towards the audience. He paused for a moment, his hand to his forehead in a gesture of concentration before announcing triumphantly "It is the five of diamonds". "Rubbish. It's the seven of clubs" claimed Mrs Ponsonby as she held the card aloft for all to see, the audience applauding loudly. "Ah, its because you weren't concentrating" suggested George. "I was" replied Mrs Ponsonby. "Well, we will try again" replied George. This time, with great exaggeration, he proffered the cards towards his volunteer, who obligingly plucked one of them from the middle of the pack. "The two of spades" announced George as he smiled confidently towards the audience. "The eight of hearts" rejoined Mrs Ponsonby loudly as she held the card for all to see. The audience applauded even more loudly and, amid cheers and whistles, Pamela Ponsonby threw the card towards the hapless Alonso the Great Magician. "Infernal nonsense" she bellowed and marched off the stage. The audience roared their approval. George then continued towards the highlight of his act whereupon he would produce several bunches of flowers from his upturned hat upon the table. The artificial flowers had been carefully concealed within the hat, in the sleeves of his coat and in the false surface of the table. George tapped the top of the hat with his cane and lifted it aloft with a flourish. Nothing. He pretended that this was just the warm-up and replaced the hat on the table as he also fiddled with the false surface and tugged at his sleeves a little. He tapped the top of the hat again and, adding additional vigour to the proceedings in order to coax the recalcitrant flowers from their hiding place, pulled the hat swiftly from the table. Unfortunately, the flowers became entangled with both the hat and the tabletop and George found himself briefly lifting the side of the table into the air before the whole assemblage fell in a heap to the floor. The audience howled their approval. The Germans were delighted, thinking George's act a sophisticated form of mock incompetence. They failed to appreciate that the incompetence was genuine. The Americans thought it nothing unusual as it seemed quite similar to their native magician acts. The Chinese snapped away happily. The Great Alonso fumbled about on stage for another few minutes, before throwing his cards into the air in a magnificent gesture, bowing to the audience and exiting swiftly back to the Rabbit and Trap for a much needed restorative. It had been a wonderful first night of entertainment concluded Ernie as he made his closing remarks and reminded the audience, in no uncertain terms, that the Boggle-on-Sea Festival had been sponsored solely by Dreadnought Consultants who, coincidentally, would be hosting a special demonstration of their computer products and services at Enterprise House the next morning, where refreshments would also be served. A cheer went up from the audience and, slowly, they began to file out of the Conference Centre to enjoy the bustling Boggle night life.

The next morning, with bunting and Festival posters still lining the High Street, visitors milled among the Boggle shops and bought whatever little souvenirs they could find, mostly at heavily inflated prices. Bert Scarlett's Fish and Chips did a roaring trade, helped along by the seagulls who ensured that all customers remained hungry, no matter how many bags of chips they bought. Similarly, Luigi dolloped out his ice cream as though there were no tomorrow. Mayor Bonking strolled around in his chain of office, shaking hands with all and sundry and everybody seemed captivated in the spirit of the Festival. At Enterprise House, Natasha and Percy were busy watering down the orange squash and serving it up in large glass jugs while visitors stood and stared as Ernie and Herbert demonstrated the various Dreadnought Consultants products and explained their services which, apparently, were unrivalled in the industrial world. Ginger the cat looked on with intense curiosity and introduced himself to most of the visitors who seemed to find his conversation more captivating than that of the Dreadnought team. The day passed all too quickly as visitors and residents alike teemed around like mice under the clear Boggle sky, darting this way and that. And then, it was time for the highlight of the Festival. The cultural event of the year, awaited eagerly by the international community. The crowd gathered outside the Conference Centre and, at the allotted time, Ernie pushed open the door to a rousing cheer as the fortunate audience hurried eagerly to their seats. The evening's entertainment would start with a musical extravaganza from the Corking twins, followed by the inaugural performance of Look Back in Wonder from the Boggle-on-Sea Players, directed by Boggle's leading impresario, Jessica Clinkworth-Sykes. The happy bustle and chatter slowly died down as Ernie rose his hand and, after thanking the previous evening's acts, announced the final programme. Without further ado, he welcomed to the stage the famous Corking Twins, Daphne and Elisabeth, who stepped smartly forward and beamed towards the audience, resplendent in their ball gowns which had been taken out of moth balls especially for the occasion. "Accompanied by that virtuoso of the violin, Mr Fred Smith" announced Ernie loudly before sliding off to the right of the stage. Fred shuffled onto the stage, a cigarette dangling from one side of his mouth, and the locals cheered wildly. "Come on Freddie!", "Let's here it for the bowls club", "Give 'em the fiddle Fred" and other such phrases of encouragement greeted Boggle's answer to Paganini. Daphne and Elisabeth smiled, cleared their throats and launched into their rendition of "What is Life" as a gentle introduction. Ordinarily, in musical terms one would expect siblings, especially twins, to sing in close harmony of a kind that could never be achieved by strangers. The Corking sisters however defied the laws of genetics by possessing voices of an individual timbre which seemed forever fixed into a contradictory key. The effect was offset nicely by Fred's playing which skilfully avoided both the tempo and underlying melody of the piece. The overall presentation gelled into a unique cacophony, not altogether unlike a group of cats fighting over an abandoned stringed instrument. The Germans had never heard anything quite like it and assumed that this must be the avant-garde of the new music they had heard so much about. They closed their eyes and, with bowed heads, listened intently. The Americans, to whom anything other than Country Music was high brow, eased back in their seats and looked knowingly towards the ceiling. The Chinese seemed to quite like it, beaming happily towards the stage, in between taking snap shots of the twins. The locals sat on the edge of their seats, grinning like Cheshire cats and waiting for the moment when they could cheer and shriek their approval. They didn't have long to wait and the sister's first offering was applauded with an enthusiasm rarely experienced at such events. Daphne announced that, as a special treat, they would follow on with their celebrated rendition of Mahler's Um Mitternacht. Fred was a little perplexed as he did not remember rehearsing this one, simply having the tunes listed as one to seven on his cuff. However, he was confident that he would pick it up as they went along and, without further ado, the sisters launched into the strains of the said work and Fred fiddled away in the background. The Germans were a little perplexed, at least initially. This was a Mahler that they had never heard before (and were unlikely to ever hear again). After a few bars, the enlightenment flooded over them. Of course, the discordant intensity and indefinable key signature must have been what the composer intended. They revelled in every strangled syllable and, when Daphne and Elisabeth finished, they gave a standing ovation, stomping and hooting their approval, the locals joining in support. "Thank you, thank you" announced Daphne, "we shall continue with Oft Denk Ich Sie Sind Nur Ausgegangen, one of our favourite Mahler pieces". They cleared their throats and, with eyes lifted towards the rafters, proceeded with another celebrated rendition, Fred dutifully improvising between the phrases, albeit in an entirely different key. The Germans were ecstatic. How could a little English town such as Boggle produce such sublime artistry? The Corking twins went on to mangle other works by Schumann and Brahms before unleashing the highlight of their performance, Brahms' Alto Rhapsody, the male parts being hummed by Fred as he accompanied them on the violin. It was a tour de force of musical prowess, the likes of which had never before been witnessed. But, notwithstanding this overflowing cornucopia of high culture, there was still more to come. This time it was Elisabeth who made the announcement. "Ladies and gentlemen, in view of the international nature of this great festival and by way of strengthening the ties across the Atlantic Ocean, we are proud to present one of the enduring classics of the international repertoire". A silence settled within the hall as the audience leaned forward in their chairs in eager anticipation. The sisters looked earnestly at each other and, after drawing a deep breath, began. "There's a hole in my bucket, dear Lisa dear Lisa, a hole in my bucket dear Lisa a hole..." The audience erupted into a spontaneous applause and, before long, were joining in with the main phrase of the song. The Americans were delighted as they thought that this classic had been written by Burl Ives, who was now taking his rightful place alongside Brahms, Mahler and Schumann. The tears rolled gently down their cheeks as they looked up towards heaven, their hands clasped tightly before them. The Germans knew of course that the song had its roots in 17th century Germany and joyfully joined in the chorus with "There's und hole in mein bucket". The locals sang along, entering energetically into the spirit of the thing and soon, the ex scouts hut was booming and shaking with pure joy as all nations came together in this wondrous celebration of the musical art. It was almost too much for the senses but, alas, all good things must come to an end and the sisters, exhausted by their efforts, glided gracefully from the stage, smiling sweetly and waving gently in acknowledgement to the audience as they received a standing ovation. Fred shuffled along behind, his violin under his arm, as he lit up another cigarette. It would surely be a hard act to follow.

A short intermission followed while Percy and Herbert erected the curtain across the stage. This consisted of two of Fenella's floral bed sheets sewn together and suspended from a long pole. This was hoisted via two pulleys, one in the centre and another in the wings, where Percy could pull on the cord and raise or lower the curtain accordingly. Behind the curtain, a bustle of activity occurred as the makeshift props were placed in position for the first scene. When all was ready Ernie strode purposefully to the middle of the stage and, raising his hand as if to quell the background chatter, proceeded to announce the recommencement of the Festival activities. He explained, once again, how Dreadnought Consultants sponsored the entire event and how they were international leaders in Information Technology, before concluding, "Ladies and gentlemen, Dreadnought Consultants and The Boggle Players are proud to present Look Back in Wonder". The audience applauded loudly while the actors for the first scene took their places. When the applause had died down a little Wally Gammer, who was playing the lead role of Bluey, looked across at Percy in the wings. "Right oh Perce, let her go!" at which point Percy pulled on the cord and the curtain juddered upwards to reveal Scene 1, at the bar in Woop Woop where Bluey and his friend Jake, played by Charlie Higgins, both wearing floppy hats with one side pinned up, are commiserating over a beer. Ernie and Herbert were brought in as extras to stand around the bar, a role for which they couldn't have been more perfectly suited "What's up me old mate, you look a bit jiggered" asked Jake. "Its me love life sport" explained

Bluey, "I'm set on marryin' me sweetheart, little Mildred, but the rellies won't hear of it, they think I'm not good enough for her". "You mean that Sheila down on the Hicks station, the one with the black wiry hair and arms like oak trees?" asked Jake. "That's the one, me little darlin' Mildred" replied Bluey sadly as he peered into his glass and sighed. "Aw she's a beaut" said Jake enthusiastically. "Give her a wad of chewing tobaccy and a pair of shears and she can put away a flock of jumbucks like a whirlwind. I've seen her sheer three sheep a minute on a good day". They went on to discuss Mildred's many virtues and how poor Bluey was smitten with her, but how Mr and Mrs Hicks had her earmarked to marry Billy Waring (played by Peter Bloggs, the printer) who stood to inherit a neighbouring sheep station and was therefore a better prospect. "What you need me old cobber is a plan" announced Jake authoritatively. "Its no good mooning around here in the bar, you need to get dolled up and pay a visit to the Hicks place". "But old man Hicks will spit the dummy if I keep going round there" explained Bluey. "Not if you dress up properly and do things by the book. You'll come over as ridgy didge and she'll be apples" asserted Jake. Bluey was not entirely convinced but Jake offered to procure his dad's best suit for him, the one he wore to funerals, and, with a little tarting up Bluey would look fine and would suitably impress the Hicks as a gentleman of rare breeding. The remainder of the scene was taken up with some advice from Jake as to what Bluey should say, while Ernie and Herbert stood around, empty glasses in hand, gazing out into the audience. The curtain juddered down again and, behind it, the props were rearranged for scene 2, down at the Hicks' station. The audience, by now fully engrossed in this dramatic love story, could hardly wait. After a minute or two, a coarse voice from behind the curtain whispered "Right oh Perce" and the curtain juddered up again to reveal Mr and Mrs Hicks sitting in their front room. A knock was heard from offstage. "Sounds like a knock on the old door Ted" announced Mrs Hicks, played badly by Emily Bonking, the Mayor's wife. "Nah, cant be Brenda, not at this time of day, there's no one around but a few boomers out on the grass" replied Mr Hicks, played by Pete Barrow from the Council Works Department. The knocking noise came again. "Are you sure that's not a knock at the door Ted?" asked Brenda. "Who would call here?" replied Ted. "After all its back of Bourke from Woop Woop and we're not expecting any visits from the rellies". The dialogue continued for a while along similar lines until, eventually, with the audience now on the edge of their seats, Ted sauntered over to the make belief offstage door and a noise supposed to sound like a door opening was made by Percy banging a few props together. Bluey made his entrance, complete with funeral suit and a bunch of dried flowers for Mrs Hicks. "G'day Mr Hicks, and Mrs Hicks". "What are you all done up wowser like for?" asked Ted Hicks. "Well, I've brought Mrs Hicks some flowers and have come to ask for the hand of your daughter in marriage" replied Bluey. "I've told you before, she's pledged to Billy Waring. He's a gent and has a sheep station of his own, while you're just a wandering jackaroo with no prospects of anything. I'm not letting our little angel throw her life away on a galah like you" snorted Hicks. Bluey drew himself up to his full height, one hand holding up the trousers of the suit which was a couple of sizes too large. "But I have got prospects Mr Hicks. I will have a station of my own one day" "Aw, maybe he will at that, he's a dab hand with the jumbucks after all" interceded Brenda. "Don't listen to her, she's gone all clucky" insisted Hicks. Some more dialogue ensued as the audience fidgeted and crunched their crisps, absorbed by the high drama being presented to them. The scene ended with Hicks shouting, "now be off with you and don't come back here bothering our little Mildred again with all your senseless yabber" "I'll go, but I shall never give up the hand of the one I love" asserted Bluey defiantly as he turned to walk off stage. Unfortunately, his trousers didn't turn at quite the same rate and, tripping over them he stumbled into the wings and crashed to the floor. "Quick, bring the curtain down Perce" a voice was heard to say and, amid tumultuous applause from the delighted audience, the curtain juddered back down. Preparations were made for scene 3 which was set down by the billabong where the story would come to a climax. The audience shuffled and chattered away until, with a flourish, the curtain was raised on the final act. Or, at least, that was the plan. The curtain rose to about three quarters of its travel and then slumped into an awkward angle. "What's up Perce" called Ernie. "The string's got tangled up in the pulley" replied Percy as he continued to fumble with it. "Well, let it down again and then raise it slowly" suggested Ernie. "I can't, it won't go up or down now" cried a frantic Percy. The audience considered the situation as all part of the experience and cheered loudly as the curtain shook and juddered to a standstill. There was nothing for it but to continue, even though, for those sitting near the back, the actors heads were obscured by the curtain when they were on the right hand side of the stage. Jessica Clinkworth-Sykes hurried to the wings and hissed to the actors that they should stay on the left side of the stage, which was of course their right side. After a little obvious confusion, which seemed to delight the loudly applauding audience, the play settled back down to the original plot. This involved Bluey and Mildred in the love scene by the billabong wherein, after the brief strains of an old record of Waltzing Matilda played from a wind up gramophone in the wings, Bluey poured his heart out to his beloved Mildred, imploring her to reconsider her planned marriage to Billy Waring and follow the true course of her heart. "But Billy has a station of his own, with a bonzer herd of jumbucks Bluey, and you are just a wandering jackaroo after all" she reminded him. Bluey got down on one knee. "But what about our love Mildred, doesn't that mean anything to you" he pleaded passionately. "Of course it does" she replied, "but a girl needs some security you know". At this point in the play, things took a dramatic turn as, following what was supposed to be the sound of a galloping horse from the wings, Billy Waring leaped onto the stage. "So, I thought as much" he snarled. "Well Bluey you've gone too far now, put em up!". Bluey was not really one for sparring but felt honour bound, in the presence of his loved one, to defend his position. He turned to Mildred and announced dramatically; "My darling little Mildred, I will defend you to the end of this world" And then, turning to Billy Waring; "Right you are sport, and the winner takes all" as he rolled up his sleeves. The two of them then undertook a dramatic charade of fighting, with much grunting, wailing and clomping around the stage until, finally, Bluey let out a groan and, very dramatically, fell to the floor, exhausted. The audience gasped in horror. But Mildred, outraged by the cruel defeat of her champion, sprang to her feet to challenge the victor. Actually, Fenella Seminovsky, who was playing the part of Mildred was quite looking forward to this moment as she always disliked Peter Bloggs, who was playing the part of Billy Waring, after he had once made a drunken pass towards her. "You brute" cried Mildred as she swung with all her might and planted a right hook squarely onto Billy Waring's chin, knocking him completely unconscious. The audience cheered wildly as Mildred helped Bluey up from the floor and delivered the last poignant line; "My darling Bluey, we shall never be parted and will forever drive the jumbucks around the billabong together". The happy couple then walked, hand in hand off into the far horizon, or at least off stage. Billy Waring, alias Peter Bloggs, remained on stage until Charlie Higgins and Pete Barrow dragged him off by his feet. The audience leapt to their feet and gave a standing ovation as the Boggle Players, minus Peter Bloggs, came back on stage to take their bows. They had to come back twice more as the audience continued to applaud wildly. The curtain which throughout all this time had remained immobile, suddenly decided to break free and fell with a crash to the floor, effectively bringing the evening's festivities to a close. The audience filed out of the hall slowly, chattering away about the wonderful play they had been privileged to witness. The Germans slapped their thighs and remarked what a wonderful social comment it was, a real people's play. The Americans thought it was better than Shakespeare as they at least understood some of the words. The locals thought it was a hoot to see Wally Gammer in a bush hat and Peter Bloggs receive his just desserts. Jessica Clinkworth-Sykes bustled about telling everyone how she had discovered and developed this wonderful piece of contemporary theatre, and all were very happy on that cool Boggle evening.

Back at Enterprise House, a drinks reception was held to mark the end of the festival. Mayor Bonking and his wife Brenda held court and shook hands with all the visitors and even some of the locals. The Boggle Players, now out of costume, signed autographs and chatted with their adoring public. The Corking twins looked in and were immediately surrounded by the Germans who pleaded with them to come and perform in Germany where, they assured them, they would be given a heroic welcome. Ernie and the boys told everyone about Dreadnought Consultants and all the wonderful new things they would be bringing to the world in the coming year. Fenella was complimented by one and all, not only on her superb acting, but on laying out Peter Bloggs with one punch. Celia Pumblepink glided from one group to another, socialising as she went. Ginger walked about among the throng and was variously petted by all and sundry. Enterprise House was fairly buzzing with exuberant chatter and goodwill and then, suddenly, the sticking door juddered and creaked open and everyone fell silent and looked towards it. There, resplendent in her best red ball gown was Natasha Seminovsky and, beside her, in an equally smart little gown, was Violet. Behind them was Liliya Seminovsky, dressed in white lace with white gloves and a tiara. "Ladies and gentlemen" began Natasha, "may I introduce you to the real architect and visionary of the Boggle-on-Sea Festival, my niece, Violet Seminovsky". There was a momentary pause as those assembled stared in brief bemusement, and then, the place erupted into eager congratulations as everyone wanted to meet the young impresario. "Three cheers for Miss Violet" shouted a voice that sounded suspiciously like Herbert and Enterprise House was rocked to its foundations with cheers and radiated good will. Eventually, the visitors started to disappear and file back to their various lodgings and homes. The Mayor's official Daimler sped off into the night, Liliya and Fenella Seminovsky took Violet home and the Dreadnought team were left alone to clear up and close for the night. As Ernie pulled closed the sticking door a lone owl hooted. "Well, it seems to have been a success" he ventured. "It was a wonderful success" agreed Natasha. "Exhilarating" confirmed Herbert. "Indeed" said Percy. "Caw" said the crow. They wandered off into the moonlight as the customary Boggle winds started to whistle up along Estuary Gardens and Ginger settled down for the night in his favourite chair.

The Boggle-on-Sea International Festival had indeed been a great success, but there was something more. A threshold had been crossed. A milestone reached. Dreadnought Consultants were no longer just another little business among Boggle ratepayers. They had become interwoven with the town and its culture. From now on, the name Dreadnought Consultants would be synonymous with Boggle-on-Sea and vice versa. The one being known for the other. From now on, when people thought of leading edge technology, they would think of Boggle-on-Sea as the incubator and Dreadnought Consultants as the instrument. From now on, when the high brow elite were preparing their calendars of social engagements, Boggle-on-Sea would invariably enter the discussions. From now on, when aspiring politicians wanted to quote leading edge technology, they would reference Dreadnought Consultants. It had been a remarkable transformation in the fortunes of Enterprise House. Ernie was proud of his achievements in steering his brainchild to such heady heights. Natasha and Herbert realised however that Violet was the real inspiration behind this success and that, without her, none of this might have happened. Indeed, without Violet, Dreadnought Consultants might long ago have shuddered and expired by the wayside like so many start up companies in the competitive high-tech field. Without Violet as a catalyst, life might have been quite different for the incumbents at Enterprise House. It was a fact that had not entirely escaped her pretty little mind.

10 MORE DISILLUSIONMENT

And so, the weeks passed by in a blur of activity as the steady stream of orders continued and Dreadnought Consultants where well on their way to becoming a household name. Violet had created a brace of genuinely useful little applications, all very nicely presented in a consistent style. They were also robust, reliable and performed well across a variety of hardware. Consequently, users were happy and looked forward in eager anticipation to future Dreadnought Consultants releases. Natasha was constantly receiving endorsements and appreciative letters from satisfied customers and, as Violet had predicted, support issues were virtually non-existent. Mayor Bonking had repeatedly suggested that the company expand and recruit more staff, but there was really no need to as everything was perfectly manageable with the existing team. It was, in fact, an almost perfect business model wherein everybody was happy and revenue streams were sufficient to keep everything on an even keel. Ernie and the boys were happy to go along with what they saw as Violet's delusion that she was running things, just as long as sales remained buoyant. However, unbeknown to them dark clouds were gathering on the horizon.

Violet was juggling her school work with the commitments of producing all of Dreadnought Consultants software as well as directing the company strategy. It was a little too much, even for one of her undoubted abilities. Fenella was a little concerned about this as she wanted a different future for her beloved daughter, perhaps as a doctor, or concert pianist or something a little more befitting a lady of substance from a distinguished family. The world of IT and computers, she considered crude and ugly. Something that crass, greedy men of no breeding might pursue, but not the preserve of a gentlewoman. The subject was increasingly being discussed at Boggleton Hall and, after much deliberation, a meeting was held among the Seminovsky family. Liliya was keen that her granddaughter should attend university and study medicine. Fenella agreed that Violet should study hard and go to university, although she was a little more open as to Violet's calling, as long as it was something honourable. Natasha was acutely aware that she was only working with Dreadnought Consultants due to her lack of a proper profession and was therefore equally supportive of the idea that Violet should be given every opportunity to do better. Violet, after listening to all the arguments and suggestions thought that she deserved a say in her own future. "I have decided..." she began, as she interrupted the conversation. "That I shall hand over my Chief Executive duties to auntie Natasha who, from now on, will run Dreadnought Consultants. I will finish the last couple of applications that I am developing and, after that I will focus on my studies, although I shall remain as a paid consultant to the company and will take a royalty on all sold products. The income will help to pay for my university fees". The elders looked at each other, a little bemused. There was no contesting the logic of Violet's proposal, although they would have preferred a clean break from this dreadful IT business. "Wouldn't you rather forget this IT nonsense altogether dear" suggested Liliya. "Exactly" agreed Fenella "We will help with your university fees. There is no need for you to worry about that". "I am not worried" replied Violet, "but the success of Dreadnought Consultants has been built upon my ideas and my software. Therefore, as long as they continue to sell my applications, I deserve a royalty on them". Natasha looked at Fenella. "She's quite right" she said pointedly. "Without Violet's input the company would still be struggling". After further discussion, it was agreed that Violet would withdraw from active participation in Dreadnought Consultants but would continue to receive a royalty on applications sold. Natasha would take over as Chief Executive and would engage Violet as a consultant if and as needed. It would all be announced at an extraordinary meeting the next day at Enterprise House.

It was a gloomy Thursday morning, the Boggle wind blowing in hard from the estuary as heavy, dark clouds marched threateningly across the sky. Ernie arrived first, leaned his bicycle against the wall and fumbled with his keys. The crow eyed him with a curious attention as he unlocked and pushed open the sticking door. "What are you looking at?" asked Ernie. "Caw" said the crow mockingly, before spreading his wings and settling back on the roof . Ernie went inside and put the kettle on and was soon joined by Percy and Herbert who, on such a bleak morning, were looking forward to their first cup of tea. A few minutes later, they were seated around Ernie's desk sipping their tea in quiet and peaceful oblivion. Percy was looking through the morning paper, Ernie was checking his email and Herbert was contemplating the virtues of digestive biscuits, wondering how much they contributed to a healthy lifestyle. It suddenly occurred to Percy that Natasha was uncharacteristically late. "I wonder where Natasha is?" he murmured, somewhat absent mindedly as he turned to the gossip column. "Probably stopped off for some shopping somewhere, you know what girls are" suggested Ernie in an equally distracted manner as he clicked on another junk mail entry. Herbert said nothing. He suspected that something was brewing in the background, having observed Natasha heading off towards Boggleton Hall the previous evening. A little later, the door juddered open and two familiar voices were heard as they hurried in from the cold. The first priority was to head for the kettle. A few minutes later, having restored their circulation and gathered their thoughts, the two ladies joined the gentlemen in the main office. "I have an announcement to make" stated Violet in her usual authoritative tone. "As acting Chief Executive I am hereby calling an extraordinary meeting of all staff". Ernie looked at Percy in disbelief. Herbert gazed attentively at Violet. "Can't it wait, I am busy now" growled Ernie. "No it can't. Pay attention" replied Violet sharply. Ernie knew better than to argue the point and so settled back in his chair, wondering what new little idea was about to be fostered upon them. "I have decided to step down from my post as Chief Executive" Ernie's attention was now engaged and a sense of glowing relief started to spread inside him. Violet leaned casually against the adjoining desk. "I am appointing auntie Natasha as the new Chief Executive and I will no longer take an active part in the running of Dreadnought Consultants, although I shall henceforth take a royalty of fifteen percent on all software sold, payable monthly into my Post Office account". Ernie choked on his tea. "Nonsense!" he exclaimed loudly. "I am the Chief Executive of Dreadnought Consultants and I will decide who does what. There will be no royalties paid on anything although, you are right about one thing, and that is that you will have no further involvement with my company". The atmosphere grew tense as a momentary silence descended upon Enterprise House. Violet crossed her little hands in front of her and took a deep breath. "I shall make it perfectly clear" she began. "It is my software that is currently providing the revenue that this company is founded upon. If I were to withdraw it immediately, the revenue stream would come to an abrupt end and you would have to start again with nothing. Existing customers would be appalled and you would lose all the goodwill that my ideas have built for the company". The boys looked worried. "She's right you know" volunteered Herbert. "We can manage without her" claimed Ernie defiantly. "I am not so sure" suggested Percy, "our finances would take an immediate tumble". "But I am not having Natasha as Chief Executive" scowled Ernie. "Yes you are. She is the only one with the necessary vision to keep things moving ahead" replied Violet. "In any case, I shall liaise only with auntie Natasha while I finish the last two software titles and, in the event of any consultancy being required, I shall deal with no-one else". The boys looked at each other in panic. Natasha decided to break the ice a little and reassure them. "Oh, it won't be so bad" she said soothingly. "It will be just like before, except that I will decide policy and set our future strategy". Ernie stood up from his desk. "No" he barked. "I absolutely will not have that. I started this company and I will run it". After a moment or two's silence, while Violet and Natasha stood gently smiling, Percy stroked his chin and said, "Well, actually, if you remember, we all came together as a sort of partnership and that is the way we have been running things". "Yes" confirmed Herbert. "And it is quite reasonable that Natasha, with her flair for marketing, should set the future policy, while Percy and I look after the financial side and Ernie looks after sales and support". "Right then, that's settled" announced Violet. "Herbert, you can set up the monthly transfer to my Post Office account and I will write the code for the accounts system to calculate the royalty and make the automatic transfers". "Oh no you won't" claimed Ernie, and the tension grew under the flat roof of Enterprise House as the dark Boggle clouds seemed to gather around it.

Of course, executive power struggles are often a feature of fast growing, first tier organisations and Dreadnought Consultants were no different in this respect. Fortunately, the rules of business allow for such matters to be resolved in a reasonably democratic manner. "Then we shall vote on it" announced Violet. "Who is in favour of Natasha taking over as Chief Executive along the terms I have suggested". Natasha and Herbert raised their hands, Violet fixed Percy with one of her stares and, almost of its own accord, his hand reached towards the ceiling. "Good, then there is no need for me to cast the deciding vote" Violet announced cheerfully and, at that moment, the clouds started to lift above Enterprise House. Natasha was relieved. Percy and Herbert thought that the whole idea was quite reasonable and workable. Only Ernie was deeply perturbed, but what could he do under the circumstances? He was not inclined to resign from what he saw as his own company, even though he had heard of other executives making such decisions. However, in their case, the decision was usually accompanied by a large pay off, something that was beyond the capacity of Dreadnought Consultants to facilitate. He would just have to go along with the new regime and hope that things would work themselves out in the longer term, as indeed, things often did. And so, Violet left for home and the team settled down to an initially uneasy regime, although Natasha assured them that nothing would really change. After all, such titles were only imaginary. In reality, the team would function exactly as before, the only real difference was the payment of a royalty to Violet on all software sales. However, as Percy pointed out, that was really quite reasonable and would not significantly impact their finances.

And so, things continued with Violet's software continuing to sell and, on the completion of the two final applications, they had a reasonable portfolio of twelve useful utilities. In addition to this, Ernie continued to offer consultancy to local businesses, often supplying them with computers which he would assemble from components bought in London and add a healthy profit margin to before passing them on. Natasha continued to develop the web site and regularly sent out press releases to whoever she could think of, often aided and abetted by Herbert in such activities, while Percy constrained himself to keeping the books. All seemed to be bubbling along reasonably well until, at one of their morning brainstorming sessions, Percy mentioned that sales of Violet's software had been dropping off a little. "Of course" said Ernie. "Its because there is no incentive for people to upgrade or buy additional applications". They pondered the situation over their third cup of tea as Herbert gazed nonchalantly out of the window at a man in overalls climbing up the ladder on one of the gasworks storage tanks. Suddenly, the solution came to him and he jumped up from his chair. "I know" he blurted enthusiastically. "We shall call in Violet as a consultant. She will surely have the answer for us". "What a good idea" suggested Natasha. "I will phone Fenella and arrange a meeting". Ernie was adamant that they didn't need help from Violet, but eventually conceded when it was pointed out that their success was mainly founded upon her ideas. However, Violet was not inclined to agree as she was no longer particularly interested in the affairs of Dreadnought Consultants and was inclined to agree with her mother that the computer industry was vulgar and that any involvement would be unbecoming for a young lady of her fine sensibilities. The team at Enterprise House discussed the matter further and concluded that, as it had been Herbert's idea to engage her, he would be dispatched to Boggleton Hall that evening to plead with her for one last bit of consultancy. And so, as the

Boggle wind whistled in the treetops around Boggleton Hall and the moonlight bathed the gravel path in its soft, benevolent light, Herbert crunched his way up to the old oak front door and swung the lion's head door knocker against the stop. After a while, Liliya Seminovsky came to the door and looked disdainfully at the visitor. "Oh, its you Mr Jingle" she said as she looked him up and down. "I suppose you had better come in". As Herbert entered the hall, Fenella popped out from the drawing room. "Oh its you Herbert. We haven't seen you for a while. Have you come to see Violet?" Herbert answered in the affirmative and he was shuffled into the drawing room where he found Violet sitting at her desk reading. "Well, why haven't you come to see me before now" she asked. "We've been so busy, I haven't had the time" replied Herbert. "Nonsense. You could have come in the evening" said Violet as she fixed him with an icy stare. Herbert explained that the Dreadnought team would like to offer her a day's consultancy in order to help them with their new strategy. "No, I am not interested in IT and computers anymore. It's a vulgar, shallow business and I don't want any part of it" replied Violet sternly. She went on to explain that she was thinking of studying medicine so that she could help people in far away places, or maybe becoming a nun. Herbert suggested that there would be time for one day of consultancy before making such a decision. Violet thought about it for a moment and then replied, "OK, I will give you one afternoon of consultancy for five hundred pounds cash, paid in advance". Herbert gulped and suggested that the price was perhaps a little too high for Dreadnought Consultants, after all, they were only a small company. "Take it or leave it. I am only making the offer because it is you who is asking" replied Violet coldly as she turned over another page of her book. Herbert reluctantly agreed to her terms as he knew that she would use the money wisely, although he also knew that the news would not be well received back at Enterprise House.

At the morning meeting, having brewed the tea and settled down into their chairs, the rest of the team were anxious to hear from Herbert how he had got on at Boggleton Hall. "Well, out with it man" cried Ernie. Herbert took a sip of tea and cleared his throat while he placed his cup on the desk. "Good news" he started. "Violet has agreed, in spite of her busy schedule, to grant us an afternoon of consultancy". "Oh, that's wonderful, well done Herbert" said Natasha. "Just a minute, just a minute" broke in Ernie. "How much is this going to cost us?". "Well, that's the best of it" replied Herbert. "Just five hundred pounds all in". "What!" exclaimed Ernie, almost choking on his tea. "It does sound a smidgen on the high side" suggested Percy. "It's outrageous. Tell the little brat to get lost" blurted Ernie angrily. "She's not a little brat" protested Natasha. "Furthermore, as acting Chief Executive, I consider the amount to represent a good investment in our future. I recommend that we proceed at the earliest opportunity". Natasha looked at Herbert with an expression which left him little choice but to second her recommendation. Percy also agreed that, in the long run, it might represent a reasonable investment. Ernie found himself out-voted once again and had to go along with the majority view. "Well, if you want to throw our money away, go ahead" he brooded although, in his heart, he also felt that Violet would probably have some insightful ideas as to the future of Dreadnought Consultants and so he wasn't really that disappointed. A date was duly set and the cash drawn out from the Boggle Mutual Bank and placed in a plain brown envelope. The day started off quite dreary with the usual Boggle mix of drizzle and light winds but, by lunchtime, the weather had cleared and a ray of sunshine came down and enveloped Enterprise House. At two in the afternoon, the door juddered open and Natasha and Violet made their entrance. The envelope was handed to Violet as arranged while Natasha prepared her orange juice and the boys settled down with their tea. As Violet sat down, Ginger jumped eagerly onto her lap and she stroked him gently. "I have written the strategy down for you. At no additional cost" Violet looked at Ernie as she made the last remark. "It is really quite simple. From now on, you will cease to sell applications and computers simply for commercial gain and will, instead, devote all your energies to supplying computers and software at no cost and in support of good causes and charitable endeavours". Percy and Ernie looked at each other in utter astonishment. Herbert looked at Violet in quiet admiration. Natasha smiled joyfully. "What a wonderful idea" she enthused. "And what are we supposed to live on" protested Ernie. "You will raise funding for all your projects and simply include your expenses as part of the financial planning" replied Violet. "It's all explained clearly in my strategy document". She handed the document to Natasha. "And we shall be bankrupt in a month" cried Ernie. "You shall certainly go bankrupt if you do not follow my plan" replied Violet calmly. "And, if there are no further questions, I shall now return home to my studies". "Wait a minute" protested Ernie. "We have just given you five hundred pounds cash for ten minutes of nonsense which we could not possibly pursue. We want a proper, feasible business plan with which to take us into the future". "You've got one" replied Violet haughtily. "And now I really must go". So saying, she deposited Ginger on her chair, wished Natasha farewell and made haste out of the building and off down the road, clutching the brown envelope under her arm. Ernie sat back down and held his head in his hands while Percy and Herbert looked at each other nervously. Natasha glanced through the document, skimming from one page to another. "You know" she said cheerfully. "I think Violet is right, we could actually make this work". "She's right you know" confirmed Herbert proudly. Percy took another sip of tea. They spent the rest of the afternoon discussing the possibilities of Violet's strategy and, the more they discussed it, the more improbable it seemed. At last, they decided to call it a day and as Ernie pulled the sticking door closed he offered the opinion that they could never make Violet's plan work, not in a month of Sundays. "Oh, I think we could" said Natasha. "Of course we could" said Herbert. "Certainly" said Percy. "Caw" said the crow. They wandered off down Estuary Gardens, four silhouettes in the moonlight, until finally disappearing over the horizon, while Ginger the cat looked on from the window. The crow settled down on the roof and the sun sank down beyond the mudflats to close another eventful day at Boggle-on-Sea.

11 ENLIGHTENMENT

Dr. Lancelot Rowbottom was a specialist at the Ear Nose and Throat department of the Boggle-on-Sea General Hospital. A tall, angular man with little hair who liked to wear pin-stripe suits and horn rimmed spectacles. He liked to keep meticulous records of all his cases and was intrigued when it was suggested to him that he could transfer all of his paper files on to a computer, thus both saving space and being able to access them quickly when he wanted to cross reference previous cases. Mayor Bonking had recommended him to Dreadnought Consultants one day while having his sinuses checked at the hospital. Consequently, one pleasant afternoon upon completion of his morning surgery, he made his way over to Estuary Gardens and, having parked his Jaguar outside Enterprise House, rushed at the door with his usual, slightly impatient air. The door was sticking more than usual that day, having expanded in the warm weather, and Dr. Rowbottom collided with it in a most unseemly manner, causing his spectacles to become dislodged. Hearing the commotion outside, Natasha pulled open the door to find Rowbottom dusting off his spectacles and adjusting his tie. "Oh, do please come in" she suggested with a smile. Rowbottom scowled and moved inside. "My name's Rowbottom. Lancelot Rowbottom" he announced, "and I'm a doctor at the General Hospital". "Oh, how nice" replied Natasha. "Yes, well, I want to talk to someone about databases" Rowbottom continued. Natasha introduced him to Ernie and left them to chat about databases and computers. Ernie explained how he could scan his paper documents and notes and keep them neatly indexed by date on the computer. Satisfied that he could achieve what we wanted, he signed an order for a computer, printer, scanner and a couple of Violet's applications, a simple word processer and a database. The equipment was duly delivered to his consulting room at the hospital and, after a little instruction from Ernie, at additional cost of course, Lancelot Rowbottom spent many a happy hour scanning in all his old notes. Not much more was thought about Rowbottom until, one day, he telephoned Enterprise House. "Lancelot Rowbottom here. Look, I need some advice about drawing in some additional data from the hospital records". Ernie was summoned and spent twenty minutes or so explaining to Rowbottom how to import data from another application. All seemed to be well until, the next day, another telephone call was received, this time from a clearly agitated Lancelot Rowbottom. "I've lost all my records" he cried down the phone. Ernie assured him that, in all probability, his records were still there. "They are not" barked Rowbottom, who demanded that Ernie come round immediately to put the situation right. Ernie made his way to the hospital and was soon sitting in front of Rowbottom's computer. "Look, all your records are there" he explained with a smile. "They are not my records" replied Rowbottom. "Yes they are" insisted Ernie. "No they are not!" maintained Rowbottom. "They are the additional records from the hospital". After a little more discussion, it was ascertained that, when the hospital records were imported, they had a similar key field of incrementing numbers. Rowbottom had received a message advising that no duplicates were allowed. As he was quite certain that there were no duplicate records, he clicked on the OK button and, lo and behold, all of his previous records with the same key field were overwritten. "You didn't explain this properly" complained Rowbottom. "Well, its obvious isn't it?" replied Ernie. "No it isn't obvious and now I've lost all my data". "Well, unfortunately, you will just have to scan it all in again" suggested Ernie. "I, can't. The original paper copies have all been destroyed" replied Rowbottom. After further discussion, the upshot of it all was that Rowbottom would be sending Dreadnought Consultants a bill for his wasted time, at his normal consultancy rate. This would amount to approximately five times the value of the equipment provided by Dreadnought Consultants. Furthermore, he would advise the hospital procurement board not to deal with Dreadnought Consultants under any eventuality. This was an unfortunate setback as Ernie had been hoping to expand to other departments within the hospital, on the back of his success with Lancelot Rowbottom. Back at Enterprise House, Ernie was disconsolate as he signed the cheque for Rowbottom's expenses, having been advised by Percy that it was best to do so rather than enter into a long drawn out argument and possible litigation which they could not possibly win.

There were one or two other situations of a not dissimilar nature which served as reminders that selling computers to the general public was a risky business. In parallel, the Internet sales of Violet's software applications had dwindled away to almost nothing as other applications came on to the market and were more aggressively marketed. The world of general purpose software was a fickle one, as many suppliers had found. With all these developments occurring, Violet's strategy had been somewhat sidelined as the team did their best to keep the wheels of industry turning at Enterprise House. However, it was quickly becoming apparent that their current business model was not going to be sustainable. Natasha was discussing the situation one day with Ginger as she prepared his breakfast when, after a he had let out a most curious gurgling sound, she suddenly saw the way ahead. "You are quite right Ginger darling" she said as she stroked his back. "We shall adopt Violet's strategy right away". At the morning meeting she reminded the rest of the team that they hadn't implemented the strategy and that that must be why they were struggling. "Haven't we got enough trouble without digging that old chestnut up again" said Ernie despondently. "But she's right you know" said Herbert. "We should put Violet's strategy into operation. After all, she was right about everything else". "Of course she was" replied Natasha, "and she is right about the strategy. We should follow it immediately. At least, that's what Ginger says". "Ginger!" exclaimed Percy. "Yes of course, he understands everything that goes on here, don't you darling" said Natasha as she picked him up to give him a cuddle. Ginger looked on knowingly as the boys looked at each other in dismay. Nevertheless, they decided to explore the idea of Violet's strategy and tried to come up with a list of charities that they could approach. However, Boggle-on-Sea wasn't exactly flush with charities, the Boggle residents always being a little careful with their hard won cash. They started to look further afield to Limewell and Sodleigh, but there were not that many there either. After spending the day rifling through the telephone directories and exhausting all possibilities, they agreed to sleep on the idea and take a fresh look in the morning. That evening back at Westminster Drive, Ernie asked auntie Freda if she had any ideas but drew a blank. Percy and Herbert asked Mrs Cravat who recommended the Women's Institute, but the idea of liaising with Celia Pumblepink filled the boys with understandable trepidation. Natasha decided to telephone Pamela Ponsonby at the Boggle Christian Association and Pamela put her in touch with an old friend, Charlotte Bunker-Hunt, whom she thought might be able to help. The next morning, Natasha rushed to Enterprise House to break the good news to the boys. "I've found our first charity and they would indeed like to computerise their operation, including a database for all their members and they would appreciate our assistance to this end". "Marvellous!" exclaimed Herbert. "Sounds just the ticket" enthused Percy. "Who are they?" enquired Ernie. "It's Charlotte Bunker-Hunt at the Donkey Sanctuary just outside Boggle" explained Natasha. The Donkey Sanctuary wasn't quite the sort of charity that the boys had envisaged, but, in the absence of any other immediate prospect, they decided that it was as good a start as any. "Now all we have to do is raise the funding" suggested Percy. "Oh, that will be easy" said Natasha. "I will start ringing around the local businesses and the Council and we shall soon have enough".

Charlotte Bunker-Hunt was a robust lady of middle years with wild ginger hair that seemed to stand on end in all directions. She dressed perpetually in corduroy trousers and old jumpers, occasionally putting on an equally tatty storm-breaker coat when conditions warranted such a precaution. She wore green wellington boots everywhere, except at home where she went barefoot around the house. Her donkeys, which were many, milled about everywhere and would routinely come into the house to find her when they were hungry or simply wished for attention. She had an old Morris Eight van which she insisted was in perfectly good order although the rust on the doorsills, wings and elsewhere suggested otherwise. This was used primarily for donkey transport and occasional shopping trips into the town. Natasha, Herbert and Ernie decided to pay her a visit, leaving Percy to hold the fort. The number three municipal bus stopped a short way from her driveway and the three intrepid consultants were soon knocking at her door which was, in any case, half open. They were not sure whether to venture inside as there was no answer and then, suddenly, a voice boomed from behind them. "What ho!. You must be Natasha Seminovsky and the boys from Dreadnought". "That's right" smiled Natasha. "I telephoned you yesterday". "Come in, come in" bellowed Charlotte as she slapped Herbert on the back with a degree of force which propelled him through the open door and, narrowly avoiding a donkey who stood watching calmly, straight into an old red armchair. "I can offer you some tea, I think" suggested Charlotte. They thanked her for her kindness as they sat and stared around them in wonder at Charlotte's living room. There were large bookcases with some very well worn books, mainly on animals and farming, a round table to one side with an oil lamp sitting purposefully upon it and some old framed photographs on the walls which, one assumed, were of previous members of the Bunker-Hunt species. Soon, Charlotte returned with an enormous brown teapot which she banged down on the table and then retrieved some cups from the sideboard. Blowing the dust out of them, she plonked them down on the table and proceeded to fill them with tea. "Milk?" she asked abruptly. "Oh, yes please" answered Natasha for all of them. Charlotte produced an old cracked jug and poured some milk into the cups before handing them around. "It's goats milk actually" she said, nodding towards the jug. "Oh, how lovely" said Natasha nervously. Ernie and Natasha explained the various ways in which they thought computers might be of value to the Donkey Sanctuary while Charlotte sat looking curiously at Herbert, her head cocked slightly to one side as she smiled at him. Herbert was becoming increasingly concerned as Charlotte looked him up and down. When Ernie and Natasha had finished explaining their proposal, Charlotte stood up abruptly. "Jolly good show" she announced as she walked over to Herbert's chair and put her hand on his shoulder. "Of course, I shall need some training" she said, smiling down at Herbert. Natasha, catching her drift replied, "Oh, yes of course. Herbert is our expert on training and he would be pleased to come and help you get set up, won't you Herbert?". Herbert gulped. "Well, there really isn't that much training required" he suggested meekly. "There will be for me" barked Charlotte as she slapped him on the back and almost sent him sprawling towards the floor. "I don't understand the first thing about computers". She grinned at Herbert, whose eyes were now wide with terror. Natasha smiled sweetly. "Herbert will be absolutely delighted and he so loves animals, don't you Herbert?" Before he had a chance to answer, Charlotte slapped him on the back once again. "Good, then that's all settled. When will I get my computer?" Ernie explained that they would order the necessary kit and test it all out before delivering to the Donkey Sanctuary, at which point, Herbert would come and give as much help as was required in order to establish the donkey database and get Charlotte up and running. Charlotte went on to explain how she rescues the donkeys and brings them to her sanctuary and how intelligent they were. "Much nicer than people" she assured them, as she gave a sideways glance to Herbert. "Although I suppose there might be exceptions" she added. The team finished their tea and, after thanking Charlotte for her kindness, proceeded back outside, Herbert stepping nervously and taking great care to keep his back against the wall. Once out into the open, Charlotte shook hands with Natasha and Ernie and, just as Herbert was sneaking past her, gave him a solid slap on the back which sent him careering across the driveway. "Look forward to seeing you soon Herbie old chap" she bellowed good naturedly. As they took the bus back to the town centre, Herbert shifted uneasily on the seat, his back still smarting. "She seemed to like you Herbert" suggested Natasha. "I am not going back there" he replied. "Of course you are" said Natasha. "She will be relying on you". "Well, I am not going there alone" he insisted. "Don't be such a sissy" said Ernie. "Think of England and your services to charity". As the bus turned by the cemetery and into the High Street the team were pleased with their success at enlisting their first charitable cause.

Charlotte's computer was soon built and configured and, this time, the boys decided to deliver everything to the Donkey Sanctuary, leaving Natasha back at the office. Everything was soon set up and plugged in and, switching on the computer, Ernie exclaimed; "There, everything is working well. We shall leave Herbert with you to explain how things work and to help you get started with your database". "Right oh!" replied Charlotte joyfully as she winked at Herbert and smiled. Herbert, with a panic stricken expression on his face suggested that he needed to get back to the office as he was expecting an important call. "Don't worry old chap, we will manage it for you" assured Percy and, shaking hands with Charlotte, he and Ernie took their leave. Looking back briefly as they walked down the drive, they saw the front door close and a terrified Herbert looking from the window. Indeed, that was all that they saw of him that day. The next morning, he was the last to arrive at Enterprise House, looking pale and shaken. "How did you get on Herbert?" asked Percy. "I don't want to talk about it" replied Herbert as he rushed to the sanctuary of his desk and plonked himself down. Around mid morning, the telephone rang and Natasha answered it. "Charlotte Bunker-Hunt here" a voice boomed down the line. "Can't get the hang of this computer thingy, you had better send Herbie around again". "Oh, he would be delighted" assured Natasha. "Right oh!. Tell him to hurry round and I will get the kettle on" replied Charlotte and the phone clicked back to the dialling tone. "Herbert" called Natasha in her sweetest, most engaging voice, and Herbert froze, his hands gripping the edge of the desk. "Charlotte would like to see you again. Quickly, you can just catch the bus if you hurry". Ernie and Percy prized him from the desk and shuffled him outside as he babbled and pleaded with them not to be sent back to the Donkey Sanctuary. "She will just come and get you if you don't go" explained Ernie. "Yes, and it is all in a good cause, after all" affirmed Percy. And so, resigned to his fate, Herbert headed off into the distance, not to be seen again that day. After a few more visits to the Donkey Sanctuary, Herbert's nerves were, it must be said, a little frayed, although he no longer feared the encounters with Charlotte. Indeed, he was beginning to enjoy their meetings in a strange sort of way that he couldn't readily explain. There were other customers now as well. Clive Wesley was president of the Boggle Birdwatchers Society, a group which was concerned with the preservation of wild birds, particularly those to be found in the marshes to the east of the town. Clive was a large, jovial man whose bright eyes flashed from above an equally large beard. He usually wore a sleeveless tunic covered in pockets, which Percy joked were full of bird seed. Around his neck were always at least two pairs of binoculars and sometimes a camera. He wore long woollen socks with his trousers tucked into the top, that reached down into the most gigantic pair of hiking boots ever seen. These were balanced at the top of the assemblage by a large bush hat adorned with various brightly coloured badges. Clive was delighted to find that he could organise his numerous photographs and notes on the computer and even more delighted to learn that he could use electronic mail to communicate with other bird watchers all around the world. Furthermore, Natasha built a web site for him where he could post details of endangered local species. Then there was Sheila Dribble who ran the Big Ears Animal Club, an organisation for the protection of pussy cats, bunny rabbits, guinea pigs and anything else that was furry and had ears. Many of her members were children and it was decided to set up three computers where they could come and learn about animals. These were set up with presentations that ran through caring for animals, feeding, first aid and other such matters, with much material provided by other organisations such as the RSPCA and the Natural History Museum. The news travelled fast and soon there were customers from the surrounding towns, including the Hedgehog Hospital at Limewell, the dogs home at Greycliff and the Feral Cats Association at Sodleigh. News even travelled to the more human charities, including the

Misplaced Orphans Society run by Captain Bertie Beaufort, a colourful ex-military gentleman with a handlebar moustache who was always impeccably dressed and spoke in a beautiful, clear English accent which was truly a pleasure to hear.

As Dreadnought Consultants attracted more such customers they found, somewhat to their surprise, that funding seemed to rise in parallel, with contributions from local government, large business corporations and a string of anonymous donations. Indeed, the level of funding was becoming almost embarrassing and the team could not give away computers fast enough, nor share their expertise wide enough. But there was something more. Everyone that they were dealing with now began not to be seen as customers, but more as friends. As no money ever changed hands, there was no need for contracts or terms and conditions and no misunderstandings of any kind. The situation was summed up nicely by Ernie at one of their early morning meetings. "You know what" he started. "All of the customers we have now are totally unlike those we had as commercial clients. They are all genuinely nice people and it is really a pleasure to deal with them". "I've noticed that as well" confirmed Percy. "Furthermore" continued Ernie. "Although I didn't always see eye to eye with Violet, I have to hand it to her, she was quite right about all of this". "I said so all along" said Herbert. Natasha simply smiled to herself quietly. Of course Violet had been right. She was untainted by the greed and pretence of the commercial world and could see beyond the shallowness of mere profit and loss statistics. Since Dreadnought Consultants had adopted her strategy, Enterprise House had become something akin to a bustling community centre, with customers calling in here and there, sometimes to ask questions about technology, often just for a chat and a cup of tea. Ginger enjoyed meeting and getting to know them all and they often brought some little tid-bit or other in for him. The Dreadnought team enjoyed hearing about the exploits of their valued customers, all of whom were characters in their own right, and all of whom were fonts of knowledge about their various interests and endeavours. The customers also got to know each other via the Dreadnought link and would often meet up at Enterprise House to discuss their plans. Indeed, it had become a hive of activity and goodwill, like a shining beacon among the dark clouds of avarice. Weeks flew by and the Dreadnought team were truly enjoying their work, to the extent that they were quite taken back when there was a public holiday and usually came into the office anyway, at least for an hour or two, just for a chat. One night, after tucking Ginger up on his favourite chair, Ernie was pulling closed the sticking door and remarked that, in spite of all their ups and downs, there was nowhere he would rather be and that he had never been happier. "I know exactly what you mean" said Natasha. "Me too" said Herbert. "Indeed" said Percy. "Caw" said the crow.

They strolled off down Estuary Gardens, their hearts full as the big Boggle moon shone down, casting their shadows behind them. A lone owl hooted somewhere in the distance and the crow slowly closed his eyes and settled down for the night.

Julian Ashbourn

12 THE NEW RISING SUN

Enterprise House had undergone a metamorphosis. It had started out as simply a business venture in the computer industry, one of many such start ups, some of which go on to make fortunes for their directors, while others are destined for better things. Enterprise House and Dreadnought Consultants had fallen into the latter category via a serendipitous route, forged by the personalities of those involved. As a result, Enterprise House was now a bustling centre where people from all backgrounds could come together to make wondrous things happen, using computers and IT as the catalyst. Charlotte Bunker-Hunt, Clive Wesley, Sheila Dribble, Bertie Beaufort, Pamela Ponsonby, Celia Pumblepink and many others made Enterprise House their second home and would often pop in for a chat and a cup of tea, sometimes holding more formal meetings when they wished to discuss a matter of particular interest. Ernie, inspired by Violet's example, had taken to developing applications for them as and when needed, and providing these freely to whoever wished to use them. One day, they were visited by Robin Figget, the Headmaster of Boggle Comprehensive, who mentioned in passing that he was dismayed that his pupils were avoiding the natural sciences in favour of the softer subjects in which they were more likely to register examination passes. "Its not right" he complained to Ernie. "We shall produce a generation who know nothing about the world and how it functions. Nothing about life and the wonders of the natural world". On that particular day, Charlotte Bunker-Hunt happened to be visiting and overheard the conversation. "Oh, how right you are" she interrupted. "What they need is exposure to the real world, the world of nature and animals. Why not run field trips to the Donkey Sanctuary, I could always find them something to do". Figget was looking unconvinced and began. "I am not sure they would take to that idea", when Natasha interrupted. "Environmental Science is becoming an important factor across the world, why not combine a study of the natural sciences with an environmental monitoring programme that students could run for themselves, thus learning about the natural sciences by practical exposure". "Brilliant!" exclaimed Herbert who, by now, had become a firm supporter of Miss Bunker-Hunt and the Donkey Sanctuary. "They could set up monitoring stations at the Donkey Sanctuary and elsewhere along the coast". "And we could create a special database in which to store and collate all the data" suggested Ernie. Celia Pumblepink had also arrived by then and, in no time, a little impromptu committee had assembled to discuss the idea, helped along by a fresh pot of tea and input from Ginger, who seemed to take a particular interest as he hopped from lap to lap. After a while, Robin Figget leaned back in his chair and, with his hands on his head announced, "You know, I do believe that such a scheme could actually work". "Of course it would work" interjected Celia sharply. "It's just a matter of proper organisation and the ability to inspire the students". "Herbert would be good at that" suggested Charlotte. "He was most inspirational when helping me at the Sanctuary". So saying, she looked admiringly towards Herbert, who blushed as several pairs of eyes were turned in his direction. Natasha came to the rescue with the suggestion that she and Herbert could make a presentation to the school and Ernie could produce some software and a methodology with which they could gather the data and analyse it as they went. "Could we involve other schools as well?" asked Figget. "Of course, that's the whole idea" replied Natasha. "Boggle Comprehensive could then act as the central coordinator, which means that the students will also learn organisational skills". "Are they capable of such things?" asked Celia, somewhat cynically. "Of course they are" replied Figget defensively. "They are all good kids, they just need a little direction". "Exactly so" agreed Percy as he joined the discussion. They went on to hammer out the details of a trial to take place at the Donkey Sanctuary, and Ernie assured them that, with input from Robin Figget, he would work on a complete methodology and provide all the supporting software, while Natasha and Herbert would work on an inspirational presentation for the students. They broke open the last pack of digestive biscuits by way of celebration and Enterprise House fairly buzzed with excitement at the prospect of another community project. A black feathered head looked in at the open window. "Caw" said the crow. "Quite right" replied Charlotte.

After much work on the project, the day had finally arrived to present the idea to class 2B at Boggle Comprehensive. 2B were a little behind in their studies generally and Headmaster Figget thought that such a project might be just the stimulus they need to reawaken their interest in all things academic. Natasha wore her business frock and Herbert, kitted out in the closest thing he had to a business suit stood nervously to one side as Figget quietened the class down long enough to announce that representatives from Dreadnought Consultants were going to treat them to a presentation about a wonderful new project. A cacophony of various sounds erupted from 2B which Herbert took as signs of derision, until by rapping his ruler hard on the desk, Figget restored a lower level of background noise, now reduced to a few subdued giggles. Herbert stepped forward and an ink pellet zoomed past his head and splattered on the black board behind him. "Now then, that's enough" warned Figget. Natasha decided to take the initiative. "Boys and girls" she began, as the class leaned back lazily in their chairs in postures of defiance. "You are all wondering why we are here and why you should listen to us at all. Well, I will tell you. We are here for you To bring you something which will help you to understand why your studies are important, and to help you to become the best students in the school. In fact, the best students in any of our local schools". A few random giggles broke out here and there, punctuated by the odd hoot but Natasha had managed to gain their attention. "Now, Mr Jingle is going to discuss the natural world and why it is so important to us". She beckoned Herbert forward and he decided to start the conversation with a question. He leaned forward and eyed his adversaries closely. "What is your definition of the countryside?" he asked. A rough looking boy in a crumpled shirt and jeans named Archie Snuffings put his hand up. "Well?" asked Herbert. "A town with no houses in it" replied Archie to the amusement of the class who shrieked their approval. Herbert rose to the challenge. "Yes, that's a fair definition" he suggested. "Given all the over-development which is occurring now, the small areas which haven't yet been smothered with houses might reasonably be called the countryside". This surprise answer got the attention of the class who now watched Herbert closely, if a little suspiciously. He went on to explain the importance of natural environments, including the land and the oceans, in regulating our atmosphere and creating the conditions upon Earth with which to support life. "Why is the atmosphere important?" he asked. The class swot, Maria Swithins explained that the mixture of hydrogen, helium, oxygen and trace gases allows for respiration while the atmosphere creates a protective layer against the excesses of the Sun's rays, including ultra violet. Amid the inevitable giggling and cheering the class bully, Nigel Brimmer called out "Without the atmosphere we couldn't breath and therefore wouldn't be sitting here listening to you". Herbert held his hand up to quieten the babble. "You are both quite right" he assured them and went on to describe weather cycles and environmental interactions. By this point, something quite strange was starting to occur. Something quite alien to class 2B thought Figget as he sat and watched. Almost unbelievably, the entire class had fallen silent and seemed to be paying attention to what Herbert was saying. Figget eyed them suspiciously, but it did indeed seem to be true. When Natasha announced that they were now going to show them a slide show presentation of an interesting new idea for environmental monitoring, there were no giggles at all, just a sea of young faces with expressions of eager anticipation. One boy, whose name was Thomas Tomlin, stepped forward to help Natasha with the projector, while Figget pulled down a screen in front of the black board. Natasha pushed the power button on the projector while Herbert fired up the laptop computer. A blank blue square appeared on the screen and Thomas, who seemed to know about such things, came and pressed another button on the projector and the image of the first slide miraculously appeared. "Thank you" said Natasha. "What's your name?". "Tommy" answered the boy with a smile. Herbert then described the methodology and showed them some screenshots of Ernie's database application, explaining how it worked and how it could be used to gain a true picture of environmental changes. After a few more slides, Natasha explained that all that was necessary to make the project a reality and produce some scientific data of value to the broader community, indeed of value to the entire world, was some intelligent observation and data gathering by a group of committed individuals who would like to manage the situation. To the astonishment of Headmaster Figget, several hands rose in respectful silence. Natasha chose one at random and a smart looking young girl named Melanie Prips asked, "Couldn't we do that?". A chorus of "Of course we could" rose up from the class. Natasha smiled. "It would mean that you would need to brush up on your other studies, including maths, science, English and more" she suggested. "And you would automatically be learning more about computer science and data analytics" added Herbert. 2B bustled with enthusiasm and Natasha noticed that Tommy had raised his hand. "Yes Tommy" she smiled at him. "If we made the database available on-line, then other schools could also contribute to it" he suggested. "That's right" interjected Herbert. "But first we need to establish the model at one location in order to prove the concept and start building the dataset". Another girl named Sharon Lewis called out, "And then we could document it and provide it to other schools". Archie Snuffings interjected, "But we shall be in charge of the whole thing". A barrage of similar comments and suggestions flowed from 2B as if by magic, temporarily stunning Figget to silence until, standing up and raising his hand he called for silence. "What we need" he suggested, "Is a small core group to manage the project overall and report on progress". Every hand in the class was raised. As Figget looked bewildered by the response, Natasha broke in to rescue him. "We shall circulate forms with details of the required roles, skills and responsibilities, and you may all bid for whatever roles you feel you are suited for". The class cheered and Natasha continued. "Then we shall draw them from a hat and the first drawn for each role shall be appointed accordingly. The remainder of the class may then contribute to the observation and data gathering". The class beamed their approval and some enthusiastic discussion ensued right through the morning break and on until lunchtime. Natasha distributed the forms and assured them that they would be collected after lunch and that the draw would take place after the first lesson of the afternoon. Herbert and Natasha packed up their equipment and headed off for lunch with Robin Figget. In the afternoon, at the end of the first lesson when, ordinarily, 2B would be rushing off for the break, they had all congregated in the classroom to witness the draw for the key posts in the new project. Melanie Prips and Maria Swithins were elected for the communications and training tasks, Archie Snuffings was elected as project coordinator and, to the delight of Natasha, Thomas Tomlin was elected as the IT support expert. Other posts were quickly filled and all students would participate in the general observation and data gathering tasks. They couldn't wait to get started and so Herbert and Natasha left them with the necessary document templates with which to classify and record information, advising them that the software would need to be set up properly as a separate task. For this, it was suggested that Thomas Tomlin spend a day at Enterprise House in order to learn both the software functionality and how to install and support it over time. A date was accordingly arranged with Headmaster Figget to release Tommy for a day in the coming week. Back at base, Herbert and Natasha explained how well their presentation had been received and how the school was looking forward to engaging with the project. "Are you sure?" asked Percy incredulously. "Yes" replied Natasha. "You *are* talking about Boggle Comprehensive?" persisted Percy. "Yes" replied Natasha. Percy drew a deep breath and sank back in his chair. "It does sound a little unlikely" suggested Ernie. "I know, but they are dead keen - really" said Herbert. And so, Ernie continued to refine the database and Natasha and Herbert produced some more documentation to aid the process. Natasha also established a dedicated Dreadnought Conservation Initiative web site for the project where other schools could register their interest.

It was on a Tuesday morning, with dark clouds looming over Boggle-on-Sea, as was their custom, when Tommy Tomlin walked up to the door of Enterprise House and wrapped loudly upon it. "Who can that be at this hour?" asked Ernie. "We haven't had our first cup of tea yet" added Percy indignantly. "Oh, it must be Tommy" suggested Natasha with a smile. Ernie looked at his watch disapprovingly as Natasha pulled open the sticking door. "Come in Tommy" she said. "Right oh!" answered Tommy cheerfully as he strode purposefully into the headquarters of that most distinguished organisation. They found him an extra cup and soon they were all sitting together with their morning tea and biscuits, discussing the Dreadnought Conservation Initiative. Ginger took an immediate liking to Tommy and jumped up on his lap, something that Natasha saw as a good sign, as they continued to chat about the project, the school and how things might develop in the future. After a while, the others left Tommy with Ernie in order that they go over the software, while they got on with their other tasks. It wasn't long before Charlotte Bunker-Hunt and Sheila Dribble popped in, both of whom were very interested in the project. Natasha explained that the school were very enthusiastic and Charlotte was looking forward to welcoming the students to the Donkey Sanctuary as a starting point for their observations. "And this is Tommy" announced Natasha as she briefly interrupted his induction process. Tommy stood up and shook hands with the ladies. "Pleased to meet you" he said with a smile. "Oh yes, I'm sure" said Sheila meekly. It was explained that Tommy would be running the computer aspects of the project and managing the database software. Upon receiving this intelligence, Charlotte warmed to him immediately. "Oh how wonderful" she exclaimed while looking Tommy up and down. "You must come round and have a look at my computer some day". Herbert, upon hearing this remark became a little jealous and coughed quietly. Charlotte went over and prodded him sharply in the ribs. "You know you are always welcome Herbie dear" she whispered, adding, "by the way, I haven't seen you lately". Herbert coughed again and pretended to be absorbed in his work. People drifted in and out of Enterprise House as usual while Tommy and Ernie discussed the database. "If you add some basic network communications functionality, we could communicate directly with other schools" suggested Tommy. "Yes, I was considering that" replied Ernie. "And if you add some basic security and privileged account management, we can ensure that others only see what they need to see" continued Tommy. "Yes, I was going to add that as well" replied Ernie who, by now, was becoming impressed with Tommy's obvious enthusiasm for the project. They went on to discuss reporting functionality and how they could provide a set of standard, pre-configured reports. The two of them spent the whole day discussing the software while Natasha, Herbert and Percy went about their business and entertained the various guests that came in for a visit. Ginger marched up and down authoritatively, as was becoming his habit, quite sure that it was he who was actually in control of affairs at Enterprise House. The day soon passed and it was agreed that Tommy, who had proved to be a most enthusiastic and useful ally, would return for another day of discussion and revision of the software before installing the same back at Boggle Comprehensive. The second day was equally productive and Tommy duly returned to the school where he installed and tested the software. He chose another classmate, Peter Perkins, to be his assistant and standby in the case of emergency and the database was properly established in no time, ready for data entry from the other students. The nest stage was to arrange the first day of activity at the Donkey Sanctuary and Archie Snuffings had arranged everything with Charlotte Bunker-Hunt accordingly.

The morning loomed dark and foreboding with heavy clouds sailing across the Boggle sky and a brisk wind blowing. There was moisture in the air which became increasingly threatening as 2B marched along the lane, past the horse trough and up towards the Donkey Sanctuary, with their clipboards and pencils in plastic bags. But providence was kind on that day and the rains held off as the eager students arrived to a cheery welcome from Charlotte Bunker-Hunt who had prepared two large pots of tea to start them off. "You might have to share a cup. I only have so many you know" she beamed as she handed round the assortment of vessels from her kitchen. 2B refreshed themselves and then, with the guidance from Headmaster Figget who was overseeing things on the first day, they set about dividing the land into quadrants, within which they would make their observations. The students were deployed in pairs and wandered off to their allotted quadrants, most of them followed by the donkeys, for whom the occasion offered some welcome distraction from their usual routine. When 2B got out their various papers and tools, including magnifying glasses, reference charts, thermometers and acidity measuring kits, the donkeys became particularly interested and were eager to help with the proceedings. It wasn't long before a cry was heard from Sharon Lewis. "The donkey has eaten my observation sheet" she exclaimed in anguish. As the others looked on and laughed, another donkey began chewing on the tails of Figget's tweed jacket. "Stop that Susie, you naughty girl" said Charlotte who had spotted it just in time, although the jacket was now of a subtly different cut. They continued with their observations as the donkeys went around nudging them and generally participating in the broader activity. One donkey, whose name was Geoffrey, was particularly curious, although he had his own idea of where 2B and Figget should be making their observations and insisted upon herding them towards the spot. "Now then Geoffrey" said Charlotte in a cross tone of voice. "I've told you before about that. Leave the class alone". Geoffrey, who perfectly understood Charlotte's every word, ignored her absolutely and continued to nudge and butt the students with gay abandon. After all, an opportunity such as this does not arise every day. Nevertheless, observations were made and noted down on the appropriate sheets. The time passed quickly and 2B and Figget were both surprised and, it has to be said, a little relieved when Natasha and Herbert arrived with some sandwiches and soft drinks for lunch. They all gathered around outside the house and it was noted that Melanie Prips seemed to be missing. A search party was organised and a disorientated and tearful Melanie was eventually found, entangled in brambles in the ditch where the donkeys had driven her. She was cut free and brought back to the house for lunch. Her ordeal was quickly forgotten as she tucked into the delicious sandwiches and orange juice. The donkeys had some little sandwiches of their own that Natasha had made for them and Charlotte brewed up some more tea to finish off with. Soon, they were all refreshed and back in the field where they continued with their scientific observations. The afternoon rushed by just as quickly and 2B were a little saddened that the experience was at an end, as were Charlotte's donkeys who had very much enjoyed the occasion. However, much useful data had been gathered and the class were eager to visit other local areas in order to enlarge the scope of their observations. Figget however, had ordained that only one day per fortnight could be devoted to field work, and this only until they had the Boggle-on-Sea area covered. From then on they would analyse the results during their Natural Science class and orchestrate the broader project during the spare periods. The trend had been set however and 2B had responded extremely positively to the whole exercise which, as intended, had whetted their appetite for the sciences and re-engaged them in their studies generally. Headmaster Figget was especially pleased with them as they had shown such enthusiasm for the project and really wanted to take it further.

Back at Enterprise House, the Dreadnought team were also very pleased as the programme represented an example of technology being deployed for genuinely useful purposes, supporting intelligent human processes. "Didn't 2B respond beautifully" exclaimed Herbert. "I knew they would" replied Natasha. "They are all good kids at heart who just need a little inspired guidance to spark their interest". "Just like all youngsters" agreed Ernie. They were also particularly pleased with Tommy who had proved to be most helpful, working closely with Ernie to refine the database and taking charge of the computer element of the project back at Boggle Comprehensive without faltering for a moment. They brewed up their last afternoon tea and sat down to reflect upon the day's activities as Ginger sat contentedly, listening to every word with interest. "You know" said Ernie, "If this project were to spread to other schools, we could provide computers and software freely to all of them and really achieve something worthwhile for the scientific community, while helping countless young students to develop their own confidence and academic understanding". "Indeed" agreed Percy. "And they, in turn, could go on to inspire others in a similar vein". "Of course" said Natasha simply as she poured them another cup. "And we could develop other projects along similar lines" continued Ernie. "All aimed at increasing our understanding of nature, the natural world and the place of humanity within it, while helping as many young students as possible, year after year". Natasha suddenly put her cup down and looked up towards the ceiling with an inspired expression lighting her features. "And not just in this country" she exclaimed, "but across the entire world". "Why not?" said Herbert enthusiastically. "We could easily organise this via the Internet". The discussion continued along similar lines, with many ideas surfacing for other projects and related computer systems, while Ginger looked on with interest. But it was getting late and the time had come when they needed to head back to their respective homes. Natasha cleared up the tea things while Percy prepared Ginger's favourite chair for him and Herbert turned off the computers. As Ernie pulled the sticking door closed behind them he remarked; "What a wonderful day this has been". "Hasn't it just" confirmed Natasha. "It certainly has" agreed Herbert. "Indeed" said Percy. "Caw" said the crow. Ernie turned the key in the lock and they sauntered off down Estuary Gardens as the sun cast long shadows across the mud flats in preparation for its own retirement for the night. The crow turned towards the east and his eyes slowly closed as the moon rose to herald the end of another Boggle day.

13 CLOUDS

As Ernie cycled along Westminster Drive, around by St. Mary's Church and along the High Street on his way towards Enterprise House, he looked up at the sky and couldn't help remarking to himself what a beautiful day it was. He whistled parts of Beethoven's sixth symphony, at least as best as he could remember them, and felt sure that the birds were joining in with him as he gaily cycled along. Past the traffic lights he sped and peddled on through the sunshine, along the sea front and on to Estuary Gardens. As he removed his bicycle clips and looked upwards once more to the big, beautiful sky with its silken white clouds drifting across a powder blue canvas, the idea suddenly came to him in a blaze of inspiration. "Of course!" he said out aloud. "Clouds. That's it. Clouds". "Caw" said the crow as Ernie turned the key in the lock. "No, really" replied Ernie as he pushed open the sticking door. The others arrived one by one as Ernie sat patiently, awaiting the moment when he would announce his new strategic initiative. All leading organisations have strategies, he thought to himself as Natasha arrived and put the kettle on. He looked around him, impressed with what they had achieved to date as Percy fired up the accounts computer and Herbert started preparing for the day. With the tea made and a new packet of digestive biscuits broken out for the morning meeting, Ernie took a deep breath and, in a grand voice that any Shakespearian actor would be proud to own, announced; "Clouds". Percy looked at Herbert, who looked back at Percy. "What of them?" he asked. "There were no dark ones this morning" said Herbert, trying to be helpful. "Indeed, they looked quite pretty this morning as I was coming along the sea front" agreed Natasha. "No, you don't understand" said Ernie. "I mean cloud computing. You know, third party architectures and all that". "Ah, those" said Percy knowingly as he opened the morning paper. Herbert stroked Ginger who had jumped up onto his lap to take a bite of his digestive biscuit. Natasha remarked that she wouldn't be surprised if Celia Pumblepink dropped in this morning and there was a message from Penelope Wilting at the Council. Ernie decided that the best approach would be to start again from the beginning and so, after taking another sip of tea, he explained the concept of cloud computing and how he saw it being beneficial to the various projects that Dreadnought Consulting might host in the future. "But why would people want to use a third party architecture when they already have their own computers. It doesn't make any sense" said Percy. "Most new concepts in computing don't make any sense" agreed Natasha. "Maybe not. But people like to use third party architectures when they need more capacity and want it provided cheaply". "But we don't charge them for their computers anyway and, if we were to use a third party cloud service, we would have to pay for it. It still doesn't make any sense" protested Percy. Herbert, who had been listening carefully, stroked Ginger on the head and cleared his throat. "In that case, why don't we create our own cloud and let others use it for free". "Oh what a wonderful idea Herbert, you are so clever" beamed Natasha as she poured him another tea. Ernie thought for a moment. "But we haven't the equipment and we should need quite a bit more funding" he mused. "Oh, don't worry about that" replied Percy. "People are falling over themselves to give us funding at the moment. Its good for them to be seen to be supporting Dreadnought Consultants and all that we are doing". "That's quite right" agreed Natasha. "And, in any case, we only have to mention it to the media and we shall be inundated with offers". Ernie stroked his chin and thought for a moment. "This is what we shall do" he said, turning over a leaf on the flip chart next to his desk. They then drew out a plan for a prefabricated extension to Enterprise House which would contain all the equipment, including their current servers, in a dedicated data centre. This would free up space in the main building which would then be reorganised as more of a community centre. As they were considering the various options, Penelope Wilting arrived from the Council and, upon hearing the plan, insisted that the Boggle Town Council would be happy to fund the new extension. As Natasha had predicted, Celia Pumblepink also dropped in and immediately lent her support to the initiative, pointing out that the Women's Institute would be pleased to hold a celebratory reception in the newly configured main office / community centre when ready. Others came and went during the day and all thought that it was an excellent plan, although most of them had absolutely no idea what cloud computing actually was or why it might be useful to anyone, but it sounded impressive enough. Stephen Spindlebrook from the Boggle Mutual bank was consulted in case Dreadnought Consultants needed a small overdraft and he immediately gave his support, adding that the bank would be proud to be one of their first customers, especially as there would be no charge for the service.

And so, the wheels were set in motion and, before very long, a new portacabin arrived and was lowered into place behind Enterprise House. Pete Barrow and Wally Gammer from the Borough Council Works Department were there to supervise proceedings. "Of course, we will need to construct an adjoining passage so that you can move from one building to the other" suggested Wally to Natasha. "Of course" agreed Natasha. "We wouldn't want to get wet when it is raining". "Tricky things, adjoining passages" said Peter. "Why's that Pete" replied Wally. "Well, we shall have to dig a proper foundation, then knock a hole in the wall of this building. Then there are the doors". "What about the doors?" asked Ernie, who had joined them. "The doors have to be hung properly, otherwise they will stick" announced Pete proudly. "And you can't have sticking doors in an adjoining passage. Never" he added, shaking his head. "Never" echoed Wally dutifully. "We shall have to call in Reg and Bill to hang the doors". "Yep" said Pete, "I reckon there's a couple of weeks work to get this all set up properly". "At least" said Wally as he lit up a cigarette and eyed the teapot hopefully. "Perhaps you had better start with a tea while you make your plans" suggested Natasha. "Very kind of you misses" said Wally as he pulled up a chair. The Dreadnought team knew very well that you couldn't rush the Boggle Works Department and that it was best to just let them do things their way. In the meantime, Ernie went about ordering the equipment that they would need. Clive Wesley had popped in and, on hearing of the plans, recommended Gerald Fuzzfig, a local electrician, to help with the setting up. Following an endearing phone call from Natasha, Gerald arrived at Enterprise House that same afternoon, his orange Ford Escort van spluttering to a halt outside and a large, awkward looking character tumbling out onto the pavement. Gerald, who wore round framed glasses with particularly thick lenses, bumbled his way into the building and crashed against Natasha's desk. "Fuzzfig the electrician, to see Mr Trubshaw" he announced cheerfully as he disentangled himself from the umbrella stand. "Oh yes, of course" replied Natasha as she eyed his crumpled trousers and heavy woollen jumper which had evidently been home to a dozen or so moths. "We were expecting you". Gerald was introduced to Ernie and, after a preliminary discussion of the plan announced, "The first thing you will need is an uninterruptable power supply. I can build one for you if you like". "That's a good idea" agreed Ernie. "Can you wire it up to the main racks?". "Yes, I should think so. Where are they?" replied Gerald. "Well, we haven't got them yet" confessed Ernie. "I had better supply those as well then" suggested Gerald as he scribbled some notes down on a pad. "Here's how it will work" he continued and, as he reached out to show Ernie the little sketch he had made, the sleeve of his jumper caught Ernie's cup and sent it flying across the desk, the tea running everywhere. Ginger, who had been sitting on the desk listening to the conversation, let out a shriek and leaped to the floor in front of Herbert who, in turn, tripped over him and fell across the desk, sending the telephone crashing to the floor. "Oh, you need another cup" announced Natasha calmly. "Would you like one as well Mr Fuzzfig?". A fresh pot of tea was brewed and the discussion continued as various locals popped in and out of Enterprise House, all eager to understand what was happening.

A week or two passed and the new data centre was finished off with a freshly whitewashed interior. Gerald had provided mains wiring to it and the two 19" racks had, with a great deal of difficulty, been manhandled through the main building and into place. It was time to toggle the main power switch to bring the data centre on stream. The rear half of Gerald Fuzzfig protruded from the little utility cupboard as, with a torch in one hand, he manfully threw the main switch. There was a loud crack and all the lights went out in Enterprise House. Gerald banged his head on the cupboard door frame before exiting rapidly and falling over Natasha, who had stepped forward to see what was wrong. Picking himself up from the floor and adjusting his spectacles, the excellent Mr Fuzzfig announced that he suspected a small technical fault and that he would have it fixed in a jiffy. He rumbled through his toolbox and, arming himself with some wire cutters, a screwdriver, some fuse wire and an electrical test meter, he picked up the torch and ventured back into the cupboard. The others stood well back, not knowing quite what to expect next. However, to their astonishment, after a quite a lot of bumping and groaning, the lights came back on and Gerald announced that all was well. Ernie and Gerald then fitted the rack mount computers into the racks and Ernie configured them in order to provide any number of discreet, usable infrastructures that their clients would be able to use at no cost. It all looked quite reasonable and, as expected Stephen Spindlebrook from the Boggle Mutual Bank was the first to take the plunge and use the environment. "It's wonderful" exclaimed Spindlebrook. "I can put all our marketing and communications stuff there and keep it away from the day to day banking accounts". Others took advantage of the readily available infrastructure and it wasn't long before Ernie had to increase both processing and storage capacity in order to meet the demand. Herbert and Natasha had the idea that schools would benefit from having this extra capacity at their fingertips and so embarked upon a communications exercise with all the local schools in order to raise awareness of the service. The take up was immediate and, as the local schools began to tell other schools, it wasn't long before Ernie had to upgrade capacity once again. A third rack was manhandled into the new data centre and Ernie, after discussion with Tommy Tomlin, configured a special Schools Cloud facility in order that any school could quickly establish an infrastructure for a particular project and then take it down again when it was no longer needed. Pamela Ponsonby popped in and Natasha explained the new Schools Cloud to her. "Oh what a marvellous idea" squeaked an excited Miss Ponsonby as Natasha poured her tea. "Does that mean we could have a Boggle Christian Association cloud as well". "Of course" confirmed Natasha. "And a Women's Institute cloud and any other clouds that we need". It wasn't long before almost everybody in Boggle-on-Sea wanted a cloud. What they wanted it for continued to be a mystery, but they were all swept up in the enthusiasm that Dreadnought Consultants had created around technology and enjoyed being part of the community that had developed around Enterprise House. Indeed, the popularity of the once scruffy old prefab had taken the Dreadnought team somewhat by surprise and they were finding themselves overwhelmed with enquiries, suggestions and new ideas from every quarter. One evening, as they were leaving Enterprise House, an exhausted Ernie announced "I think we had better call an emergency meeting tomorrow morning to discuss how we are going to move forwards". "Yes, a good idea" said Natasha. "Indeed" said Herbert. "Indubitably" said Percy. "Caw" said the crow. They trudged off slowly into the moonlight, looking a little like a miniature refugee column as Ginger watched from the window.

The next morning, with spirits revived, they gathered early at Enterprise House and quickly set the tea going while Percy arranged the chairs for their meeting. "Better shut the door so we are not interrupted" suggested Ernie and Herbert duly obliged, giving the sticking door a good shove. However, when Natasha brought in the tea, she noticed that there seemed to be one too many of them. "Oh, I think we need another cup" she said apologetically. Percy looked around and, with his quick accountant's brain, realised that there were now five of them. "Just thought I would pop in before class and see how the schools web site is coming along" announced Tommy cheerfully. "Well, I suppose you had better join us for the meeting then" suggested Ernie. Equipped with tea and biscuits all round, they proceeded to discuss the dilemma that their popularity had landed them in. "What we need is some structure" suggested Ernie. "And a way of fielding enquiries efficiently" added Percy. "Why don't you have a weekly scheduled meeting, that anyone can attend, especially to discuss new ideas and suggestions" said Tommy. "Oh, that's a wonderful idea" agreed Natasha. "We will get the Women's Institute and the Salvation Army to provide tea and cakes". "And we could hold it in the Conference Centre" chipped in Herbert enthusiastically. "It would mean that we would have to close Enterprise House early" said Ernie. "And that might mean that we would miss enquiries". "Not if we have one of those automated telephone systems like the Council have" suggested Percy. "You can have special IP phones now of course" added Ernie. After a little more discussion, it was agreed that they would indeed schedule a weekly public meeting at the Conference Centre and Natasha quickly contacted Pamela Ponsonby and Celia Pumblepink for support, the latter introducing her to Maud Willets and Florence Blacket from the Salvation Army. Charlie Higgins popped in on his way to work at the refuse tip and also suggested that they have Bert Scarlett's Fish and Chip van outside at every meeting. "It will go down well with the Salvation Army stewed tea" suggested Charlie. A few more telephone calls, plus contributions from various visitors to Enterprise House and the concept of weekly public meetings was firmly established. In parallel, Ernie had started looking at new telephone systems and, after a particularly enthusiastic sales pitch from Willy Billet at nearby Greycliff Communications, he ordered half a dozen of the new Tornado T21 IP phones and the associated CallPerfect software control system. The equipment arrived early the next day and, as Ernie was busy developing the new Dreadnought Consultants Universal Database application, he called in Gerald Fuzzfig to install the new telephone system. A little later, Gerald's orange Ford came to a spluttering halt outside Enterprise House and the effervescent Fuzzfig tumbled out onto the pavement. The rear door of the van screeched loudly as Gerald prised it open in order to retrieve his battered old toolbox and head inside. Unfortunately, just as Gerald was giving a cheery hello to all assembled, Ginger ran forwards to welcome him and, not observing his furry friend, Gerald tripped over Ginger, his toolbox bouncing ahead of him, distributing its contents far and wide. "Good morning Gerald" announced Natasha calmly as she stepped over him. "Er, good morning Miss" replied Fuzzfig as he fumbled with his spectacles while still rolling around on the floor. Celia Pumblepink had also arrived and was gingerly picking her way among the scattered tools. "Don't worry, its only Gerald" Natasha called reassuringly from the kitchen area. After his first tea and some biscuits, Gerald quickly regained his composure and set about his task, strewing out wires across the floor like a demented spider spinning its web. An hour or two later, after much banging and tacking, Gerald announced that the telephone system was now up and running. Natasha picked up the nearest phone and attempted to make a call. "It doesn't work" she complained, as Gerald was collecting his tools together. "You have to log in to it" explained Gerald. "How?" asked Natasha. "With your password" replied Gerald. "What password?" asked Natasha. "They have to be set up in the software system" explained Gerald. "Well, haven't you done that?" asked Natasha. "I don't know how" claimed Gerald. Herbert, upon hearing the exchange, came up and asked if he could help. "Gerald hasn't installed the software properly" exclaimed Natasha. Herbert looked quizzically at Gerald. "I'm an electrician, not a blooming software engineer" explained Gerald as he thrust some papers into Herbert's hand. "Here, you have a go". Herbert had a look at the requirements and, in consultation with Ernie, they soon had the CallPerfect software installed on the office server and the staff details entered accordingly while Gerald looked on. "That should do it" claimed Ernie as he picked up the nearest phone and entered his password. "There, I have a dialling tone" he exclaimed triumphantly. "Well, that's all right then" exclaimed the venerable Fuzzfig. "I will be on my way now". After colliding once more with the sticking front door, Gerald's orange van soon spluttered into life and wobbled its way back along Estuary Gardens, leaving the team to experiment with the Tornado T21 phones. Natasha entered a variety of 'sorry we are out' messages into the software and, in general, they were pleased with their new communications system, although callers would find it an altogether more challenging proposition. But then, that is the thing with technology, as Ernie was quick to explain, it no longer had anything to do with making people's lives easier, it was all about providing ongoing opportunities for technology suppliers. As users, they simply had to make the most of it, as best they could. However, Charlotte Bunker-Hunt, Clive Wesley, Sheila Dribble, Robin Figget, Bertie Beaufort and others who had embraced the Dreadnought Consultants model, were all very pleased with how the technology had enabled them to do other things. In particular, the Environmental Monitoring programme introduced at Boggle Comprehensive had proved a godsend for engaging young students with the natural sciences and had now been adopted by several other schools. Ernie now planned to introduce a universal database, founded upon what had been learned with this project, which could easily be applied to almost any situation. It would come with a predefined schema, allowing users to simply change the names of the existing fields according to their particular requirements. Everything else would be ready built, including predefined reports. Tommy had also had an input to this and was fast becoming a useful member of the team.

The weekly meetings were introduced with great success and served to embed Dreadnought Consultants even more deeply into the community. Bert Scarlett had never sold so many Fish and Chips in his life and the Boggle seagulls were equally delighted. In fact, it seemed like the seagull population at Boggle-on-Sea was expanding exponentially and so, Dreadnought Consultants were inadvertently supporting the natural world with their technological deliberations. Maud Willets and Florence Blacket, or 'Maud and Flo' as they quickly became known, joined fully into the spirit of things and, as a result, the Salvation Army also benefitted from the weekly meetings. Celia Pumblepink was usually present to keep an eye on things and Penelope Wilting from the Boggle Council Community Affairs department was a regular attendee, as was Charlotte Bunker-Hunt who enjoyed seeing Herbert speak at the meetings and often brought along one or more of her donkeys for the exercise, leaving them outside the main door, although their curiosity would sometimes get the better of them and they would occasionally wander in. All things considered, the meetings were a great success and served as a community meeting place where all manner of situations were discussed, whether or not related to technology. However, there was usually a technology angle somewhere and Ernie and the team were quick to understand the associated opportunities. Jessica Clinkworth-Sykes from the Rotary Club suggested that, at every meeting, they should have a 20 minutes presentation from someone in the community, in order to share their experiences with the broader assemblage and spark discussion upon different topics. Charlie Higgins quickly volunteered to be the first and the idea was accepted, at least for a trial period. At the next meeting, after working with Natasha on some electronic slides, Charlie, kitted out in his Council overalls, stood proudly on the stage. "Quiet everyone please" squawked Jessica who, as originator of the idea was given the honour of chairing that particular meeting. "I would now like to present Mr Charles Higgins from the Refuse Department who shall provide an overview of his activities in our historic town". The audience greeted this announcement with cheers and hoots as Charlie steeped forward and began his presentation. "Well, er, I thought you might like to know how the refuse collection actually works" explained Charlie nervously as Natasha fired up the first slide, a beautiful picture of a dustcart, stopped in one of the Boggle streets, blocking the traffic, while its crew manipulated the wheelie bins. "You see, we first have to assemble at the depot every morning at six o'clock" continued Charlie, who went on to explain how they checked the dustcarts for fuel and basic operation before moving off onto the streets. He then explained the finer points of tipping into the Earth-fill sites and offered some anecdotes of their experiences, including the time when they accidentally backed into, and completely demolished, the vicarage wall while undertaking a complex manoeuvre with the dustcart and had to leave a note for the vicar who was, at the time, giving a sermon at St Mary's on loving thy neighbour. Then there was the time they collected a huge amount of sacks from outside the charity shop only to discover later that they were full of precious donations. They rose to the challenge by providing the location of the Earth fill site, enabling those concerned to go and pick about among the rubbish, an activity which, as Charlie gleefully acknowledged, uncovered even more donations. Natasha clicked away, throwing up numerous interesting pictures of piles of rubbish and dustcarts from varying angles, while Charlie continued with his stories. Ernie, Herbert and Percy looked at each other in disbelief and were concerned that it might have been a mistake to let Charlie be the first presenter of the series. However, to their astonishment, at the end of his 20 minutes, Charlie was enthusiastically cheered and applauded by the audience who had evidently enjoyed his presentation very much. "Thank you Mr Higgins" exclaimed Jessica in warm tones, clapping away herself, before returning the meeting to the original agenda. Charlie's presentation had set the tone for the event and the inhabitants of Boggle-on-Sea were to receive many more enjoyable little diversions from a variety of townsfolk, all of which served to knit their community ever more closely together. Dreadnought Consultants, in turn, continued to provide their technology and services freely to anyone who would benefit from them and everybody was happy with the arrangement. The

Dreadnought Cloud Services concept was going extremely well, with new people availing themselves of the facility almost every day and, based upon this success, the team expanded their expertise into various new areas, including mobile technology, identity management, certificate services, web site hosting and much more. However, Enterprise House had become a centre for something much more than simply the provision of technology. It had become a community asset in the best sense, bringing people together and becoming the incubator of ideas and projects which served a genuinely useful purpose. In addition, many Boggle-on-Sea residents whose paths would otherwise never have crossed, had met and forged enduring friendships, collaborating across societal barriers in a manner which seldom occurs. The Dreadnought team themselves had developed into this new and somewhat unexpected role and were enjoying their work like never before. In addition, upon learning that Tommy would soon be leaving Boggle Comprehensive and had no immediate plans, he was invited to join the team. A suggestion that all were pleased with and which Tommy quickly agreed to as he was enjoying his relationship with the team. Dreadnought Consultants were now uniquely placed for their strategic trajectory into a technological world into which they would bring a special distinction. Ernie's dream was now coming true, albeit in a different manner to which he had originally supposed. Similarly, Natasha, Herbert and Percy found themselves on career paths that had not been originally anticipated. Ginger curled up in his favourite chair each evening as the team pulled closed the sticking door and went their various ways. The crow would look on knowingly. It was as if he alone knew all along what Enterprise House would develop into. He had made it his home also, settling down on the flat roof each evening and coming and going during the day as he pleased. Real life had come to Boggle-on-Sea from all parts of the compass and had converged upon a magical spot, upon which an old prefabricated and unloved building had blossomed into something quite special.

14 LOVE STORY

Life continued at Enterprise House as the team became engaged in many projects, all of benefit to the broader community. The Environmental Monitoring project had spread to other countries, still being managed by Boggle Comprehensive who coordinated things centrally, their own students benefitting enormously from this activity and the additional opportunities for communication that it provided. Indeed, the academic standing of the school had increased proportionally and it was now considered a leading academic institution. Other students visited from far and wide and special introductory sessions were established for them, including a visit to the Donkey Sanctuary, an activity in which Charlotte Bunker-Hunt took great delight as she introduced her own work and often received contributions for the upkeep of the sanctuary. The donkeys also greatly enjoyed the steady stream of visitors and new friends. Other community projects were equally successful, as was the annual conference, the Boggle International Festival and other events in which the team were engaged. In parallel, Dreadnought Consultants continued to be at the forefront of technology, introducing many new concepts and building an international reputation as innovators in their own right. However, running like a thread throughout all of this activity were undertones of a quite different nature. It was as if there was another force, outside perhaps of mortal control, which was nonetheless operating in the background, bathing Enterprise House in its unseen benevolent rays. A force which had no doubt been attracted to the vicinity by the absence of greed and selfishness to be found within the walls of that establishment. A force which, unknowingly at first to those involved, was gently manifesting itself within the environs of that erstwhile broken down building and elevating it to an entirely new position among the Boggle community. It was now about to focus its influence directly upon the lives of some of those involved.

Charlotte Bunker-Hunt and Herbert Jingle had, from a somewhat shaky start, developed a mutual respect for one another as they collaborated on the various events associated with Enterprise House. In particular, Herbert had developed a love of the natural world and had increasingly been helping Charlotte with her donkeys. The donkeys, in turn, had also got to know Herbert well and would come to him whenever he visited the Sanctuary, as if to tell him all their news of recent days. He knew them all by name and would talk to them freely, often bringing them little treats that he had picked up from the vegetable market on the way. Charlotte would look on with a smile as Herbert chatted with his donkey friends, stroking their heads and asking them how they were. Even the mischievous Geoffrey had come to like Herbert and would often be the first to notice his approach and to trot up to welcome him. In the evenings, Herbert would often be found at Charlotte's house, helping her with the donkey database and with the numerous enquiries that they were now receiving from around the country and even one or two from overseas. Charlotte would make some of his favourite Irish stews or Shepherd's pies and they would often share an evening meal together. At weekends, the Dreadnought team would always know where to find Herbert. He would invariably be up at the Donkey Sanctuary. Charlotte, for her part, became a regular visitor at Enterprise House and contributed many ideas for the various associated events. Even some of the donkeys would occasionally be seen either outside Enterprise House or at the Conference Centre. Visitors would interact with them accordingly and either Charlotte or Herbert were always on hand to ensure their safety and wellbeing. Ernie, Natasha and Percy had of course noticed this gradual coming together of their two friends and, indeed, it wasn't long before Charlotte and Herbert were increasingly being mentioned in the same breath by the inhabitants of Boggle. A little of the force had been sprinkled, like star dust, upon their lives and was slowly working its magic upon them. Everybody had noticed this, although Herbert and Charlotte themselves never mentioned it. It was as though, to them, it was a perfectly natural progression which fate had had in mind for them all along. Of course, as Natasha had once observed, Herbert had always been something of a dark horse and it was interesting that he, more than the others, had been influenced by Violet and had remained loyal to her throughout. Charlotte had obviously observed these same qualities. She explained once to Natasha how, on a quiet evening up at the sanctuary, Herbert had revealed that he had once, in his earlier years, visited New Mexico and was moved by the open land and visions of the night sky in the little area where he had stayed, close to Rio Rancho. He had written a little verse for Charlotte in order that she would understand his feelings upon the matter.

In Cielo Norte's clear night sky
We watch the stars as they stroll by
Looking down upon our world
And all the sands of time unfurled
To reveal our long times past
And all the things we thought would last
But there's so much we fail to see
For all our great humanity
And so we gaze upon the scene
And think of things that might have been
Our lives will serve to document
The best of all our good intent
And all the things that we hold dear
To show the stars that we were here

It was typical of Herbert that he had said nothing of this to his colleagues at Dreadnought Consultants and it indicated a special trust that he had developed with Charlotte. She in turn had revealed a highly knowledgeable interest in both the natural world and the arts which had astounded Herbert and caused him to look upon her quite differently. They had found, in their companionship, many shared interests and an understanding of life which ran far deeper than mere material considerations. They had become soul mates in a world obsessed by the frivolous.

One late summers day, as Ernie turned the key in the door of Enterprise House, a sudden warm wind blew down Estuary Gardens as if to herald the coming of a special event. Ernie turned and looked down the road. "Caw" said the crow. "It's nothing" replied Ernie. "Just a passing gust of wind". But the crow knew better. Slowly, the others arrived and, after their morning tea, proceeded about their business as usual. Tommy was feeling a little tired as, the previous evening, he had attended his evening classes at the University where he was studying the natural sciences. The Dreadnought team had offered to sponsor Tommy to formally study computer science but, as he already understood computers, he thought he would much rather study the natural sciences in order that he be able to understand the workings of the world and contribute more fully to the community. It was interesting that Tommy was showing distinct leanings in this direction, realising that there was more to life than simply technology and commerce. Nevertheless, on this particular morning he was a little restless. It wasn't just that he was tired, he couldn't seem to focus upon his work in the usual way and found himself easily distracted. And then, all of a sudden, Ginger got up and walked towards the door, as though expecting someone to enter and Tommy looked expectantly in that direction. Sure enough, the sticking door juddered open and who should make an appearance, but Violet. She had been away for quite a while at University and had now grown into a beautiful young lady who was already becoming distinguished academically. "Violet!" exclaimed a delighted Natasha. "How lovely to see you. We had not been expecting a visit". "I was visiting Mother and decided to look in and see how you were doing" replied Violet as she walked forwards and then caught a glimpse of Tommy. She stood motionless for a moment. Tommy was transfixed and couldn't avert his gaze from this vision of loveliness that seemed to have descended out of the blue. Natasha noticed the poignancy. "Oh, and this is Tommy" she announced smiling. Tommy stood and took Violet's hand into his own. "Pleased to meet you Violet" he said quietly. Violet blinked and smiled back at him. "And you Tommy" she said, equally quietly. Ernie came up and explained their Environmental Monitoring project with the school and that Tommy had been so helpful that they gave him a job. "Indeed" said Violet. "I should like to speak with him about that". Some fresh tea was brewed and after Ernie and Herbert had provided a run down of recent activities and Percy had provided an overview of their financial standing, Violet and Tommy sat down together at Tommy's computer and discussed various matters, the others pulling back tactfully and going about their business. Celia Pumblepink popped in, as did Sheila Dribble from the Big Ears Animals Club and one or two others. They all noticed Violet and would like to have paid their respects, but Violet and Tommy noticed none of them. They gelled together from the first moment and it was obvious to all that something more than a technology exchange was occurring. Violet had spoken of the need to protect the natural world and natural ways of life from the onslaught of overt materialism, supported by the wrong sort of technology. Tommy agreed but felt sure that, if implemented in other ways, technology might actually be able to help. He enthusiastically explained the school project as an example and, the more he talked, the more Violet began to admire him. For his part, he was smitten with Violet from the start. At lunch time, Violet announced that she would, reluctantly, have to return home but that she would be staying at Boggleton Hall for another week at least and smiled sweetly at Tommy, who escorted her to the door and watched as she walked away down Estuary Gardens. As he came back in the others were standing, all smiling at him. "Where's Boggleton Hall?" he asked anxiously. "Don't worry, we shall show you" replied Natasha, taking him by the arm. Tommy was filled with a new energy and, grabbing up a pad, started to make notes of several new ideas which had been sparked by his discussion with Violet. No one had expected such an occurrence, but they were all deeply touched by the innocence and sincerity with which both Tommy and Violet had conducted their meeting. A meeting which was, as expected, to become one of many that week. When Violet returned to University, Tommy visited her at every opportunity and they spent many weekends enjoying each other's company, either on campus or back at Boggleton Hall. It was a fairy tale relationship which endured throughout that year and into the next, with no sign of waning. Indeed, the more they were together, the more Tommy was inspired and the richer the flow of his ideas. For her part, Violet was noticeably more contented and settled into her own studies, quietly excelling in almost every subject that she tackled. Tommy was also well on his way to obtaining his degree in the Natural Sciences that he had set his heart on. Everyone at Enterprise House was delighted. Perhaps the unseen force was sprinkling a little more of its magic among the inhabitants. Who could say? Certainly not Ernie. As he pulled closed the sticking door one evening he remarked quietly to Natasha that it was nice that Charlotte and Herbert had become so close and that it looked like Tommy and Violet would follow suite. "I suspected it all along" whispered Natasha as she patted Ernie affectionately on his arm. "Really?" he replied. "What's that?" said Herbert as he overheard them. "Nothing" said Ernie. "Caw" said the crow. Ginger curled up in his chair and the crow watched as the Dreadnought team walked slowly into the moonlight, casting long shadows across Estuary Gardens. The sun sank low on the horizon and the crow shifted his stance a little and rested his eyes. All was well with the world.

The next few months seemed to wiz by in a blur, with a steady stream of people coming in and out of Enterprise House, a run of successful meetings at the Conference Centre and now it was time to think about the next Dreadnought International Computer Science Symposium and of course, to be run shortly afterwards, the Boggle-on-Sea Festival, both of which were now considered as essential annual fixtures for the town. It would be a busy time ahead and would take a good deal of organising. However, this year, they had the help of a brace of local people, all of whom were willing and eager to help. Indeed, it all started to fall into place beautifully as Ernie and Natasha found themselves managing the preparations for both events. The Dreadnought International Computer Science Symposium was however shaping up to be quite different from the previous event, mainly due to the nature of the proposed presentations as many Dreadnought Consultants clients wanted to come and speak about their own experiences. Indeed, there were more potential speakers than could comfortably be accommodated and Ernie and Natasha quickly reached the point where they had to conclude the agenda. The town of Boggle-on-Sea was also better prepared with respect to accommodation this time around, with several new guest-houses opening in the vicinity of the Conference Centre and sea front. Mrs Cravat now had competition from Rachel Gubbins and Sally Bobble, both of whom had houses on the sea front, as well as others in the town. George Thorogood at the Rabbit and Trap had also converted his upstairs store rooms into three very small rooms, all sharing a bathroom, and had placed an American flag behind the bar. Bert Scarlett had invested in a larger fish and chip van in anticipation of the coming season and Luigi, the ice cream man, had introduced several new flavours including the Boggle Sundae and the Boggle Surprise at especially adjusted prices, geared towards tourists. Indeed, the whole town was looking forward to the summer season of activities at the Conference Centre. As the Dreadnought International Computer Science Symposium approached, Boggle-on-Sea was a hive of activity with people bustling about everywhere in preparation. Enterprise House seemed to never close as all manner of people drifted in and out, much to Ginger's delight as they invariably brought him little gifts of catnip and colourful toys. Gerald Fuzzfig had been brought in as technical support for the conference and Peter Bloggs, the printer, had printed a substantial number of programmes and posters advertising the event. All was ready and, soon enough, the great day arrived.

Mayor Bonking arrived in the official Daimler and parked it beside Bert Scarlett's new Fish and Chip van in order to get his free bag of chips before giving the opening speech. The Conference Centre was packed to capacity as Bonking welcomed all nations to what he called the 'Boggle Computer Science Symposium'. The delegates gave him a hearty round of applause as Ernie stepped up to announce the agenda for the day and introduce the first speaker, Robin Figget from the Boggle Comprehensive School. Figget gave an overview of the Environmental Monitoring project and how Boggle Comprehensive was now coordinating a network of thirty seven schools, including eleven overseas schools of varying descriptions. This resulted in the creation of a broader environmental picture and, as this was their third year, they were already producing valuable data around natural evolutionary trends. All of this was of course enabled and supported by the freely supplied software developed by Dreadnought Consultants. Figget received a rousing cheer from the delegates, augmented by a similar vocalisation from the sixth form, most of whom had packed into the back of the hall in order to hear his presentation. Next up was Charlotte Bunker-Hunt who gave an overview of the Donkey Sanctuary and the Donkey Database which now held records of all stray and abandoned donkeys in England. Charlotte and Herbert had now provided this database model freely to other countries who had contacted them via the associated website, screenshots of which were provided. Charlotte enhanced her presentation towards the end by bringing in Geoffrey and Murgatroyd, two of her favourite donkeys who had been waiting patiently outside. This was a great hit with the audience who cheered and clapped most enthusiastically. Unfortunately, Geoffrey, who was always a little unpredictable and clearly had a distinct sense of humour, took advantage of the situation and rushed into the assembled delegates, knocking some of them from their chairs and rifling through their pockets for any signs of sweets. This sent the delegates into an uproar of laughter and applause which was enjoyed by all, but especially by Geoffrey and Murgatroyd. Charlotte had seen it all before of course and calmly called her companions back to order before leaving the stage to a thunderous applause. Sheila Dribble continued the animal theme with an overview of the Big Ears Animal Club, supplemented with a batch of photographs of various furry, cuddly creatures, all of which drew an elongated 'ahhhh' from the audience. She went on to explain how the Dreadnought Consultants supplied software had helped her to organise her members and put together an attractive newsletter which had proved most interesting. Soon, it was time to break for lunch and the happy delegates filed out of the old Scouts Hall and crowded around Bert Scarlett's Fish and Chip van, Luigi's Ice Cream van and Maud and Flo's tea and coffee facilities. The Boggle seagulls were by now well practiced in the art of swooping down and relieving the delegates of their Fish and Chips in a systematic aerial combat manoeuvre of which the Royal Air Force would have been proud. This was orchestrated via strategically placed 'spotter' gulls who gave directions to squadrons of 'grabber' gulls who would scramble and quickly assume attack formations in order to dive down upon the hapless delegates, most of whom were lucky if they got to eat one or two chips from their packages. The seagulls saw this as a perfectly natural development whereby they continued their fishing, but with an added step in the process which exploited the human capability of frying up the catch and adding a few chips. Bert was struggling to keep up with demand and Luigi, likewise, was dishing out ice cream at an alarming rate. Maud and Flo were busy rinsing out cups in the horse trough and refilling them with what passed as tea and coffee, each iteration of which became more luke warm than its predecessor. But of course, the delegates were well acquainted with the ritual by now and loved every minute of it. Geoffrey and Murgatroyd mingled with the crowd and thoroughly enjoyed the opportunity to socialise with the visitors who, in turn, shared whatever they had left of their fish and chips and ice cream. Murgatroyd was particularly partial to Luigi's Boggle Sundae and sought out delegates who had purchased the same with uncanny accuracy. Filing back in for the afternoon session, the delegates were treated to a special 'warm up' presentation from Charlie who had, over previous iterations of the symposium, become a firm favourite with his tales from the world of refuse collection. As usual, he was announced as Professor Charles Higgins and received a rapturous welcome from the delegates. Further presentations followed, from Clive Wesley and Bertie Beaufort and, all too soon, the first day of the symposium was over and the delegates dispersed around Boggle-on-Sea, some of them back to their lodgings, others to stroll along the mudflats in the wind and rain and, a privileged few, to attend the evening reception at Enterprise House, an item which had also become a mainstay of the event. To the Dreadnought team's delight, Bethany Bugalberg had come over from America once again and was telling everybody, in a loud voice, how the Computer Science Symposium was the highlight of her professional calendar and how she wouldn't miss it for the world. She quickly appreciated that Herbert's affections were now spoken for, and so turned her attention to Percy, who she quickly cornered and homed in on, ensuring him that she would so appreciate his financial advice with regard to her own consultancy business. Percy felt quite flattered and soon, the two of them had established a rapport and were gaily laughing and chatting away, oblivious to what was occurring around them. Enterprise House was packed to capacity with a hubbub of joyous activity which ensued late into the evening. It was working its magic on the delegates, just as it had done with everyone else who was fortunate enough to cross the threshold of that sticking front door. Ginger had a wonderful time, being petted by all and sundry, and the Dreadnought team enjoyed every moment until, sadly, it was time to clear away the orange juice and biscuits and pack up for the night. "They just get better and better" said Ernie as he turned the key in the lock. "Don't they just" said Natasha. "They do indeed" said Herbert. "Absolutely" said Percy. "Caw" said the crow. And off they wandered into the pale moonlight as the red sky gazed down upon the mud flats of beautiful Boggle.

The remaining days of the Computer Science Symposium went extremely well and everybody had a wonderful time. The Boggle shop keepers renewed their acquaintance with the visitors, swapping stories about their various home towns and previous adventures. Mrs Cravat had now developed a hardcore of regular visitors who wouldn't stay anywhere else but at her guest house, although there were still plenty of clients for Rachel Gubbins, Sally Bobble and the others providing accommodation in the town. The delegates slowly drifted away after the event and it was time to start planning the Boggle-on-Sea Festival. Everybody seemed to want to be involved and there was much discussion with Celia Pumblepink, Pamela Ponsonby, Jessica Clinkworth-Sykes, Penelope Wilting, Clive Wesley and others, all of whom had a wealth of ideas for the Festival. It was agreed that the Boggle Players would mount a special production of Hamlet and that, this year, the Boggle Comprehensive music class would perform an abridged version of Orff's Carmina Burana under the direction of music teacher Olivia-Rose Winkle. Gerald Fuzzfig would rig up a special, remote controlled lighting system for the stage and everything seemed quickly to be taking shape. Old favourites such as the Corking Twins and Aloysius Browning were enlisted once again and Councillor Penelope Wilting was in charge of organising the carnival procession which had become a popular feature of the event. It was one afternoon in Enterprise House, when Herbert and Tommy were up at the Donkey Sanctuary and Percy had gone to the bank, that Ernie and Natasha found themselves uncharacteristically alone. "Everything seems to be going quite well" suggested

Ernie. "Everything is going wonderfully well" replied Natasha with a smile. Ernie thought for a moment. "You know Natasha, you and I are quite good at this sort of thing. I mean, working together to get things organised". "Well Ernie, we've been together in Enterprise House for a while now" replied Natasha as she sidled up to him. Time seemed to stand still for a moment or two, and then Ernie thought again. "You are right, we do make a good team". They looked at each other and both felt an involuntary smile spreading across their features as a warm glow enveloped them both. The crow came and sat on the sill of the open window, spreading his wings in the sunshine and peering inside. Ernie thought again. "You know Natasha" he began nervously as he shuffled some papers. "Maybe you and I should think about getting married". Natasha, after a brief pause, embraced Ernie warmly before pulling back a little, her eyes filled with tears. "Shall we?" said Ernie, as he looked deep into her eyes. "We shall" replied Natasha. "Caw" said the crow happily, shifting from one foot to the other in a sort of dance. Enterprise House had worked its magic once again.

The others returned later and, when all were assembled, including Celia Pumblepink who had dropped in, Ernie announced that he had some news for them. "That's funny, so have I" suggested Herbert. "I have some news too" said Tommy, looking around nervously. Percy smiled. "One at a time now please" he joked. "Well" started Ernie as Natasha came up beside him and took his arm. "I am proud to announce that Natasha has agreed to become my wife". There was a pause. "You are getting married?" gasped Celia. "That's right" confirmed Natasha with a delightful smile that illuminated the room. "Well, that's strange" interceded Herbert. "What's strange about it?" asked Ernie. "Well, because that is my news too. Charlotte and I have decided to get married". "That's wonderful" exclaimed Natasha, we shall have a double wedding. They all laughed and shook hands and then, remembering that Tommy had some news, Natasha turned towards him. "What's your news Tommy?" she asked. Tommy looked shy for a moment. "It's just that I have been talking with Violet". "And?" asked Natasha impatiently. "Well" replied Tommy quietly. "We have also decided to get married". "What!?" exclaimed Ernie joyously. "Then we shall have a triple marriage" suggested Natasha, and they all cheered gaily and embraced one another. "What about you Percy?" asked Celia earnestly. "You seemed to be getting along rather well with that American lady". Percy looked temporarily taken aback, although he was not offended by the suggestion. "Not yet!" he replied with a smile. "But who knows? maybe one day" he added. "Of course you will Percy" said Natasha, and she kissed him on the cheek. That evening, they all assembled in the Rabbit and Trap to celebrate the news and, after discussion with some of the locals, they decided that it would be lovely to hold the triple wedding ceremony as a fitting end-piece of the Boggle-on-Sea Festival. They would of course have to agree the idea with the Mayor and the local council and a meeting was arranged accordingly. When Claude Bonking and Penelope Wilting heard the suggestion, they were absolutely delighted and agreed that it would make the festival an even more wonderful event than usual. They also advised that St. Mary's Church now had a new vicar, Mervin Longbottom who, they felt sure, would relish the opportunity for such an event. The next day, an appointment was made with the vicar and, the following Sunday after the morning service, the three pairs entered St. Mary's for some instruction on the procedure and to agree exactly how a triple wedding might take place. Mervin Longbottom was a very serious minded man, balding and yet elegant looking, who fitted in perfectly with the musty interior of St. Mary's which hadn't changed much over the last few centuries. Indeed, the church was one of the first buildings which served to define the original village of Boggle, together with some farm cottages. The town that is now Boggle-on-Sea grew systematically around the original settlement. Longbottom seemed to blend seamlessly into the wooden pews and main altar of the church, as if he had always been there. He eyed his visitors cautiously for a moment or two. "So, you all wish to be married" he stated quietly while still holding his bible. "That's right sir, we do" replied Ernie confidently. "In a combined wedding" continued Longbottom. Natasha smiled sweetly and, just as she was about to speak, Violet interceded. "It's quite simple really" she explained. "We shall all stand in a row and take the vows together and you shall ask us one at a time whether we agree to the union". Longbottom raised his eyebrows, unaccustomed as he was to having someone explain to *him* how he was going to run his service. But Violet continued. "The aisle is quite narrow, so we shall approach singularly, Uncle Ernie, Thomas and Uncle Herbert will arrive and take their places at the front and then Natasha, myself and Charlotte shall walk down the aisle in that order, before branching off to stand next to our partners. There is plenty of room here at the front of the church. When we have taken the vows, we shall return up the aisle in reverse order and meet in the vestry to sign the records". Longbottom recovered his composure and thanked Violet for her suggestion. "That's essentially how we shall do it" he agreed. "However, you will need to understand and rehearse the service itself. And then there is the question of choosing the hymns". Herbert coughed. "Actually, I have one or two suggestions in that respect" he ventured while unfolding a paper and handing it to the vicar. Longbottom, having raised and lowered his eyebrows again, studied the paper. "How Great Thou Art, Abide With Me, Jerusalem, Love Divine, All Love Excelling" he whispered quietly to himself. "Well, these should do as a starting point if you are all agreed" he suggested. Actually, Ernie hadn't thought much about hymns but Natasha winked at him and he realised that some prior discussion had ensued among the girls and

Herbert, and he was pleased to accept their choices. After this initial meeting, they congregated outside the church entrance and wandered together along the winding path through the cemetery. There were some very old tombstones, including one or two un-named 'pirates' graves featuring a simple skull and crossbones chiselled into the stone. Herbert paused and looked around him. "This church has been the centre of the community for a very long time" he mused. "It is fitting then that we should all be married here" suggested Charlotte with a smile as she clung to his arm. A gentle peace seemed to come and settle upon them all as they strolled slowly through the church yard and out onto the adjoining lane. They had become such special friends that it seemed perfectly natural that they should all be married together. Back at Enterprise House, preparations were made for the Boggle-on-Sea Festival, with the wedding planned for the day after. Invitations would be sent to their closest friends and Liliya Seminovsky had absolutely insisted that she would host an evening reception for them all at Boggleton Hall, after which, they would leave for their respective honeymoons, although this part had not yet been planned.

And so, the first day of the Boggle-on-Sea Festival finally arrived and it was a beautiful morning as the Mayor assembled the carnival participants and the procession duly moved off down the High Street and around towards the sea front. Crowds lined the street, both locals and visitors and it was a wonderful start to the festival proper. Joss Finkle from the Boggle Examiner ran alongside the procession taking numerous photographs while Juliette Slinkbottom interviewed visitors for the feature that they would run after the event. Visitors and locals alike were treated to a wonderful variety of entertainment over the course of the next two evenings, while they enjoyed the town and surrounding areas during the day. As had now become customary, the Boggle-on-Sea Festival was a great success with everyone engaged in the spirit of communal goodwill and, as a consequence, thoroughly enjoying themselves. But this year was subtly different. There were rumours circulating. Wherever people gathered together, it wasn't long before whispers were heard and startled expressions would briefly skirt across the faces of those around. Alongside Bert's Fish and Chip van, at breakfast within the various guest houses, down on the mudflats in the evening, within the High Street shops, in the snug at the Rabbit and Trap, the rumours spread like wildfire wherever folk congregated. Meanwhile, the Dreadnought team were reflecting upon another successful Festival and preparing for their own special day at St. Mary's. They had kept knowledge of the event contained among just a few close friends and family, ensuring that the wedding would be a relatively low key affair that would pass off quietly within the town. On the morning of the great day, Ernie arose and breakfasted with Auntie Freda at Westminster Drive, even though he had his own apartment in town now. Freda was a great help in ensuring that Ernie was properly dressed and was well rehearsed for the occasion. Herbert was assisted by Percy in a similar manner at Mrs Cravat's boarding house and Tommy was being groomed by his family for the occasion. Up at Boggleton Hall, Natasha and Violet were similarly being groomed and prepared, together with a visitor in the form of Charlotte Bunker-Hunt. It made sense, as Liliya Seminovsky had observed, to prepare all the girls together and, aided by Natasha's sister Fenella, she was orchestrating the affair upon a grand scale and enjoying every moment of it. Herbert and Ernie had hired a brace of limousines from Johnnie Crocker at Crocker's Transport Services, to collect the various parties and deliver them to the church on time. Ernie looked in the mirror and took a deep breath. The car was waiting outside and it was time to go. With a fond farewell to Auntie Freda, he got into the car and they headed off to collect Herbert and Tommy. At Boggleton Hall, the brides were looking absolutely beautiful and Liliya and Fenella had to fight back a tear as they made the last minute adjustments to the dresses and ensured that everything was just so. Violet was like a star from heaven, Natasha was looking gently serene and Charlotte had been transformed from the Donkey Sanctuary eccentric to a most beautiful lady. They were all radiating love and goodwill as they filed into their own limousine and headed off towards the church. As Ernie's limousine turned into church lane, the car was momentarily brought to a halt as it had to slowly pick its way through the crowd. "What are all these people doing here?" asked Ernie. "Don't they know that the festival is over". "Perhaps they are just sight-seeing, on their way down to the sea front" suggested Herbert. Tommy looked out from the window and, all of a sudden, there was a tumultuous cheer which reverberated throughout the crowd. The cheering continued as the car finally reached the church and the grooms alighted and headed towards the front porch. The boys turned around and were greeted by the extraordinary sight of what appeared to be almost the entire town, plus visitors from the festival, all crowded into the church yard. Ernie instinctively raised his hat and there was another enormous cheer from the crowd. Herbert, Tommy and Ernie looked at each other, but could not say a single word. They were completely overcome by this extraordinary display of affection and support. Moving inside, the church itself was packed to capacity. As they walked slowly down the aisle, all of their friends were there; Celia Pumblepink, Clive Wesley, Sheila Dribble, Pamela Ponsonby, Stephen Spindlebrook, Robin Figget, Maud Willets, Gerald Fuzzfig, Florence Blacket, Jessica Clinkworth-Sykes, George Thorogood, all smiling cheerfully as the boys passed by and there, on the front row, was the entire Boggle Town Council with Mayor Bonking sporting his chain of office. On the other side stood Charlie Higgins and the immediate relatives. Even if they had been allowed to, the boys would not have been able to utter a word at this juncture, they were all choked with emotion. Having been quietly welcomed by Mervin Longbottom they stood at the front and waited. After a few minutes, there was the sound of sustained cheering from outside the church and they knew that the girls had arrived. With baited breath, everyone inside waited and then, with a sign from the vicar, Harold Beaversmith, the church organist, launched joyfully into the wedding march and three visions of loveliness glided slowly down the aisle as heads turned on every side. The brides assembled next to their respective grooms and Liliya Seminovsky shed a tear as she watched two generations of her family wed their chosen partners. Percy, who was the communal Best Man, stood proudly and watched as his friends took their vows. Longbottom navigated his way through the service and, all too quickly, it seemed to be over and they were walking, arm in arm, back up the aisle to the sound of the organ playing and the sight of a sea of smiling faces, each one of which radiated love and goodwill. They assembled in the vestry to sign the documents which, guided by Longbottom, they all performed solemnly and then, they headed outside where there was much cheering and confetti throwing. Joss Finkle from the Boggle Examiner had been engaged to take the wedding photographs and Juliette Slinkbottom orchestrated the whole affair against a backdrop of the prettiest corner of the church, with a tree on one side. Everyone wanted to be in the photographs and the session ran on for the best part of an hour while Joss snapped away with his impressive looking camera gear. More cheering ensued, together with a good deal of hand shaking as the happy couples walked, smiling, through the church yard and then re-entered their cars and drove slowly away down the lane. Meanwhile, Gerald Fuzzfig, who felt uncomfortable dressed in his one and only, ill-fitting suit which, it should be noted, had been bought fifteen years earlier, was shifting about uneasily among the crowd when one of his trouser legs got caught on the base of a jagged tombstone and launched a startled Fuzzfig into a batch of unsuspecting visitors. Oaths were enunciated in several languages as people sprawled over the tombstones in a domino effect. Joss Finkle snapped away happily, capturing the moment for posterity. Claude Bonking, resplendent in his chain of office sought to take charge of the situation, after all he was the Town Mayor. Leaning forwards and proffering a helping hand towards a heap of assorted arms, legs and distressed expressions, he suddenly found himself being pulled into the mêlée by his official chain which, not being quite as substantially made as its appearance might suggest, immediately snapped, showering its various medallions in all directions. Bonking thrashed about wildly as he attempted to gather up the missing pieces of his chain of office, while being generally pushed, shoved and trodden on as the assemblage rolled around among the tombstones. Those not caught up in the fiasco stood and looked on approvingly while Finkle continued to snap away. Eventually, the distressed managed to regain a vertical position, all looking at each other suspiciously in an attempt to apportion blame for the incident. Fuzzfig said nothing, but limped away quietly, his torn trouser leg flapping in the breeze. A group of German visitors found the incident most interesting and made notes accordingly, while the Americans thought it must be part of an old English tradition, having been fed a brace of equally unlikely stories by the good townspeople of Boggle. The crowd then dispersed back into the town, still in the Festival spirit as they bought their last batch of fish and chips and ice cream, before settling down for the afternoon. The seagulls, sensing that this would be their last opportunity for full scale operations for some time, had been waiting patiently and now scrambled their various squadrons in order to liberate what they saw as their rightful property.

Up at Boggleton Hall, cars arrived, one after another, depositing the carefully chosen guests who assembled in the lobby where Fenella offered them all a celebratory drink while her mother and herself changed and readied the main dining hall. After twenty minutes or so, a maid who had been hired for the occasion, announced that it was time for them to move into the main room which, initially, was in semi darkness, the window shutters being closed and the lights turned off. When all were assembled, Liliya Seminovsky gave the order and the lights were switched on to reveal a long oak table piled with various delights of fancy pastries, savoury items, fruits, chocolates and much more, all on silver platters and punctuated by two large silver candelabras with large red and blue candles which Fenella quickly lit. There were decanters of various wines and sherries with silver hearts tied around them, with the names of the happy couples and the year of union. On another table were three gigantic wedding cards which all the guests were encouraged to sign. In the corner of the room sat a baby grand piano which had been moved in from the study. One of Violets university friends, Candice Cherryweather, kitted out in a beautiful powder blue frock, sat down and played a selection of Chopin waltzes and nocturnes. Everyone wanted to wish the brides and grooms their very best wishes and comment on what a wonderful day it had been. Among the joyous hubbub, Charlotte squeezed Herbert's arm gently. "Thank you Herbert" she said simply. Herbert smiled and kissed her gently on the cheek. Tommy held Violets hand throughout the evening, as if frightened that she might disappear if he let it go. Ernie gazed gently at Natasha. "You do look beautiful" he said. "Did you think that this would ever happen when we first met at Enterprise House?". Natasha took his arm. "Of course darling, I knew it all along" she said with a smile. Everyone present was happy and content in the warm embrace of an evening among friends and of course, there were many toasts to the happy couples, many of them proposed by Percy who was somewhat overcome with emotion to see his good friends so happy. Eventually, the evening drew to a close and the guests paid their respects to Liliya, Fenella and the wedded couples before, one by one, drifting away into the pale Boggle moonlight. Those remaining had a quiet celebratory drink of champagne on their own before turning in for the night. As Herbert and Charlotte ascended the stairs, Charlotte noticed through the window a particularly bright shining northern star. "Look Herbert, that must be our special star" she whispered excitedly. Herbert looked through the glass and smiled. "It *is* our star" he said. "And it will shine over us for all our days on Earth". The next morning, the newlyweds would depart for their honeymoon breaks while Liliya and Fenella restored Boggleton Hall to its usual status. The wedding day had been a special day for everyone in Boggle-on-Sea, including the visitors to the Festival who, by now, regarded Boggle as almost a second home. For the newlyweds, it would of course be a day that they would never forget and which would open a new chapter in their respective lives. That evening, a particularly beautiful red and violet sky stretched out over the mudflats of Boggle-on-Sea, while the pale yellow moon bathed Enterprise House in a lovely soft light. The crow folded his wings and sat contentedly on the roof. All had come to pass.

Enterprise House

15 EPILOGUE

When Ernest Trubshaw first came to Boggle-on-Sea, it was almost as if he was a refugee from the big city in which, no matter how he tried, he was destined never to succeed. Similarly, Herbert Jingle and Percy Proudfoot had never succeeded with their practice in the city, as they were just not cut out for the dog eat dog existence that prevailed there. Natasha Seminovsky had been a talented designer with many good ideas, but equally had failed to make much of an impression. When they found themselves thrust together at Enterprise House, something gelled and, very soon, their previous ambitions and energies returned as they joined forces as Dreadnought Consultants. Initially, they dreamed of becoming successful and wealthy entrepreneurs, with all the material trappings that such status provided, just as many in the world of IT had done before them. But, under the benevolent auspices of Enterprise House, they had become something much more important. They had become human beings. Their wealth was not measured in money, but in the currency of friendship. Their success was not in predatory business expansion, but in the joy that they had brought to others. The gentle, benign influence of Enterprise House had slowly worked its magic on them and, when they needed a little extra guidance, an administering angel was provided in the form of Violet. She illuminated the path ahead with her goodness, innocence and clear thinking, bringing out the best in Herbert, Natasha and the others. Her star would remain shining gently within Enterprise House even after she had left for other things.

What Ernie had originally feared as failure, turned out to be their wonderful success. The more they gave to others, the more secure they felt in themselves and the more the waves of warmth and goodwill would reverberate back to them. It is an odd thing that some people understand this, while so many do not, especially those politicians, business entrepreneurs and criminals (the distinction is a weak one) for whom material gain is the sole meaning of life. The tragedy is that they are not necessarily born with such a conviction, but that they inherit it via the influence of the universal culture of greed and corruption which prevails among humanity. The pattern has existed since the dawn of civilisation whereby, the truth has always been there, for those who will see it, while others prefer to turn a blind eye. That understanding had been encapsulated within the prefabricated walls of Enterprise House, itself a somewhat unlikely building which might be considered a misfit among the pretentious glass towers of the average city or the soulless look alike buildings of suburbia. And yet, like many misfits, there was a heart within Enterprise House which allowed it to exert a benevolent influence upon its inhabitants. It had weathered the storm of neglect and indifference and finally blossomed in its later years when a particular combination of people came to appreciate it. In this respect, it was not unlike many human beings. And, like some human beings, it was imbued with a special magic which it could wield on behalf of others. Those who entered through its sticking front door, found themselves bathed in a warmth of goodwill, a little piece of which they took away with them with every visit. That previously broken down building that nobody really wanted became the centre of a community that had found its own special place and time. A community that had reached out beyond Boggle-on-Sea to welcome friends from far afield. And, at its centre, lay Dreadnought Consultants. Were they the architects of this community, or were they simply the instrument of Enterprise House? If we asked the crow, he would surely tell us, but then crows are more intelligent than we care to believe. In any event, Ernie, Herbert, Percy, Natasha and later Tommy, would all come to learn the truth about life within the walls of Enterprise House. It stood like a shining oasis in a desert of grim mediocrity. A mediocrity and pretence that sapped the souls of those who embraced it, attracted by its shallow glitter.

Sergey Seminovsky, Liliya's late husband, used to say that we have an obligation to leave something good behind us, regardless of the situation in which we find ourselves. It was a philosophy that became embedded in the hearts of Liliya and her daughters, Fenella and Natasha and was in turn passed down to Violet. A philosophy that found a ready home in Enterprise House. Herbert assumed a little of that philosophy in a verse that he wrote for Charlotte at the Donkey Sanctuary.

Enterprise House

We dance on this Earth but for a short while
Our feelings of mirth raise many a smile

But what of the folk who suffer and toil
Destined to choke on life's mortal coil

The lonely and frightened and those who don't see
The time honoured truth of that which will be

And all of the creatures at sea and on land
So cruel is their justice received at our hands

But what of the brave and the gallant and true
Who light the way forwards for me and for you

Theirs is a light which shines in the dark
A jewel in the distance that must leave its mark

So we must remain, clear straight and true
That much ordained in all that we do

And love is the key, our compass and guide
Though stormy the sea, from truth we shan't hide

And so the way forwards is clearly defined
For those who are wise, and gentle and kind

And this much I pledge, to you my dear heart
To follow that path, till death do us part

And now, dear friends, it is time to leave Enterprise House for a while. "Farewell" say us. "Caw" says the crow.

AUTHOR BIOGRAPHY

Julian Ashbourn has wide interests ranging from leading edge technology to the natural world. He has spearheaded various initiatives with respect to conservation, education and specific technological areas. In addition, he is an accomplished author and photographer with publications in various sectors including Computer Science, the Earth Sciences, Poetry and some works of fiction such as The Homesteaders and Enterprise House. His uniquely broad experience brings a special perspective to all of these works.

Enterprise House

Enterprise House

Printed in Great Britain
by Amazon